Material Evidence

"…a fine debut with intense plotting, strong characters and just the right touch of acid in the dialogue…"—Aberdeen Press and Journal

"Add to the cast of characters a good sense of pace and an excellent plot that kept me guessing and you'll see why I liked this book." —Cathy G. Cole

Rough Justice

"…a thoughtful and thought-provoking book… It ought to bring Bill Kirton the attention he deserves." —Sunday Telegraph

The Darkness

"…clever, tightly constructed, immensely satisfying and peopled with a cast of completely believable characters, who don't let you go until the final word." —Michael J. Malone

"…a dark, intense ride … a book that keeps you guessing right until the exciting conclusion." —P. S. Gifford

"…a wonderful, thrilling, dark, compassionate book." —Gillian Philip, author of *Firebrand*

Shadow Selves

"…a thoroughly engrossing medical mystery with a surprise ending that was totally unexpected." —Chris Longmuir, author of *Dead Wood*, winner of the Dundee International Book Prize

Coming soon: *Unsafe Acts* (book 5 in the Jack Carston series)

Historical Mystery/Romance

The Figurehead

"…an exciting, page-turning murder mystery … interesting, thoughtful and thoroughly absorbing." —Mary O Farrington

"…a splendid romance of … exquisite tenderness, *The Figurehead* satisfies on every level, giving the reader authenticity, characters to care about, a mystery, and a romance."
—Diane Nelson, author of *Dragon Academy*

"The Figurehead deserves a 5-star rating because it's artfully written and leaves the reader wanting more." —Jean Henry Mead

Children's Books (writing as Jack Rosse)

Stanley Moves In

"Stanley in all his obnoxious glory … it's hard not to like Rosse's charming tale of this out-of-the-ordinary fairy."
—Melissa Conway

Coming soon: *The Loch Ewe Mystery*

Bill Kirton

THE SPARROW CONUNDRUM

PfoxChase

PfoxChase, a division of Pfoxmoor Publishing
4972 Lowhill Church Road
New Tripoli, PA 18066 USA

www.pfoxmoorpublishing.com
www.pfoxchase.com

The Sparrow Conundrum

Print ISBN: 978-1-936827-04-6
Digital ISBN (PDF): 978-1-936827-05-3
Digital ISBN (ePUB): 978-1-936827-06-0

FT
Pbk

Cover by Sessha Batto

First Pfoxmoor Publishing electronic publication: March 2011
First Pfoxmoor Publishing print publication: March 2011

Published in the United States of America with international
distribution.

DEDICATION

My thanks to all my online friends who gave such useful
feedback.
This book is for them.

PROLOGUE

They were desperate to get rid of their virginity and this was the night. They'd been skulking about near the video shop for half an hour, too scared to admit they fancied any of the women they saw. It was the right part of Aberdeen and they'd checked on the internet, knew how much it was going to cost, talked about it a lot. In fact, they rarely talked of anything else. At the library where he worked, Derek was known, behind his back, as Ed, short for erectile dysfunction. Tony worked in a bank and was simply called wanker. To his face.

In fact, they're both mere statistics in this story. Derek is the first of its many casualties. He and Tony just happened to be there when it began, so they deserve their moment of fame before they disappear completely.

They knew prostitutes cost anything from ten to two hundred pounds, depending on where they looked and what they wanted them to do. Tonight, they'd pooled their funds: forty-one pounds seventeen pence between them.

"Should be enough," said Tony.

"Depends. What d'you want?"

"Plenty," said Tony, implying he had some specific perversions in mind but hoping Derek wouldn't ask for details.

They tossed a coin to decide who'd go first. Derek lost.

"Away you go, then," said Tony.

"Where?" said Derek, pushing away the need to act.

Tony flicked his head towards the woman across the street. She'd been standing in the semi-darkness of a doorway ever since they'd arrived.

"Her," he said, in a hard whisper.

It was good timing. The woman took a step out into the light and looked up and down the street. She was tall, fair-haired and gorgeous.

1

"Bloody hell," said Derek.

"Aye," said Tony.

There was a pause before Derek asked, "Think forty-one pounds seventeen's enough?"

"Course it is," said Tony.

"But..." Derek paused. "...what if she doesn't like me?"

'She doesn't have to bloody like you," said Tony. "Just get on with it. She's only a bloody woman. Anyway you're paying. What's not to like?"

Derek had been hoping they wouldn't find what they were looking for, but there was no dodging it this time. And she really did look incredibly sexy. He took a deep breath, pulled his coat more tightly around him and crossed the street.

****

Out of the corner of her eye, the woman saw him coming. She knew what he'd want. So far, she'd had six approaches, all of them thinking she was on the game. It was absurd. If they hadn't all been wired up with hormones, they'd have realised she was far too elegant to be selling herself in a doorway. If she had been in the business she'd have been sitting in some fancy granite villa in the West End taking bookings on a platinum mobile from oil men, MSPs, City Councillors and men of the cloth. Her class didn't belong with back seats and back streets; it suggested leather and harnesses designed to relieve urges generated at Gordonstoun, Fettes and the like. But she was here to do a job. It had to be this street at this time. There was no choice.

As Derek began his sidle towards her, she was ready with the same polite rejection she'd given the other six. But circumstances were against him. Across the street, just along from where Tony was watching, a door opened and a figure came out. The woman froze. Derek, mesmerised by the fact he was about to graduate from librarian to stud, noticed nothing. His breath came faster; his excitement rose. His idea was to start by saying what a nice evening it was, but she was so bloody gorgeous that all thoughts of subtle small talk vanished as he came up beside her and started to say "How much?"

He didn't get beyond "H—"

Her eyes stayed fixed on the man across the street as her knee

2

jerked sideways into Derek's groin and, simultaneously, the edge
of her right hand chopped into the front of his throat. He collapsed
against the wall in agony but at least relieved of the need to try to
get an erection.

The woman didn't even watch him fall. She'd recognised the
face of the thick-set man in the green, service-issue combat jacket
who'd come out of the building opposite. Her eyes followed him
as he hurried along past a street lamp and the doorway in which
Tony was hiding, scared shitless by the woman's unprovoked
assault on Derek. The man got into a green Renault Laguna. The
woman noted the registration number and drew back into the
shadows as he drove away. That was it. She'd confirmed he was in
Aberdeen and active. There was no need to follow; he wouldn't do
anything tonight. According to her boss, things wouldn't start
happening until the next morning.

She stepped out of her doorway and looked down at Derek,
feeling sorry that he'd been unlucky enough to arrive at exactly the
moment when she'd needed no distractions. She bent down and
reached towards him to see if she could help. He screamed. It was
a combination of fear and what he would later recognise as
ecstasy. The woman didn't have time for this. She patted his
cheek, blew him a kiss and went quickly to where she'd parked her
white Mercedes 200SL. She got in, flicked open her mobile and hit
a button.

"Hey, Big Snake," she said when she was connected.

"Yo. What's happening, Birdwatcher?" The voice was throaty,
not much more than a whisper.

"Just to say. I've clocked the Sparrowhawk."

"Where?"

"The docks. He's just driven off."

"OK. Keep in touch."

The woman closed the mobile, took a deep breath, started the
growling engine, and accelerated away. It had begun.

****

Tony waited for her to vanish then crossed the street to his
sobbing friend. He helped him up and the two of them caught a
number nineteen bus back to the flat they shared. Neither spoke a
word the whole way and, when they got there, Derek went straight

3

to bed with a mug of instant Horlicks, and Tony watched an American football match on Sky Sports One.

It was the last time they went hunting for sex. Thirteen days later, when Derek could once more walk without limping, he brought home a pizza. He and Tony sat on the couch, watching *Star Trek*, the pizza between them. As Captain Picard flicked his finger and said "Warp factor three. Engage," they reached simultaneously for a slice. Their hands touched and they fell into one another's arms and began sloughing off life's frustrations in a series of unspeakable embraces.

CHAPTER ONE

The postman was out of luck. It wasn't his usual beat. One of his colleagues was on holiday and he was just doing his round for a week. It was a posh bit of town. People there had standards. You didn't jump over the walls dividing driveways, however low they were. You had to go back down one to the pavement and up the other. Boundaries meant properties, respect.

He didn't know that.

He put his right hand on the wall separating numbers twenty-two and twenty-four, did a little skip over it and landed on the edge of a newly-dug rose-bed. The explosion as his foot touched the ground spread him and his bag of letters over the garden and the pavement.

That's the price of ignorance.

Chris Machin, the owner-occupier of number twenty-two, was just coming out of a side street when he heard the bang. The shock made him jump and drop some of his shopping. He guessed right away that the explosion was something to do with him. Over the past few weeks, scary things had been happening.

His body prickled with fear as he ran to the corner and looked towards his house. Smoke and dust were still whirling; neighbours were already converging on his newly excavated garden and all his fears were confirmed. He wasn't a brave man and the evidence that there'd been an attempt on his life made his legs feel boneless. He leaned against, then sat on the garden wall of the corner house, letting more articles slip from his shopping-bag. An upstairs window opened and a loud voice shouted, "Oi! Go and sit on somebody else's wall, you drunken bastard."

He struggled weakly to his feet and brushed the egg-yolk off his shoes. He was shaking very badly, but the mechanical process of scraping the remains of his shopping together helped him to focus. He had to react fast. They needed to know about this. He had to phone them.

He didn't have his mobile and certainly didn't fancy trying to use his home phone, so he walked on his watery legs back past bits of shopping until he came to a group of three telephone boxes. Only two of them were out of order. In the third, he took out his diary, dropped it from fumbling fingers, picked it up again, found the number he wanted and dialled. A cool female voice said, "Benton Exporting. Can I help you?"

"Yes," he said. "Quick, it's an emergency. I want to speak to Mr…"

He stopped. They didn't do it that way. He didn't even know the guy's real name.

"Hullo caller. Can I help you?" repeated the woman.

"Yes. Just a minute. Er …"

He couldn't remember his code-name. He flicked through the pages of the diary.

"This is Starling. No, Sparrow," he said. "I want Eagle. It's an emergency. They've blown up my garden."

There was a silence.

"Hullo. Are you there?"

The woman's voice came back. Cool had become frosty. "I'm sorry, caller, I think you may have the wrong number."

"No, I haven't," he shouted. "It's Sparrow here. I want Eagle."

"I'm sorry, Mr Sparrow, we have no one of that name here."

"Not Mr Sparrow. That's my code-name. I'm…"

He stopped as he heard the click which disconnected him. He swore, checked the diary again and redialed. The same voice said, "Benton Exporting. Can I help you?"

He took a deep breath, trying to control his panic and the break in his voice.

"This is Sparrow. I want Eagle."

But this time the click had come as soon as he said "Sparrow", and even in his frenzy he knew it was futile. They'd told him, "Don't phone us, we'll phone you," and they meant it. He leaned forward against the coin-box and tried consciously to decelerate his pulse as his mind jumped frantically over the alarms of the past few weeks. He couldn't pretend it would go away now. He was well and truly involved.

****

Across the street the thick-set man in the green, service-issue combat jacket squatted in the bushes which were just inside the park railings. Out of a black holdall, he took a Glock 17 pistol fitted with a Jupitereye Suppressor. After his two days of training, this was his first job. He was excited, primed and ready. He looked again at the figure in the phone box and dropped forward onto the grass to steady himself for the shot.

As his left elbow came down, it was all he could do not to scream. His arm had jabbed straight onto the jagged edges of a broken bottle. He dropped the gun and, almost fainting with the pain, pulled with his right hand at the stump of glass protruding from his elbow. As it came away, blood flowed immediately and copiously down his side and onto the grass.

He got to his feet, tore open his left sleeve, and tied it as best he could round the top of his arm to act as a temporary tourniquet. As he gave a final tug at the material he stumbled, stood on the gun, and fired a bullet which took off the end of his right shoe and two of his toes. By the time he'd cleared up some of the mess in the remains of his shoe, his target had left the phone box and disappeared.

The tall, fair-haired woman had been watching every move from behind the wheel of her parked Mercedes 200SL. She put away the Beretta which had been trained on the man until his elbow found the bottle, and reached for her mobile again.

****

Joey McBride died because he was too ambitious. His organisation was one of those which had missed out on the bread and butter business of drugs and prostitution and needed to diversify. Their attempts at a protection racket coincided with the beginning of the credit crunch, their industrial espionage efforts failed because of the decline in manufacturing and, as his options diminished, Joey needed to become more creative.

He'd seen *Casino Royale* and liked the idea of having a network of agents causing mayhem and skimming profits from whatever they encountered and so, like many others in Aberdeen, he'd looked to the oil industry.

Despite the gloomy prognoses, the revenues continued to flow.

7

The oil giants themselves had decided they couldn't be bothered getting the remaining pockets of oil and gas out of reservoirs which were nearing the end of their life cycle, so smaller independents and some service companies were moving in. They took over the assets, ran them, and paid the big boys for the privilege.

Joey had no expertise in anything much, but he'd watched enough movies to know that image was everything. The gang of chancers he'd gathered knew little about oil but they wore the right sort of suits and, being mostly from broken homes and abusive backgrounds, they were so riddled with insecurities that they always retaliated before there was any provocation. It was a powerful mixture which, for a while at least, impressed the genuine businessmen to whom they offered their support.

Joey had decided long ago to call the office block from which they operated "The Cage." Nobody knew why; it was just a good tag. It went with all the Bond-inspired code names they'd dreamed up to give their set-up street cred.

Joey loved *Reservoir Dogs* but thought the names—Mr Orange, Mr Pink and the rest—were limited. They worked if you just had a handful of guys but, when you were set on building an empire, you'd have to get into Mr Puce and so on. There weren't enough colours. He couldn't remember who'd come up with the bird idea but he liked it a lot. As boss, he called himself Eagle and, by the time he died, he'd gathered quite a flock around him.

He passed away, far from peacefully, on a Tuesday afternoon. He was walking along in Union Grove, trying to guess the bra sizes of the women he passed, when a number 23 bus mounted the pavement and crushed him against the wall of a Pizzeria.

It was driven by one of Tony Belazzo's boys, or maybe one of the new Russians—no one ever found out. But it meant that The Cage needed a new Eagle, and quickly. So Joey's deputies looked around for someone they could manipulate, and they came up with a Texan with a fat bank account and the right sort of contacts Stateside.

He moved into the fifth floor office and took over Joey's name and function. In fact, it was soon obvious that it would've made more sense to call him Thrush, which was both an unpleasant fungal infection and a bird of the genus turdus. But they were stuck with him now and he looked down on Aberdeen harbour from his room with a sense of power and fulfilment.

He was a small man in his fifties. His thick grey hair sat like a fat Brillo pad on his square head and his eyes squinted meanly at a world he didn't really understand. Way back, the late Joey had installed a computer so that he could have a continuous loop of music playing while he sat behind the desk or looked out over his operational patch. In those days, the room was always filled with the themes from *Braveheart*, *Rob Roy* and *The Godfather*.

The change of management had brought a change of style. For the 17th time that afternoon, Dolly Parton took over from Emmy-Lou Harris. The new Eagle wanted everybody to know who they were dealing with, someone whose heart belonged to the land and the misery of country music.

Above the door, a red light started flashing. It indicated that someone was standing on the pressure-pad outside. Eagle, still squinting at the supply ships moored alongside the quays, was unaware of it, and it was not until the final chorus of *Nine 'til Five* that the man standing in the corridor decided to knock.

It was a mistake. As his hand touched the door, he was jolted to the soles of his feet by a massive electrical charge. The second pulse threw him back against the opposite wall and an alarm tone began its furious warbling inside the room. When the man looked up, the door was open and the Browning in Eagle's outstretched right hand was aimed at his forehead.

"Hi, Jim," shouted Eagle over the keening noise. "New fail-safe alarm. Cool, eh?"

The man smiled and nodded as Eagle helped him to his feet and supported him into the room and onto a steel-framed chair beside the desk. He closed the door, reactivated the alarm, and turned back to his trembling caller.

"You'll feel as useless as a dodo's dick for a while. Soon wears off though. When you feel up to it, get yourself a Jack Daniels. I'll have one with you."

Jim, or Hawk as he was officially designated, knew of old that "when you feel up to it" meant immediately, and so, as Eagle resumed his survey of the harbour, he staggered to his feet and moved to the drinks cabinet. Bottles clinked and whiskey splashed as he poured the drinks, but Eagle remained unmoving until his glass was handed to him by his grey-faced boy.

He grunted his thanks, slurped back a mouthful and washed it round his tongue and teeth before swallowing it. Hawk remained standing beside him, shaking too much to raise his own glass to his lips. Eagle gave an "Aaah" of pleasure, and, still without turning, said, "Well, Jim, what's happening?"

Hawk took a deep breath.

"I just came up to tell you," he said, "The Cowboys are trailing. The Patriots got a turnover and two touchdowns in the third quarter."

"Shit," said Eagle, "What was it? Fumble? Interception?"

Hawk knew nothing about American football.

"Interception," he guessed.

"Godammit," grunted Eagle, his small eyes piercing even more sharply. "Yankee bastards."

"Indeed," said Hawk.

Another wave of nausea surged through him and he added, "Is it OK if I sit down?"

Eagle turned, an expression of mild surprise on his badly-assembled face.

"What's up? Not feeling so good?"

"Och, it's nothing. It'll … it'll pass."

"Good, good," said Eagle, turning back to the harbour.

Hawk remained standing, gathering his wits.

"By the way," Eagle went on, "while you're here, what's your handle on Sparrow?"

"Who?"

"Sparrow."

"Never heard of him."

"Phoned this morning. Total asshole. Didn't know the signs, his coding, nothing."

"Really?" said Hawk.

"Unbelievable," said Eagle. "You should check it out."

He went to his desk and pressed a button on his phone. His secretary answered.

"Mary honey, bring in the file on Sparrow, will you?"

"Right away," said the intercom.

"Weird bastard. I thought so from the start," went on Eagle, back at the window once more. "Shouldn't have given him a coding. Bad move. Did you meet him?"

"No," said Hawk, recovering all the time. "I don't touch them till they've hatched. Kestrel deals with eggs."

Eagle nodded.

"Yeah, well. We'll look it over while you're here. See if you can get an angle on him."

"Sure," said Hawk, starting as he saw the red light flash again. There was a knock at the door which brought fierce electric memories to him and prompted Eagle to shout "Yes." The door opened and his secretary came in carrying a buff file and wearing rubber gloves and wellington boots.

"Thanks. I appreciate it, Mary," said Eagle as the tall, bearded ex-petty officer handed over the file. Eagle tried to look and sound like a Deep South version of Robert de Niro but his deviant idiosyncrasies were against him. He was the only one in The Cage who didn't acknowledge that Mary was a man.

"While I'm here, sir…" said Mary.

"Yes?" said Eagle.

"Well, they got the contract."

"Who did? What contract?"

"The one in the Norwegian sector. They've commissioned a wellhead protector platform and they're going to lead a line from it to an FPSO."

"What the fuck are you talking about?" said Eagle.

"FPSO, sir. A Floating Production Storage and Offloading vessel."

Eagle looked at Hawk and pointed at Mary. "Have you any idea what she's on about?" he asked.

Hawk, being one of those who'd decided to make his career in management and therefore knew almost as little as Eagle, simply shrugged.

Mary scratched his dark beard.

"They pump the crude to the vessel, process it on board and store it until the shuttle tanker comes alongside," he said.

"So?" said Eagle.

"Well, sir, they're going to need new electro/hydraulic multiplex control distribution hardware—dynamic and steel tube static umbilicals, subsea control modules, sensors…"

"Well don't stand there talking about it. Arrange it, organise it, do whatever it is you do to fix it. I can't run this bloody mess if I have to do your job too."

"Of course not, sir. Sorry to have interrupted," said Mary.

As he saluted and went out, Hawk thought he was smiling.

"They expect you to baby them," said Eagle. "Learn from that,

Jim. Hands-off management. Encourages initiatives. People take responsibility. Lets me get on with running the show."

"Yes, sir," said Hawk.

He'd joined Benton Exporting, which was The Cage's official designation, thinking it would maybe give him the chance to travel. It had come as a surprise to him to find he was part of a sort of commercial double helix.

On the surface, its structures were those of any other company or organisation. There were two tiers of management controlling a workforce whose activities they barely understood. The financial director e-mailed their accounts from the Isle of Man, and there were tenuous links with oil-related outfits in and around Aberdeen and in Houston. But underneath that lay a murky, dangerous web of activities which he tried not to notice and which scared the shit out of him.

He'd quickly come to realise that Eagle and his management team were simply tolerated by the people who did the real graft. He suspected that the occasional nuggets of arcane terminology from Mary were designed to remind Eagle and the others where the real power lay. Hawk and the rest were there to give an aura of normality, if not quite respectability, to the firm. The continued use of code-names and pseudo-espionage procedures helped them to maintain the impression that they did indeed belong.

In truth, they didn't.

Eagle, still muttering about "that bastard Mary—she'll have to go" began to free the tapes which held the Sparrow file.

"Sit down, Jim," he said. "Get this."

Gratefully, Hawk obeyed the instruction and waited. Eagle looked closely at the sheets he'd taken from the folder.

"His name's Christopher Machin. Some sort of teacher. Seems he was a student at Aberdeen. In the nineties. Had a little sideline in cannabis to supplement his grant. And guess who his buddies were."

He waited. Hawk shrugged.

"The Belazzos."

Hawk whistled and nodded slowly. Eagle mirrored the movement. They faced each other, like two play-dogs on a parcel shelf.

The Belazzo brothers and their mob were The Cage's main rivals. Unlike Benton Exporting, they made no pretence at legitimacy. The family started out making ice cream in the city but, as appetites changed and people started earning the sort of money that let them progress to other substances, they expanded their product range. In a city where the wind blew in off the North Sea, there were obviously better things to trade in than Cornettos.

That's when they realised the real profits lay in companies which had the balls to go looking for oil and gas in the trickier high pressure, high temperature wells. The arrival of post-communism Russians on their patch and the continuing strength of The Cage were combining to question their supremacy in the field.

Eagle was still rustling the papers and reading.

"Seems this guy Machin worked in the student union or something. Had a little wacky baccy thing going with them. Finished up owing them. Now, seems they're calling in the markers. They've realised he's still around and want him back on the payroll. Lord knows why."

"What's our connection with him?" asked Hawk.

"He did a couple of jobs for Joey about a year ago. Small stuff. Joey needed somebody to speak some French. This guy teaches it."

"So he's on our payroll?"

"No," said Eagle. "But Joey gave him a code name, numbers, stuff like that. He craps his pants just thinking of the Belazzos. Ever since they put that guy through the plate glass window, then took him to the next window and did it again."

"But why are the Belazzos back on his case?"

"Who knows?"

"Maybe…" Hawk stopped.

"What?"

"Maybe it's because he's a teacher."

"What's that got to do with it?"

Hawk was recovering slowly and always grabbed any chance to impress.

"Well, plenty of the kids leaving school still think there's money sloshing about in the oil business. You still need the roughnecks at the sharp end."

"Cannon fodder, eh?" said Eagle, who tried to use what he saw as quaint British expressions every now and then to demonstrate his wit.

"Exactly," said Hawk. "Ready supply. Maybe this teacher could spread the word. Maybe that's what the Belazzos are after."

"Hey, you could be right," said Eagle, who was always

13

impressed by anything that sounded like thinking. "They sent him an email about a month ago, saying they'd be in touch. The guy went apeshit. Tried to contact us. Our guys told him to cool it. Now, though, it's getting serious."

"Why?" Hawk continued.

"Why what?" asked Eagle.

"Why's it getting serious?"

"Somebody blew up his garden. Worse than that, though, he's messing up the codes. Look at this."

He handed over one of the sheets. It was a transcript of Machin's abortive phone-calls. Hawk read it quickly and whistled.

"Bloody hell," he said.

"Right," said Eagle.

"But does it tie up?" asked Hawk. "I mean, has his garden been blown up?"

Eagle perked up. "That's an idea. We could find out. Kinda check out his story. Good thinking Hawk."

Hawk was pleased to have become Hawk again. He didn't like the chief's familiarity when he called him Jim, mainly because his name was Henry, but also because, given the chief's proclivities, familiarity might to be the overture to love.

Eagle was back at the window. It was Glen Campbell's turn on the tape with *Rhinestone Cowboy*. Several moments passed. Eagle suddenly asked, "Who'd know if his garden had been blown up?"

Hawk allowed the regulation gap to pretend he was thinking about the question and then said, "The police, maybe?"

Eagle thought for a bit.

"You could be right, Hawk. Check it out, will you?"

Hawk stood up, put down his untouched whiskey and turned to go, only to be stopped by Eagle's voice, which contained something almost like amiability.

"Hawk."

"Yes, Chief."

"I'm glad you came up. You've got a good brain. That's worth a lot to me."

"Thanks," said Hawk and, his nausea eased with pride at the praise, he walked to the door with the fluidity of a Pinocchio.

"Hawk, don't forget…"

But Eagle's warning was too late. Hawk had once more been thrown across the room by the fail-safe alarm.

CHAPTER TWO

The following day Machin was standing near his crater-garden. Policemen and gas engineers were still sifting through the heaps of rosebed, masonry, fence, letters, and bits of postman in an attempt to pinpoint the cause of the blast. Their methodical pursuit of the evidence which would confirm that the fault lay in a fractured gas-main irritated Machin. His house was all electric. Why didn't people see the simple things?

According to Machin, life consisted of appetites. OK, their satisfaction only postponed the onset of the next hunger but that was irrelevant; there was nothing he could do about it. That's how he'd got into the present mess in the first place.

Through the fears of the past few weeks he'd struggled to recall the circumstances of his involvement with the Belazzos. He remembered Tessa Lyall very clearly; she was tall, fair-haired, and had beautiful legs. She seemed to like thrills of all sorts, so Machin had pretended to be part of the drugs scene.

The significant change came about on the night he managed to persuade a drunken Tessa to leave the club and come up to his room. She groped her way up the staircase, said goodnight to a wall poster of Greta Garbo on the first landing, and eventually, when he'd steered her into his room and onto his bed, she was sick on his pillow. The smell of the bed-linen ensured the survival of Tessa's virginity for the rest of the term.

Somebody must have believed his drug-dealer fantasies, however, since, as if by magic, Tessa's place was filled, with little effort on his part, by a nurse from the Aberdeen Royal Infirmary.

Inge was foreign—Finnish he'd thought—and brought to the Aberdeen of the nineties a healthy sexual exoticism. She indulged his love of straight sex and there was never any need to invent excuses to get her into his room. When the appetite rose it was immediately satisfied. She obliged in cars, pub passageways,

15

parks, and once, with discretion, under the desk at an extra-mural lecture on Joseph Conrad.

Typically, he didn't question his luck, and when she began hinting that he might like to come on a trip to Europe with her and bring back some "presents" for some friends of hers, he jumped at the chance. He was never thinking any further ahead than the next orgasm, which Inge was always careful to ensure was urgently needed whenever she wanted to broach the subject.

His entanglement with the Belazzos' import-export business was gradual. He and Inge had made several trips to and from Amsterdam before he noticed that the bootleg cigarettes and booze they'd carried at first had been replaced by bulky packets of white powder. By then, of course, he was deep in debt to them.

Luckily for him, the gang at the Dutch end of the operation was busted without any repercussions for the Aberdeen connection, but he was left in no doubt that his future was heavily mortgaged and that, one day, they'd call in his markers. At the time, he didn't let it bother him. Inge's expertise made his present blissfully secure. He could ignore the claims of an uncertain future and give himself unreservedly to an undergraduate career of perpetual coition.

On graduation, with uncharacteristic foresight, he chose to become a teacher, reasoning that a member of that profession would be of no value whatsoever to criminals and of only minimal interest to society anyway. He settled dozily at the chalk face and so, when the Belazzos' email arrived, it came as a bit of a shock. His youthful scams were suddenly calling for paybacks at a time when shagging Inge was no longer available as a displacement activity.

He felt used, insecure, and utterly terrified of the world which he was being asked to re-enter. He knew that the only people who'd understand his problems were those at The Cage. When Joey had used him for the translating job, he'd been well paid and there'd been no risks. So, after sleepless nights and jumpy days spent locked in his dilemma, he'd eventually phoned Benton Exporting.

And now, here was the police force constructing and labelling little piles of debris and wilfully choosing to believe the explosion was caused by a leaky gas-pipe rather than the sinister and all-too-evident actions of some homicidal third generation Italians. One of the men came out of the house and saw Machin standing on the bloodstained path.

"Ah, there you are, Mr. Machin. I didn't realise you were back."

"No, I've just arrived."

"Right. Well, this was delivered by hand this morning."

Machin immediately felt the now habitual slide of apprehension as he took the envelope. On it was his name and initial. No stamps. No address.

"Who brought it?" he asked.

"Not the postman, certainly," said the policeman, with a little laugh.

"Who then?" insisted Machin.

"Oh, just an ordinary bloke really."

"Couldn't you describe him?"

"Not really. Didn't take much notice."

Machin was angry.

"What branch of the force are you in?" he asked.

"C.I.D.," said the man.

"I thought so," said Machin heavily.

He stamped into the house through the hole in the wall. The policeman shouted after him, "Make yourself a cup of tea, sir. You're distraught."

One of the sifting constables looked up at his colleague, a frown on his face.

"Distraught?" he said.

"Yeah. What's up with that?"

"You don't hear that on *CSI*."

"Fuck off."

Inside, Machin fumbled as he tore open the white envelope. It contained no message or letter, just a ticket. Machin was baffled, but he knew it was another push along the path he didn't want to take. There was no other explanation as to why he should be sent an expensive ticket for a front-row seat that same evening at the Aberdeen Conference and Exhibition Centre to watch the wrestling. This must be what they called a "meet".

His bafflement settled closer to abject fear; things were no longer theoretical. But he had no idea how to behave, what to expect. He'd have to get on to The Cage again. Surely they'd know the form, they could advise him. More important, they could

17

protect him and rescue him from this nightmare. He felt alone, vulnerable and not in the least reassured by the police presence he could see through the hole in his wall.

At first, in his self-absorption, he scarcely noticed the man in the green, service-issue combat jacket who was turning with difficulty onto his garden path. The man's progress was made painful by a heavily bandaged right foot and the fact that he could only use one arm for his crutch since the left arm was in a sling.

As he came up the path, a policeman who'd been levering at a piece of masonry suddenly succeeded in freeing it. It toppled from its insecure position and fell heavily against the side of the newcomer's right leg. From the way he fell and the scream he gave, it was obvious that it had at least torn the tendons of his right knee and probably dislocated the joint entirely. The hypodermic syringe he'd been carrying was knocked from his grasp and lay unnoticed, obscured by some earth in the part of the garden under the kitchen window which the police had sifted, sorted and finished with.

As the man fell, the white Mercedes 200SL which had been pulling up opposite the house, suddenly accelerated away.

Machin, momentarily shaken from his reverie by the accident, went out to see if he could help. But the man was unconscious and the policeman who had delivered Machin's wrestling ticket was already using his radio to call for an ambulance. He smiled at Machin, pointed at the dislocated cripple and said, "Not his day, is it?"

Machin, appalled, went back inside thinking to himself that Thomas Hardy didn't know the half of it. The relief afforded by this literary association was cut short by the sound of the telephone. Automatically, Machin picked up the receiver and gave his number. A toneless voice said, "Sparrow, from Eagle. Millet and Cuttlefish 0207-326-9590. Acknowledge."

"What?" said Machin, and then, "Oh, it's you. Thank God for that. Listen. I've just received…"

The voice cut him off.

"Acknowledge."

"No, wait a minute. Things are hotting up. There's…"

But once again the click indicated their lack of interest in anything he had to say. He swore and began pleading under his breath for someone who knew how to stop his helter-skelter thoughts. These enigmatic little contacts were all he had; he'd need to make the most of them. They wouldn't bother to ring him again, though. Not with the way he cocked it up every time.

He was getting cosily into his self-pity when the phone rang again. Fighting his combined panic and desperation, he picked up the receiver once more. Thank God. It was them.

"Sparrow, from Eagle. Millet and Cuttlefish 0207-326-9590. Acknowledge."

He wrote the message on the back of the envelope which he was still holding, noticing how the numbers were immediately smudged with his sweat. Despite the urge to plead once more for help, he forced himself to say, "Sparrow. Acknowledge." And any chance at a postscript was denied by the same loud click. The smudged message was before him, curt and enigmatic, but at least it was contact. Now he had to find out what the hell it meant.

****

The unfortunate man who'd just met with the bizarre accident at Machin's house had been taken by ambulance to Accident and Emergency. The doctors were surprised to see him readmitted and at once started worrying about being sued for whatever it was they'd done wrong for him to be back so soon. They diagnosed extensive damage to the cruciate ligaments of the right knee, and noted that the fall had caused his other wounds, to his right foot and left elbow, to reopen.

Later, on his afternoon rounds, the doctor who'd reset the knee and restitched the reopened wounds was concerned to find his patient more feverish than his condition, grave though it was, warranted. The man was babbling the drivel typical of delirium, his particular variation of it stressing the words "fledgling" and "armadillo." Having made all the usual checks on pulse, temperature, blood-pressure, reflexes and the rest, the doctor was still unable to account for the man's fever.

He stood at the bottom of the bed with the ward sister.

"Beats me," he said. "That analgesic should be bringing his temperature down."

"What analgesic?" asked the sister.

"The one I prescribed."

The sister shook her head, consulted the patient's notes and pointed to the medication she'd been administering to him. The doctor scanned it quickly and it was his turn to shake his head.

"This is for Mrs Drayson," he said.

"What, the pregnant diabetic?" said the nurse.

"Yes."

"Oh, she's in maternity. Her labour started this morning."

"But you've been injecting this stuff into him?"

The nurse nodded.

"We'll stop now, though," she said. "Give him analgesics if you like."

"I think that'd be better," said the doctor, relieved to have discovered the mistake.

It explained why the patient's condition had deteriorated so quickly and set the doctor's mind at rest as he set off for an afternoon of consultations with his private patients. He knew that the full effects of the mistake wouldn't be evident until the man regained consciousness, which wasn't very likely now. In any case, the error was less career-threatening than it might have been since, to judge from the accent in which his ravings were delivered, the man was a foreigner.

****

On the fourth floor of The Cage, Hawk and Kestrel were in conference in the lavatory. This was their habitual meeting-place since the strict Cage hierarchy always gave a slight edge to the occupant of any office in which meetings were held, and neither Hawk nor Kestrel was willing to accord higher rank to the other. As far as they knew, the choice of Eagle's successor, when the old man was eventually certified or rubbed out by the Belazzos, was down to the two of them and both were ambitious. The Cage may have been a criminal organisation but it took care to observe bureaucratic rules of precedence.

It also mirrored the managerial structures and practices of regular companies in its preference for arcane terminology. In ordinary commercial and industrial contexts, management-speak resonated with meaningless buzz-words and phrases. There was a proliferation of "win-win situations", people "walked the walk", "talked the talk", and sometimes did both at the same time. Line management at The Cage had its own avian variations on these eternal themes and mastery of them was a prerequisite of success.

Hawk was on the defensive because Kestrel had come in wearing wellington boots and rubber gloves. Either the grapevine had already spread the sad story of his own recent fracas with the fail-safe alarm, or Kestrel had been forewarned. If the latter was the case, the warning could only have come from Eagle, since Mary and the other men were notoriously taciturn. Which in turn implied that Kestrel enjoyed a precedence greater than Hawk's. Making a mental note to dress more effeminately, Hawk continued his gentle probing of Kestrel's current operations.

"And, apart from him, any more fledglings being fed?"

Kestrel knew Hawk's intentions and knew where the conversation was leading, but until it came to the crunch he was prepared to play along.

"Only two. One in Stonehaven, called Robin, and the other in Inverness, called Grebe."

"I thought we already had a Robin in Banchory."

"No. You're out of date. He flew."

Hawk couldn't remember for the moment what "flew" meant. Jargon was fine if it stuck to essentials, but it could be a bit too obscure at times. Kestrel saw the hesitation, realised its source, and took advantage.

"I suppose you've heard Shrike's droppings were addled?"

Hawk pretended surprise.

"Really?" he said.

Kestrel nodded, turning to hide the involuntary smile which the success of his invention prompted. Hawk noticed the turn. His mind raced. He said, "After-effect of plover turbulence, I suppose."

It was Kestrel's turn to doubt. He took refuge in a shrug that expressed nothing. Simultaneously both men tacitly agreed to come out of code. Hawk returned to the point.

"So Sparrow's been on his own in training?"

"Hasn't had any. I've had ringers in Stonehaven and Inverness working with Robin and Grebe. There's been no need to bring them here yet."

"So you've dealt with Sparrow yourself?"

Kestrel knew this was dangerous.

"No. You know bloody well, Hawk, he's not normal. Came to us by default."

"So what's the latest then?"

"I've sent him an M and C," said Kestrel.

Hawk had been long enough at The Cage to be at home with initials. M and C said one thing to him: "Millet and Cuttlefish."

"Isn't that giving a lot away to somebody you're not sure of?" he asked, sensing an opening.

"It's a Mark II M and C. We'll see how he reacts and take it from there.

Kestrel was covering his tracks; a Mark II M and C was one which conveyed information which was either completely false or, if a subsidiary coding technique were applied after the first decoding, completely true.

There was no point continuing the fencing. Nothing more would be known until they'd seen Sparrow's reaction to the M and C. Each man looked for a closing remark to enable him to leave feeling he'd won, but their efforts were wasted as the washroom door swung open and Eagle walked in with Mary.

****

Machin had been ordered by Kestrel during their brief session together to memorise the basics of the two decoding systems and immediately destroy any written reference to them. As he sat in his ruined kitchen finishing his lunch, he was glad he'd ignored the order. Without notes he would never have succeeded in translating the M and C into meaningful terms.

As it was, it had taken him over two hours of hard reading, complex cross-references and half a small exercise book to elicit the necessary information from the elliptical "Millet and Cuttlefish 0207-326-9590."

If his calculations were correct, it meant he had to be outside the main entrance of Marks and Spencer at three-thirty that afternoon. There he'd see a man carrying a copy of the abridged volume of Gibbon's *Decline and Fall* in the Book Club Associates edition.

He was to follow him, note the number of the third shop he entered after switching the book from his left to his right hand, subtract that from his own telephone number and remember the answer. The man would then catch a bus, the number of which was to be added to the total already arrived at.

22

When he eventually got off the bus, he would leave his book on the seat for Machin to retrieve. Inside the fly-leaf there'd be a number by which he should multiply the previous total. This would give him another number containing twenty-seven digits and, by a process of selecting every third digit, doubling it and dividing it into the two which had preceded it, he'd arrive at a series of page numbers. By turning to the pages thus indicated (in reverse order) he'd find words underlined which would together form a sentence.

He then had to apply the second of his decoding procedures to the sentence in order to discover the time, place and method of his contact with the personnel of The Cage.

He marvelled at the concision the code-makers had achieved. He knew he must follow the instructions to the letter or his only chance of receiving help would be lost.

He looked at his watch, jammed the exercise book into his inside pocket and hurried out past the big policeman whose face carried a broad grin because he'd just picked up a new piece of evidence: the postman's thumb.

At the same moment, two miles away in a hospital bed, a patient with a strange accent screamed "Armadillo!" and lapsed into a coma.

CHAPTER THREE

The woman had finished editing the photographs she'd taken outside Marks and Spencer the previous afternoon and was passing the time saving them into separate files as she waited for the call she was scheduled to receive at 1400. The room around her was muted, unadventurous. Over the years she'd cut herself off from everything, material things and emotions alike, to achieve the mental and physical flexibility she needed to stay safe.

The white car was her one luxury, a present from an American oilman. Her rejection of his demands had been so comprehensively ball-crushing that he gave her the car. He was terrified that, if he didn't, she'd broadcast a story that would severely undermine the machismo he worked at with such diligence.

Her musings were interrupted by her mobile's trill. She flicked it open, saw the words Big Snake and listened.

"Birdwatcher? What's happening?"

"Not much," she said.

"What about Sparrowhawk?"

"Up at A and E. In a coma."

"Cool. Well, maybe it oughta be made permanent."

"If that's what you want."

"Just as well. Could be untidy else."

"OK."

"Fine BW. Gotta go. Need to talk to Two-toes."

The woman lobbed the phone onto the bed and started thinking about the job she'd been given. The man in the hospital bed had to be eliminated.

****

By a nice coincidence, as the woman switched off her phone, Hawk and Kestrel met in the corridor outside Eagle's office.

"What's happening?" asked Hawk.

"Search me," replied Kestrel. "I just got a status one."

"Me too."

"OK, let's find out then."

They knocked simultaneously on the door, Kestrel grinning at the new rubber gloves which Hawk had bought at Boots. The door opened almost immediately and Eagle stood looking at them. There was a silence. At last he said, "Well?"

They looked at each other. It was Kestrel who took the initiative.

"We just got a status one."

Eagle frowned, but almost at once his features brightened. "Ah yes, that was me. Come in, come in."

They did so and waited as he made his way to the window. He looked out. Then, with his back still towards them, said, "Paul, this Sparrow thing. What about it?"

Neither of them knew to whom he was speaking because Hawk, whose name was Henry, he usually called Jim, and Kestrel's real name was Colin. With a quick flick of his head, Hawk indicated to Kestrel that he must be Paul. Kestrel took the plunge again.

"What exactly did you want to know about it?"

Eagle turned.

"Damn it, Paul," (Hawk had been right) "you've sent him an M and C haven't you? For this afternoon."

"That's right, sir. Three-thirty."

"Mmm. Who's going?"

"Pigeon, sir."

"Yes, I've been thinking. With this explosion and everything, I think we should maybe play it a bit tighter."

"In what way?"

"Well, make sure it stays in the nest."

Kestrel didn't really understand.

"Pigeon's OK. We can rely on him," he said.

"Yes, I know. But I'd like a first-hand report, and I can't have pigeons up here on the fifth floor."

"Well, who do you suggest?"

"You, Jim."

Hawk couldn't conceal a hot rush of surprise.

"But it's a straight messenger job."

"Maybe, maybe not, Jim. Either way, it's got to be one of us. He knows Paul, and I'm not going. I'd freeze my balls off out there. So that leaves you."

Hawk was visibly annoyed, the more so when he saw Kestrel's

25

smile.

"Well, I suppose if that's what you want."

"I do, Jim. But listen. It's only because I want it to be a good job. I know I can trust you."

Kestrel's smile waned and Hawk straightened. Eagle looked out of the window again.

"When you get back, come straight up here. I want to know everything about the drop, how he reacts, what he's wearing, everything."

The "what he's wearing" struck a discordant note and both Hawk and Kestrel wondered about the real nature of Eagle's interest. Their suspicion was dashed, however, when Eagle turned again, looked from one to the other, and said, "This whole business is getting a bit tricky. I had the chief superintendent on the line this morning. He thinks there's something going on. And Sparrow may be a part of it."

The chief superintendent in question, Donald McCoist, had been on The Cage's payroll since his days as a sergeant. He had a bank account on the Isle of Man and Eagle made sure the monthly deposit was always on time. He'd smoothed the way for them on many occasions and was worth every penny they paid him.

An unaccustomed gravity settled on the three men, which even the rubber gloves and wellingtons did nothing to lift. They looked from one to another and down at the carpet like television actors, then, hardly daring to break the spell, Eagle said softly, "So off you go, Jim. And get back as quick as you can."

"Aye, OK," said Hawk, and he and Kestrel turned purposefully towards the door as, from the computer, came the voice of Johnny Cash singing *A boy named Sue*.

****

Detective-Inspector Lodgedale was baffled. Not by the case; his devious mind could find clues even when there weren't any. In just a few hours he could turn the most innocuous traffic offence into a major civic disturbance. No, what puzzled him about the explosion at Machin's house was how the hell he was going to get any promotion mileage out of such an absurd event. The nearest gas main was on the other side of the street, the chance of a seismic or volcanic explanation was slim, and no self-respecting terrorist group would claim the credit for destroying twelve rose bushes and a relief postman. All he could do was invent a solution, file it away and forget it.

He hated unmemorable cases; his record of arrests and convictions proved it. There was the old woman he'd arrested for shoplifting and who got twelve years for manslaughter and arson. And the youth-club leader questioned after complaints from the parents about his activities in the changing rooms who finally confessed, under Lodgedale's incomprehensible but insistent interrogation, to seven murders in Sicily. But the inspector's own favourite was the case of the bigamist nun.

As Hawk and Machin were on their separate ways to Marks and Spencer, he was wandering morosely around the site of the explosion. He'd already planted packets of cannabis in the bedroom and some downstairs cupboards (a precaution he took in all his cases), and arranged for everything in the house to be fingerprinted, but he had no idea yet how he was going to turn the whole thing to his own advantage.

The house yielded nothing apart from a framed print of a sailing-ship which he thought would look nice on his own bedroom wall. As he carried it out to his car, the scene outside looked no more promising. Along the path was a series of black rubbish bags. Each was labelled, from the largest, which said "masonry" to the smallest, which said "postman", and Lodgedale knew the next part of his task was to examine the contents of each so that he could start creating clues.

One of Machin's neighbours had come out and was tidying up her garden, over which the blast had scattered assorted bits of garbage. Lodgedale looked at her. She was small, mousy, and comprehensively unattractive.

"Oi," he shouted. "Come over here."

The woman looked up.

"Hurry up," yelled Lodgedale.

She looked around, established with a gesture that she was the person he was shouting at, and came down her path and along the pavement to where he was putting the print into the boot of his car.

"Did you call me?" she asked, pushing her glasses higher on her nose.

"Yes. You live here, do you?"

"Yes. Mhairi McBean. Number 26."

"What d'you know about the chap who lives in number 22?"

The woman looked at the house.

"Nothing really. I keep myself to myself. I've hardly ever seen him."

"You must have seen him now and then."

"Well, yes. Once or twice, but I don't know him. I don't think I've ever spoken to him even."

Lodgedale slammed the boot and started rummaging through her pockets as he asked, "What sort of chap was he?"

The woman was flustered.

"I've just said, I don't know… What are you doing?"

Lodgedale had opened her housecoat and was looking for pockets in her dress. Her bewilderment changed to fear mixed with a certain excitement; no man had unfastened any article of her clothing for a very long time. Then, as she made to close the housecoat again, she dropped the dustpan she was carrying. Soil and pieces of plaster spilled out of it onto the pavement. Lodgedale looked at it.

"What's this?" he said.

"I was just clearing up my garden," she said. "That explosion spread stuff all over the place. The soil here's very poor and if you…"

"Shut up," snapped Lodgedale as he retrieved the dustpan and its contents. He called to one of his men. "Fraser, over here."

A constable came across. "Yes sir?" he said.

Lodgedale handed him the dustpan. "Bag this and take it and her down to the station."

"Yes sir," said the constable. "What's the charge?"

"Withholding information and concealing evidence."

The woman looked amazed, and folded her housecoat shyly around her as the constable reached for her arm. Lodgedale saw the gesture.

"And resisting arrest," he added.

The constable, glad to be away from the tedium of sieving Machin's garden, led the woman to a squad car. She sat close to him in the back seat and quite enjoyed the pressure of his left side as they were driven off to the station.

As Lodgedale watched the car disappear, the little satisfaction the arrest had caused had already begun to dissipate, and he was forced back to his musings on the crater and the row of black bags.

That evening, with the help of his wife, he would concoct some scheme to get the neighbour put away for a couple of years—he couldn't really hope for much more—but before then he had to decide in which direction he should push the enquiries surrounding the main event in order to manufacture a real case.

****

Amongst the shoppers outside Marks and Spencer at 3.28 the pressure was beginning to tell on Machin. He'd already seen four men with copies of Gibbon's *Decline and Fall*, but only one of them carried a single volume. Machin had bumped into him and knocked the book onto the pavement but it wasn't the edition he was looking for.

As he'd picked it up to give it back, he noticed that it did have underlinings on certain pages, but he presumed either that the man was a legitimate scholar specialising in Roman history or that Marks and Spencer's main entrance was a sort of cross-roads for clandestine oil-related activities. He handed the book back. The man stared hard at him and said, "Swallows rarely fly at sunrise."

"Really?" said Machin.

"Shit," said the man, before snatching the book back, tucking it carefully under his left arm and resuming his wanderings around the pavement.

Another man who'd been standing at the entrance when Machin arrived was looking at his watch more and more frequently and, at 3.32, began to shout, "Fulmars are migrating early." The shoppers changed course to steer well away from him, but he continued looking round at their faces and shouting his enigmatic information until a nondescript little woman carrying a bible approached him and said, "I'm a Jehovah's Witness, friend. Come with me."

The man gave one more desperate look around, recognised there was no other salvation available, threw the copy of *Stone Circles of the British Isles* he was carrying onto the pavement, shouted "Bugger Kestrel", and went off with his new-found friend.

Machin was so fascinated by the incident that he almost missed the tall individual with the receding gingery hair who hurried by the entrance carrying the Book Club Associates edition of the volume he was looking for. Hawk, for it was he, had approached the store just as the distracted man was shouting about fulmars. Hearing an unscheduled contact phrase being screamed to a crowd of Aberdonian shoppers, he'd panicked and increased his pace, caring little whether Sparrow had identified him or not.

But Machin had recognised the cover of the book and, with relief and gratitude, he ran after Hawk, pulled at his sleeve and said, "Excuse me, is that a Book Club Associates edition of Gibbon's *Decline and Fall?*"

Grossly embarrassed, Hawk muttered, "Yes it is," and strode on, while Machin, with something like a smile on his face, fell in step about a yard behind him.

It was a long time since Hawk had had any street work to do, and he couldn't believe things had changed so much since his day. The clinical observation which Eagle had required of him was difficult to achieve with Sparrow walking immediately behind him, literally shadowing him and whistling nervously and very loudly.

For Machin, the whistle was intended to indicate relaxed abandon, a signal to the other passers-by that he was just out for a gentle little stroll. His hyper-activated nerves prevented him noticing that in fact it had the reverse effect, so that almost everyone they passed looked at him and had all their suspicions about care in the community confirmed.

Hawk was sweating profusely and, wishing to terminate the exercise as quickly as possible, he shifted the book very theatrically from his left hand to his right, improvising as he did so, just loud enough for Machin to hear, a little musical phrase. He sang, "I'm moving the book from my left hand to my right."

Machin heard him and stopped whistling to sing very loudly, "So I notice", whereupon Hawk dived into a shop for relief.

When he came out again, he found Machin looking into the window and whistling at a volume that had attracted a small crowd around him wondering whether they should report him to someone. Hawk continued up the street, almost at a run, and Machin followed.

The increased pace had the advantage of rendering Machin too breathless to whistle, but the stares of those they passed or overtook were now focused on two men walking at Olympic pace, with one barely two yards behind the other. Hawk looked at the numbers of the shops as they flashed by. He was breathing heavily and needed another rest. He stopped at the next shop, gave Machin a furious stare as the latter cannoned into him, and strode inside. Three minutes later, he came out, carrying a tea-cosy which he'd been forced to buy. Machin was sitting on the pavement, still breathing heavily.

"Keep your distance, you idiot," hissed Hawk.

"I wouldn't touch you with a barge-pole," said a man who was coming out of the shop behind him. Hawk smiled at him, glared at Machin, and continued on what was becoming something of a nightmare. Machin set off again, determined to be more discreet. He caught up with Hawk and as he walked for a moment beside him, he muttered, "What does the tea-cosy mean? That wasn't in my instructions."

"Nothing, you fool. Ignore it," said Hawk, having to accelerate once more. He was grateful that the shop number he was looking for was near and, on reaching it, he stopped, turned very deliberately to look at Machin, hesitated in the doorway, pointed above his head, and walked in.

Machin looked up, saw the number and hurriedly took out his exercise book. He had already written his phone number on the top line and now, beneath it, he wrote the shop number and performed a rapid, neat subtraction which he continued to check and double-check while waiting for Hawk to reappear. When he did so, Machin looked up and said, "Hullo again. So far, so good, eh?"

Hawk had had enough. Careless of how many of Belazzo's boys might be in or near the tobacconist's from which he had just emerged, he thrust the book into Machin's hand and said, "Here, take this. I'm going to catch a number 37 bus."

He laid ultra-heavy stress on the "37" and, without waiting for a reply, he turned away and hailed a taxi.

Machin was rather alarmed at this departure from the suggested programme but at the same time grateful it was all over. He clutched his book and walked back the way they'd come. As he passed Marks and Spencer he ignored a small Chinese man who approached him and said, "Peregrine, at last. Where the hell have you been?" and continued to where he'd parked his car.

He didn't even open the book until he got back to his own house. It was well past five. The police had gone and the street was empty except for Mhairi McBean's husband, who was standing in the doorway of number 26, looking up and down the

31

street and then at his watch over and over again.

Machin went inside and made straight for the kitchen. He needed the stimulation of a cup of coffee before tackling the arithmetical and investigative tasks which still had to be performed. He felt sweaty and tired, and desperate just to sit down and collect himself.

As he took down the coffee jar, a slip of paper fluttered off the shelf with it, and his adrenal glands began pumping away once more. In the whirlwind of the afternoon's adventure he'd forgotten his date, if that's what it was, at the wrestling match. The ticket was inescapably there, the first bout was at half past seven, and he knew it would be perilous for him to stay away.

As he considered the prospect, however, he was surprised to discover that his apprehensiveness was somewhat muted. He felt an edge of excitement and anticipation.

He made and drank his coffee very quickly, put the book on his bedside table for attention later, showered and dressed and, at 6.15, was ready for action again. Before leaving the house, he dialed The Cage. When the female voice answered he said, "Eagle from Sparrow. I'm going to the wrestling tonight. Acknowledge."

The voice duly said, "Acknowledge" and, with a sense of achievement, Machin picked up his ticket and walked out of his house and down the street past the man at the front gate of number twenty-six who was shouting "Mhairi" into the evening. He climbed into his car, failing once again to notice the woman in the white Mercedes which had never been far from him in the past four weeks.

CHAPTER FOUR

The man in the hospital bed was crawling slowly up the slope of his coma towards mere unconsciousness. Dull-coloured mists fogged his mind, laced occasionally with a bright streak of pain from his foot, elbow, knee, or one of the many internal organs which had been irreparably damaged by the medication he'd received. Through the irradiated mist there would loom occasionally the grey face of his boss, slowly, intently, briefing him for a job. The big mouth formed the word "fledglings" and was still again before spitting out as if in a rage, "Armadillo."

These images were confusing and tended to provoke the flashes of pain, so it was like the application of a balm when the mists parted to reveal the oval face and high cheek bones of a beautiful woman. She smiled at him from a garden he knew so well, and on her lap her wee girl cuddled into her and looked at him with little chuckles in her eyes. How absurd that his work should force him away from them, that he should be so racked with pain when he could so easily be holding them in his arms.

But life was universally unfair. Even if he'd been back in Dundee with them, her husband would arrive home in the afternoon and he'd have to return to his own house, next door, and to the flat chest and bristly chin of his own wife, to her sexual demands, impossible to fulfil with her prominent hip bones lunging back at him like blunt breadknives.

Even in his unconsciousness, the vision of his wife's scrawny necessities clawing at him stimulated the reflexes of his trade. His fists clenched, his feet stabbed, his hands chopped invisible planks of wood and piles of bricks. One of the jabs hit the intravenous drip attached to his left arm and pulled it from its bottle. It hung unnoticed beside the bed as his blood began to seep down it onto the tiled floor of his room.

After having terminated the meet with Sparrow in such an unprofessional way, Hawk, as he cooled, realised his report to Eagle was going to leave a lot to be desired. Sparrow might well have been in touch with Kestrel, or vice-versa, and no time would have been lost in that quarter in laying before Eagle a dazzlingly lucid account of every facet of his inefficiency. He would have to tell the truth, and it was unlikely that Eagle would take it with much equanimity. To make it worse, the Cowboys had eventually been beaten by the Patriots 42-6.

As Machin set out to watch the wrestling, Hawk's interview with Eagle was still in progress. This in itself was remarkable since it was past six and Eagle rarely stayed at The Cage beyond four. For someone running an ethically challenged service operation, he kept strangely conventional hours. Even more remarkably, the interview had gone splendidly and Hawk felt confident that he'd eased well ahead of Kestrel in the pecking order.

Not that Eagle was pleased with the details of the encounter with the fledgling, but his displeasure was completely offset by the effect of a touch of inspiration from Hawk, who'd decided, before returning to The Cage, to go home and change.

The outfit he was wearing, which he'd bought specifically for this purpose but which hitherto he hadn't dared to wear, was a source of ineffable delight for Eagle. The cream silk trousers were tucked into high boots of light tan suede fringed with small gold chains. A kingfisher blue smock was gathered loosely at the waist and held by a broad tan belt with the Waffen SS insignia for a buckle, while the cream chiffon scarf at Hawk's throat moved with a crisp whisper every time he shifted his position in the leather chair which Eagle had brought out for him.

Eagle had been kneeling eagerly on the floor at the foot of Hawk's chair for some time without speaking a word. Hawk was used to his boss's silences but not to the close scrutiny to which he was now being subjected. He began to feel more and more embarrassed.

"Well, what do you think, boss?" he asked at last.

Eagle's small eyes flashed from their fleshy little caverns. "Delightful, my dear, absolutely delightful."

"No. I mean Sparrow."

"Oh, Kestrel can take care of him."

"But you did say he might be mixed up with the Belazzos. Isn't that a bit too important to leave to somebody like Kestrel?"

As he said this, Hawk knew it was an important pawn to be playing so he accompanied the question with a gesture which made his loose shirt billow at the armpit and send a cloud of heavy musk deodorant towards the kneeling Eagle. Eagle's breathing quickened momentarily.

"Maybe you're right. Maybe you should deal with it yourself. You'd like that, wouldn't you? To be in total command. To do whatever you like, give orders, walk all over people. Literally. Yes, literally. And beat them, and grind their grovelling guilty faces into the mire. The loathsome mire which is their element as they wallow grotesquely..."

Eagle was by now prostrate on the carpet and Hawk, who had at first experienced a gush of power as his boss had eased his neck under the suede boot, suddenly sat upright as the red light over the door flashed.

"Boss, the lights. There's somebody outside," he gabbled.

"I don't care. I don't care," moaned Eagle from the carpet. "Faecal matter, that's all I am. And I deserve whatever you're gonna do to me."

Hawk was near to panic. He leapt to his feet and stumbled over to the door, not yet used to the heels on his boots.

"Just a moment," he shouted.

Eagle, abandoned by Hawk, was sobbing and clutching at the recently vacated chair, sniffing for traces of after-shave.

Hawk called to him, "Boss... Eagle... There's someone outside."

There was only a half-response from the wretched Eagle. Then Hawk's desperation inspired him to say, "It may be about the New England Patriots."

The effect was instantaneous. The words "New England" reminded Eagle that there were, after all, people to whom he would never be inferior, and the thought that some damn pisspot Yankee liberal was about to enter his room restored his old intolerable self once more. Seeing the transformation, Hawk muttered, "Actually, I'm not sure who it is," and at once opened the door.

Immediately, Mary entered, his gloves and boots superfluous since the aggressor function of the fail-safe alarm had been disconnected. Eagle, on seeing him, stood up and turned towards the window. Mary's years of naval training proved invaluable as he took in the scene and reconstructed, from personal experience, what must have been happening just before his arrival. He simply smiled, saluted and put a piece of paper on the desk.

"Thought you should see this," he said. "Phone message from Sparrow. Just received it."

Eagle turned angrily.

"Why in God's name bother me with that stuff?" he yelled.

Mary didn't flinch. "You said, since the chief inspector's phone call, you wanted to see everything that came in relating to Sparrow."

Eagle was unmoved.

"I know that. I know that," he shouted. "It still seems to me you're getting a bit above yourself, Mary. Making too many assumptions. You're not indispensable, you know."

Mary smiled, remembering the letters Eagle had sent him and how much they'd be worth to the *News of the World*.

"Sorry", he said before turning away and strolling out. As he passed Hawk, he pursed his lips at him in a mock kiss and, with another smile, muttered "Bitch."

The spell had been sufficiently dissipated for Eagle to go to the trouble of picking up the message Mary had left. He read it, turned towards the window and said in amazement, "Goddam, what d'you make of that, Hawk?"

Hawk was glad of the respite from Eagle's fetish.

"What?" he said quietly.

"The message. From Sparrow. Weird or what?"

Hawk apologised. "Er ... I haven't actually seen it."

Eagle, without turning, held his arm out behind him, offering the piece of paper. Hawk took it and read, "Eagle, from Sparrow. I'm going to the wrestling tonight."

"What's it mean?" he asked.

"God knows," said Eagle.

"It's not ... er ... it's not one of our back-up codes, is it?" asked Hawk.

"Don't think so," muttered Eagle, and then he continued, "You know, Hawk, this Sparrow's getting to be a bit too devious.

Wonder where this wrestling is."

"We could try the evening paper," suggested Hawk, realising too late that he could be landing himself with another assignment.

"Good idea," said Eagle. "Find out where it is and go along. See what the hell he's getting up to. You know what he looks like, don't you?"

"Yes," admitted Hawk with some reluctance. "But I'm not exactly dressed for wrestling, am I?"

And again, as he heard himself forming the words, Hawk's regret at his indiscretion was too late to save him. Eagle turned round, his hormones stampeded by the sudden memory of Hawk's ensemble. His breath caught in his throat as the SS buckle stared at him from beneath the little fold of flesh it was creating in Hawk's stomach.

"On the contrary, my dear. On the contrary," breathed Eagle, his demeanour altered once more. "And you know what? We'll go together. Let me take you. Please."

Hawk knew that refusal would only ensure they remained in the office while Eagle swooned under the infinitely delicate caresses of what he imagined to be Hawk's disdain. The prospect of an evening at a wrestling match dressed as he was and accompanied by a fawning Eagle was horrific, but still preferable to an evening as the Queen of Sheba.

He said, "Perhaps that would be best."

Eagle took his arm in a savage grip.

"Come along then, Helen. You don't mind if I call you Helen, do you?"

Hawk, being propelled out of the office, could only shrug his acceptance of what he was afraid were going to be many unacceptables that evening. Eagle smiled, put his arm round Hawk's waist, and said, "Good. You can call me Donna."

****

After dinner, Lodgedale fetched the black rubbish bag from the hall where he'd left it and began taking things from it and arranging them on the coffee table. There were bits of bone, some with flesh or tendons still adhering to them, shreds of uniform, some letters more or less intact, and a few very recognisable anatomical fragments. His wife Ella was just bringing two cups of coffee through from the kitchen as he laid the last of the items on the table.

"Where am I supposed to put this coffee, then?" she asked.

Lodgedale said with a leer, "Don't tempt me," and she chuckled and laid the two cups on the carpet beside the table. She looked at the gruesome collection spread before her husband.

"I've told you before, Arthur," she said, "you shouldn't bring work home with you. You ought to relax more."

"No. I've got to think about this one, Ella," he said. "It's a bit of a puzzle."

"What is it, anyway?" she asked, vaguely indicating the mess on the table.

"You mean who is it," Lodgedale quipped. "Some of the evidence we found today. There's bags of stuff lying about there. I could only manage this one. It's the postman."

"Well endowed, wasn't he?" said Ella slyly.

At first, Lodgedale pretended not to understand, but a nod of her head and a deliberately directed glance showed him what had prompted her remark.

"That's a part of his intestine," he said reprovingly, and added, "I think."

(Ella had her doubts and the interest the object had quickened in her was sustained through the evening by more surreptitious glances. For a change, when they eventually did go to bed, Lodgedale's regular sexual requirement was actually pleasurable for her too.)

"No, the problem is," Lodgedale went on, almost to himself, "none of this makes sense. I mean, the house, that street, the bloke Machin who lives there—they're all too ordinary to rate any sort of explosion. I should think it's a major disaster if they have a power cut."

His wife gave a little smile.

"You'll think of something, Arthur. You always do."

"Yes, I know," said Lodgedale, "but it's got to be reasonable. I mean, bigamist nuns are all right when you're just starting out, making a name for yourself, but the force has got its image to think of. The public are used to crime nowadays. They expect it to make sense. I've got to make this one good."

"You will, Arthur," said Ella.

She sat on the sofa beside him.

"Can I help?" she asked.

Lodgedale was still surveying the evidence.

"Not sure yet," he said. Then, remembering, added, "Oh well, there's one thing, just for a start."

"What's that, love?"

"I had one of the neighbours arrested today. No real evidence. Bit of a flimsy case. Trouble is, she's totally innocent. D'you think you could get one of your book club lot to identify her as one of that mob who did the Sainsbury's cashier?"

"I didn't know there were any women in the gang," said his wife.

"There weren't," he said. "But I can't just let her go, can I?"

His wife gave him a grin and a nudge and said, "You know, you're a bit of a genius on the quiet, Arthur."

"I know," he said seriously. He smiled at her, but his gaze quickly moved back to the coffee table as he added thoughtfully, "I'm going to have to be to sort this lot out."

His eyes moved from item to item, looking for the inspiration, the slightly incongruous detail from which he would construct his case. He leaned forward, his mind lumbering, his coffee forgotten, and a thumbnail flicking reflectively against his lower lip.

It was as he became aware of this latter experience and realised the thumbnail belonged to the postman's thumb which he'd picked up, that the first idea, and one which should have been obvious, occurred to him. He would get the fingerprints of the dead postman and somehow implicate him in the affair.

Perhaps indeed it had been a secret intuition below the level of his awareness which had prompted him to choose to bring home that particular bag. (Although the subliminal truth was that he suspected the sort of effect that the piece of intestine might have on his wife and welcomed anything nowadays that lifted the nightly sex above the humdrum.)

Whatever the motives, hidden or subconscious, the embryonic case was forming. The postman, an innocent trigger of the whole affair, no longer able to defend himself, would soon be as inextricably entangled in the spirit of the case as he was in its body.

The study of the coffee table became more purposeful. From the rags of body and function rose the presence of the postman; not the actual presence he'd projected in life, but a new sinister

39

presence which had somehow used the post office, the nondescript residents of Machin's street, and an innocuous clump of roses to strike at the moral fibre of British society.

After all, postmen were notorious for the things they brought into one's life. News of undreamed-of events, bereavements, disasters, all manner of catastrophic information came tumbling into a placid breakfast scene thanks to these infiltrators of privacy. And how many of the bombshells they dropped through your letter box, he continued with an inward smile at the pinpoint relevance of the metaphor he had chosen, were unsolicited?

The justness of his imaginings was suddenly so glaring that he wondered why he'd only just thought of it. His case was made. The postman was guilty. And, with a little chuckle of delight that surprised his wife who was looking once more at the piece of intestine, Lodgedale seized on the keystone of his evidence; the corner of an envelope, unharmed by the blast. It no longer carried an address or any letter, but there, blatantly, was the mark which convinced Lodgedale he was right. It had been posted in Dundee.

CHAPTER FIVE

On his way to the Exhibition and Conference Centre, mildly inebriated by what appeared to be a developing taste for clandestine activities, Machin had tried to anticipate how the "meet", if that's what it was, would take place. He knew there'd be lots of noise and a considerable crowd, both guarantees of cover for any surreptitious communications.

On the other hand, although he wasn't certain what sort of people went to watch wrestling bouts, he felt uneasily that they would all be of a particular type and he, and presumably his contact, might be all too identifiable as different.

He made his way to his seat trying, unsuccessfully, to imagine that the waspish or ballooning women who seemed to predominate in the front rows were part of the Belazzo set-up. As he sat down, he noticed, and assumed it was significant, that the seats on each side of his own were vacant. The rest of the places in the front rows were filled and as the wrestlers in the first bout climbed into the ring, the absence of immediate neighbours made Machin feel rather vulnerable.

He supposed his contacts would come in once the fighting was under way and, using darkness as a cover, convey to him whatever was to be conveyed. But if that was the case, why pick a seat which was glaringly illuminated by the lights over the ring?

And a second perplexing question occurred to him. Why two seats, one on either side? He imagined finding himself flanked suddenly by a pair of goons built like prop forwards and being lifted helplessly up the aisle and out to a waiting Alfa Romeo, or alternatively being skewered by a pair of stiletti and left there so that at the end of the evening the caretaker would find a wrestling fan firmly and literally transfixed into a state of perpetual ringside attentiveness.

By the end of the first bout the questions were still

41

unanswered. Machin had seen little of the wrestling since his attention had naturally been tuned to the vacant seats, but apparently the small man now pulling on the seaweed-trimmed cape with "Charlie Neptune" embroidered on the back had butted his opponent, Jimmy "The Ferret" Casey, so effectively that the latter had submitted twice when trapped in some sort of nose hold.

The women all around the ring were screaming abuse at Charlie whose response was simply to clutch both hands to the genital lump in his trunks and make to lunge the parcel at them. Thereupon, the screams redoubled, some sets of underwear became slightly soiled, and the process of simulated hatred spiralled. "The Ferret" was helped solicitously up the aisle by his seconds to sympathetic cries of "Never mind, Ferret, you'll get the bastard next time." And altogether the evening seemed to have got off to a good start.

The contestants had disappeared and relative calm had returned to the hall. Machin still looked, although less nervously, for the people who had reserved the three seats of which his was the middle one.

The crowd turned its attention expectantly to the top of the aisle down which the next fighters would come. As they did so the curtain obscuring the entrance was flung back, a spotlight operated by a startled electrician swivelled to illuminate it, and there, in solitary splendour, was Hawk.

Machin, as impressed as all the other spectators at first by the daring incongruity of the kingfisher shirt and cream silk trousers, felt his heart rate increase as he recognised the man he had followed that very afternoon. Surely this couldn't be his contact. Why arrange this when they could have done whatever it was in the throng outside Marks and Spencer?

And anyway, did operatives about to make a "meet" dress in so outlandish a fashion and enter a crowded hall with a spotlight trained on them? Machin decided it was all some kind of double-take and his senses were extra sharp as he watched Hawk duck back out through the curtain again to the disappointed "Oooohs" of the crowd.

***

It had, of course, been a mistake. Hawk had needed all his tact

42

and training in the taxi on the way to the Conference Centre to keep Eagle at bay. When they'd arrived, Eagle, free of the confines of the cab, had no longer felt the need or ability to suppress his exuberance. He'd clutched Hawk's arm, and hustled him past the main entrance until they came to an alleyway which disappeared darkly up the side of the structure. Hawk's protests were ignored as Eagle pushed him up into the darkness, panting more heavily.

"But what about Sparrow?" pleaded Hawk.

"To hell with Sparrow," was the hoarse reply.

"But boss ... Eagle ... Donna."

The progressive exclamations followed the course of Eagle's attempted caresses until Hawk, appalled at what he guessed the next development would be, shouted, "Stop that, you filthy swine! You're just a vile degenerate."

Eagle gave a whoop of delight and slumped into the gutter with a triumphant scream of "Way to go. Aaaaw-right!"

Hawk took his chance to duck into an open door. He heard Eagle coming after him and rushed down a passage. And it was precisely that passage which led him to his brief but very dramatic appearance in the spotlight.

As he ducked back from the glare he expected to be clutched by his boss, and was relieved to see the latter's attentions had momentarily been diverted elsewhere. One of the contestants for the next bout had come out of a dressing-room just in front of the slavering Eagle and, given the latter's degree of arousal, the apparition was almost too much for his overloading system.

The wrestler was black and wore the flimsiest pair of satin trunks in which bulged everything that Eagle had ever dreamed of. The man looked mean and cruel and on the flame-coloured wrap clinging to his massive shoulders was the legend "Bad Boy Jackson."

Eagle tottered weakly against the wall as the man walked on up the passage, past the embarrassed Hawk and out into the hall to an immediate barrage of jeers. Hawk went back to Eagle.

"Are you all right, boss?"

Eagle looked at him, his eyes failing to focus or stay on one spot as they looked into the air around him for the vision of Eden he had just been granted.

"What? Yeah, yeah, of course... Fine." Then, with a clutch at Hawk's by now superfluous shirt, he whispered, "Did you see that?"

"You mean the wrestler?" said Hawk, still embarrassed.

"He was a god," said Eagle.

"Yes. Perhaps," said Hawk, and then, to try to bring the evening back within its intended bounds, he added, "Shall we go in and watch him wrestle?"

Eagle couldn't believe such ecstasy was possible and looked at Hawk, his whole face a childish question. Hawk answered the unspoken request.

"Yes. He's next on the bill. Come on. We'll go in."

As they moved slowly towards the hall Eagle whispered feebly, "Hawk."

"Yes?" said Hawk.

"Be gentle with me."

And Hawk, with a smile, was gentle with him as they made their way to their seats.

****

In the front row, Machin was still trying to see a justification for Hawk's earlier appearance. He hardly noticed the whistles and the cries of "Black bastard" which greeted Bad Boy Jackson's arrival, and was only made aware of the entrance of his opponent Eric the Emancipator by the distinctly sexual tone and content that entered the cries of the ringside women. Eric was big and blonde and altogether represented the archetypal Aryan liberator from the satanically unnameable that inhabited Bad Boy's dark body and darker soul.

Machin searched for Hawk, but without success. As the lights in the auditorium dimmed out again he felt his vulnerability return. The seats were still empty, and now, somewhere in the dark behind him, lurking in the depths of the lapping sexuality of the crowd's responses, was a definite contact—dressed, it was true, like a drag-artist, but all the more dangerous for such a cavalier disregard of all the rules.

The wrestlers lunged and grunted, butted one another in the face, unleashed kicks to the groin and pokes in the eye which should have finished the fight instantly, but which, strangely, merely resulted in equivalent grunts, momentary staggers, and miraculous recoveries. Their histrionics could not, however, hold

Machin's attention. He knew himself to be involved in a more serious game.

And then, suddenly, the two worlds coincided.

Machin's eyes were on the fighters as Eric began picking Bad Boy up and slamming him spine first into the canvas. Each slam was accompanied by the imagined sound of newly-splintering vertebra and a groan from Bad Boy, which in turn provoked orgasms of delight—some of them literal—from Eric's fan club.

At the ninth or tenth slam, Eric changed his tactic, picked Bad Boy up once more and began to spin with the black man across his shoulders. After a few spins he released his opponent, helping him on his way with an extra shove. Bad Boy fell across the top rope, tumbled out onto the edge of the canvas, and ricocheted from there straight into the front row of seats and almost onto Machin's lap.

Machin was terrified. He was sure Bad Boy must have broken his back on the edge of the ring. He leaned forward to help him up and was astonished when Bad Boy said, "Next Tuesday, at noon. Be hitch-hiking on the Alford road. Near the turn-off to the crematorium. Don't accept a lift unless the driver says 'Armadillo'. Got it?"

Machin was unable to speak, and indeed Bad Boy had conveyed his information just in time because, almost at once, over Machin's shoulder came a handbag which began flailing at his head as its owner climaxed to her own cries of "Filthy bastard!"

Bad Boy climbed feebly back into the ring and at once gave Eric seventeen forearm smashes which gradually knocked him out.

Machin's numbed state of disbelief prevented him reacting in any positive way to the victory, or to the spectacle of the square-headed man with the Brillo pad hair who subsequently leapt into the ring, fell at Bad Boy's feet and began shouting, "My God, you were wonderful. Like something from the Divine Marquis."

And his feeling of alienation became total when he saw his contact of that afternoon at the ringside pleading with the fawning man, "Please, let's go now, boss. There's nothing more we can do here. Please, Donna. Please."

****

At the hospital, the next morning, the receptionist watched the tall but stooped old lady come through the big glass doors and stand for several minutes looking around her with the archetypal bewilderment of the aged. The receptionist called to her, offering assistance. The old lady turned towards the direction from which the voice had come, and the receptionist waved a hand, then an arm, then both arms to help the visitor to home in on the reception desk. The old lady smiled, waved back, and made her inelegant way across the lobby.

"Hullo, my dear," she said when she eventually arrived. "I wonder if you could help me. I'm looking for my nephew."

"Of course," said the woman. "Which ward is he in?"

The old lady, most of whose features were hidden behind a handkerchief she was holding to her nose, conveyed some anxiety through those that were still visible. "Oh dear, that's the trouble. I don't really know. You see, he had an accident yesterday and they just brought him in."

The young woman smiled reassurance.

"That's all right. He'll have been in A and E. If you'll just tell me his name and what sort of accident he was involved in…"

There was an almost imperceptible hesitation before the old lady answered.

"Christopher Machin. And he had rather a nasty fall. A lump of concrete fell on his leg actually."

The girl wrote down the name and said, "If you'll just wait a moment, I'll find out where he is for you."

The old lady smiled and turned away, still dabbing at her nose as the receptionist picked up the phone and dialed. As she waited for an answer she looked at the old lady's back and was suddenly aware of an incongruous lack of wrinkles on her neck. She had no time to pursue the thought however since the receptionist in A and E answered her call.

"Hullo, Doris," she said, "I've just got a relative of Mr Christopher Machin with me. He was admitted yesterday. Can you tell me which ward you've put him in?"

She listened to the reply and her face registered slight surprise. She asked Doris to hang on and spoke again to the old lady.

"Excuse me, you did say yesterday, didn't you?"

"Yes," said the old lady, and the girl explained to Doris that the patient had been admitted the previous day. She went on to describe the nature of his injury and Doris's reply this time caused

46

her even greater surprise. Once again Doris had to hang on while the receptionist consulted her visitor.

"Er ... excuse me, but was your nephew in the day before that with a lacerated left elbow and gunshot wounds in his right foot?"

The old lady smiled brightly and said, "Yes, that's him. Careless little devil."

The smile which the receptionist returned was a little weak and she took refuge in the telephone and Doris once more. Eventually she replaced the receiver and said, "I'm sorry, but it's all a bit strange. You see, the first time he was admitted he told us his name was Campbell."

"He's always playing practical jokes," said the old lady.

"Yes," said the receptionist. "Doris said he certainly didn't sound like a Campbell with an accent like his."

The old lady gave a little blast of laughter.

"Oh no," she pealed, "he hasn't been doing his accents to you, has he? He's incorrigible. I'll chastise him thoroughly when I see him. Er... Where can I find him then?"

The receptionist gave her the necessary directions and watched her make her apologetic way past patients and visitors as she negotiated the main hallway. She went up to the third floor and along a corridor which was flanked by rooms each containing one bed.

She squinted at the numbers on the doors of these rooms and, after two false entrances, one of which occasioned profuse apologies to the patient and the female visitor whose head was under his blankets, she found the door she was looking for and went in.

The delirious patient was very pale since the effect of his karate chop on his drip-feed hadn't been discovered until the arrival of the night shift. He'd been swiftly reconnected and the overflow from his cardiovascular system had been mopped up, but the doctors' tests had revealed that the combined effects of trauma and blood loss had caused irreparable brain damage.

His mind no longer contained thoughts of fledglings or armadillos, and he would never again be in a condition to cherish, or even identify, the oval face with the high cheekbones which his neighbour was kissing at that very moment in the garden in Dundee.

Unfortunately for him, his visitor knew none of these things.

Once inside the room she moved quickly, taking from her handbag a tiny hypodermic syringe. She carefully peeled back a corner of the dressing on his left elbow which lay outside the blankets. Then she used the syringe to inject into his bloodstream, via one of the minute punctures caused by the stitching of his wounds, a substance which almost instantaneously induced a fatal coronary thrombosis.

The final spasms were still twitching the body as she replaced the dressing with the care she had used to remove it. After a last look around, she went out of the room and back along the corridor.

When she found a door with the little black silhouette indicating "Ladies" she went in and was never seen again. In her place there emerged the tall elegant woman with fair hair. She moved softly along the corridors until she found an emergency staircase which led her out to the car park, where the Mercedes waited to take her away.

****

While this was going on Machin was still asleep. The marathon decoding session and the evening at the wrestling had combined with the previous day's explosion and the jog around the city centre with Hawk to drain him entirely. He slept long and dreamlessly well into the following morning.

He didn't hear a sound from the figure who'd been creeping round his garden in the small hours, looking silently for an easy entry. In fact, the only real noise the figure made came as he was crawling on hands and knees under the kitchen window.

He suddenly gave a small yelp which was instantly succeeded by an intake of breath, then his lifeless body slumped down onto the earth with a sound not much louder than that of a brief crumpling of clothes.

There was considerably more noise when two constables arrived to take the occupant of number 26 into custody for causing a breach of the peace. His calls for his wife had gone on rather too long and too late for the liking of Mrs Simpson in number 28 and she'd rung the police. The occupants of the nearest patrol car had been having a quiet night so they rushed delightedly over and provoked the man into a full-scale fight with them which Mrs Simpson watched until they took him away to be charged.

As he ate his late breakfast, Machin was unaware of these fresh pebbles in the pond of the previously placid street. He was looking, with the new excitement that his refreshed mental state allowed, at the book which contained the details of his next appointment with an inmate of The Cage.

He had completed the required arithmetic and was about to start assembling the word sequence when the door-bell rang. He left the book and his pencil beside his plate of cereal and went through the hall. He opened the door and saw a large raincoat surmounted by a terrifying smile. Its owner said, "Good morning, sir. Detective Inspector Lodgedale, C.I.D. Might I have a word?"

Machin looked at the brief flash of identification card and back at Lodgedale's evil features.

"Well, I was just having breakfast actually," he said.

Lodgedale tutted.

"Bit late for that, isn't it? I had mine ages ago."

"Nevertheless, that's what I'm doing, so if you wouldn't mind…"

But Lodgedale was already past him and on his way through to the kitchen. Machin, angry, followed him.

"Look, I'm trying to tell you, it's not convenient at the moment."

Lodgedale helped himself to some toast and began to butter it.

"It is for me, sir. Just a few questions, that's all. It won't take long."

He sat at the table and took a bite of toast. Machin accepted the inevitable and made to sit down with him. A gesture from the policeman froze him.

"Er, just before you start making yourself comfortable, I'll have a cup of coffee. This bread's a bit dry."

"Why don't you just move in here?" asked Machin.

Lodgedale looked around the kitchen and back at Machin, wrinkling his nose.

"Not civilised enough for my tastes," he said, and Machin inwardly acknowledged that the rapier of his wit would never penetrate a skin over which a steamroller of mockery could drive without leaving a blemish. Gracelessly he scooped instant coffee into a mug and switched the kettle on.

"How many sugars?" he asked.

"Seven," replied Lodgedale.

Machin turned to see if this was a joke, but Lodgedale was flicking through the pages of *Decline and Fall*. He looked up and caught Machin's glance.

"Read a lot of dirty books, do you?" he asked.

"What do you mean?" said Machin.

Lodgedale indicated the volume he was holding.

"This," he said, "Roman Empire. All perverts, weren't they? Orgies and that. I've seen them on the telly."

Machin poured water onto the pile of sugar in Lodgedale's cup. He carried it to the table and placed it in front of the policeman.

"Is it all right for me to get on with my breakfast?" he asked.

Lodgedale waved him magnanimously into his seat. Machin sat and picked up his spoon. As he scooped up some cornflakes he said, "What exactly are you here for?"

Lodgedale leaned forward and with a sudden movement flashed his hand from his coat pocket and thumped it onto the table, releasing from its grasp as he did so the postman's thumb.

"This," he said, staring hard at Machin.

Machin looked at the object. The end nearest to him was the jagged base of the thumb from which bone and tendons protruded. It looked like a small, bald, disembowelled mouse wearing a flat, pink crash helmet.

The colour drained from his face as he put his untouched cereal back into the plate. Lodgedale noticed his reaction and immediately deduced guilt. He settled back, confident of success, and took a sip of coffee, which immediately provoked a grimace.

"Ugh!" he said, "Not enough sugar."

"It's not been stirred," stammered Machin, fighting back nausea.

Lodgedale looked for a spoon, saw none, and picked up the thumb instead. As he dipped it into his cup and began to stir, Machin leapt up from the table and just got to the sink before the cereal he had eaten in the tranquillity before Lodgedale's arrival fought its way up his throat and back out into the world. After further, less productive retching, he wiped his mouth and turned to look once more at the smiling monster that had invaded his kitchen.

"Look, what the hell do you want?" he said weakly.

"Like I said," replied Lodgedale, sucking coffee off the thumb, "just a few questions."

"Well ask them, for God's sake," said Machin, desperate to be rid of him.

"Let's start with your postman then," said Lodgedale. "D'you know him?"

"Not really," said Machin, "I mean, I see him now and then, when he delivers parcels and things, but that's all."

"So you don't know much about his private life then?"

"Of course not. Why?"

"I'll ask the questions," said Lodgedale, and it was a threat.

"No idea where he lives or anything?" he continued.

"No," said Machin. "Why don't you ask him yourself?"

"Don't get funny with me," snapped Lodgedale, thumping his hand on the table.

"I'm not. Honestly," said. Machin.

"Oh no? Well, what sort of answers d'you think I'm going to get from a thumb, a few bones and bits of spleen, eh?"

"No, no. That's not him," said Machin, indicating the thumb.

"What d'you mean?" asked Lodgedale.

"Well, he was only a relief postman. The usual one's on holiday. Inverness, I think. He told Mrs Simpson about it. She mentioned it last week."

Lodgedale's features were horrifying as they struggled to maintain the hostile suspicion that was being directed at Machin and simultaneously conceal the delight at this new complication which would add such complexity to his case.

He probed on, wearing down all Machin's resentment of his unwelcome presence by combinations of totally unrelated questions, barely veiled threats and absurd juxtapositions which would have convinced a professor of philosophy that logic was an illusion.

After only twenty minutes he'd learned a variety of facts about all Machin's neighbours and the two postmen and was just about to concentrate, via the previously concealed cannabis, on Machin's involvement in the world of hard drugs, when his perambulations stopped by the window.

Outside in the garden he thought he saw a familiar piece of material. He opened the window and leaned out, only to bring his head sharply back in again and spin furiously round towards Machin.

"You murdering bastard!" he hissed, before leaping and pummelling away at him with a heavy fist. Machin cowered foetally against the onslaught but his forearms and shoulders still had to endure the effects of Lodgedale's temper. He tried screaming, "What's the matter with you? What the hell's going on?"

Eventually Lodgedale had tired sufficiently to answer him.

"What's going on? What's going on?" he screamed back. "I'll bloody tell you what's going on, you evil bastard. Murder's what's going on. And you know bloody well that's what it is, too."

Machin was too sore and astonished to reply. All he could manage was, "Murder?"

"That's right," said Lodgedale, "And don't come the innocent. You're going to have a job explaining this away."

"Explaining what away?" asked Machin, rather timidly since he had no wish to provoke a second assault. Lodgedale grabbed his upper arm and propelled him roughly out of the house and round the back where the garden dipped under the kitchen window. There he jerked Machin to a stop, pointed, and said, "Talk your way out of that one."

On the earth before them lay a crumpled, dislocated heap. It was the individual who had been trying to effect an entry in the early hours as Machin had slept so soundly. Machin was horrified.

"Oh my God!" he said. "Look, inspector, this is horrible. But I don't know anything about it. Honestly. I've never seen the man before."

"Well, I have," said Lodgedale. "Once upon a time, that twisted little pile was Detective Constable Baxter. I sent him round here last night to keep an eye on things. I knew you were a nasty bugger, but I never realised you'd go this far."

His anger at the loss of his colleague provoked him to punctuate his final remark with the traditional knee in the groin, which floored Machin and reduced him once more to a silence laced with incomprehension and pain. He curled beside the erstwhile Detective Constable Baxter, clutching himself together to fight the waves of agony that washed through him, and fully expecting some more attention from Lodgedale's boots. But Lodgedale had noticed another piece of evidence and was examining it with satisfaction.

Protruding from below Baxter's left kneecap was a

hypodermic syringe. Lodgedale was not to know it belonged to the man with the service issue combat jacket (deceased) and was rather surprised that Baxter had allowed any assailant to get so literally under his defences.

But then, of course, Lodgedale realised the murderer must have been, again literally, lying in wait and must have stabbed at the constable's leg as he passed. That being the case, the guilty party would be covered in filth.

And suddenly a small crack opened up above Lodgedale's chin, indicating that he was grinning to himself. He looked again at Machin and the dirt that had accumulated on his clothes as he grovelled in his distress beside the corpse. The evidence was beginning to look overwhelming.

CHAPTER SIX

Kestrel was already standing at Eagle's office door when Hawk arrived. The previous evening had taken its toll of Hawk's pallor. His face looked like wet dough into which two small, dark marbles had been dropped. Kestrel, on the other hand, had slept well, and on seeing Hawk, decided his condition invited exploitation.

"Morning, Hawk," he said loudly, and was pleased to see Hawk flinch at the volume and merely raise a slow hand in greeting.

"Aviary's teeming with finches," yelled Kestrel. "Eagle will want you to arrange migration, I expect."

Hawk's wits were greedy for sleep and completely incapable of interpreting Kestrel's jargon. Kestrel, pleased at his fabrication, and feeling even more refreshed by Hawk's evident dullness, turned briskly to lead the way as the office door clicked open.

"Morning, boss," he said keenly, and was instantly alerted by a "Can it, you noisy bastard," from an Eagle whose condition was obviously even worse than that of Hawk.

The wire strands of his hair were uncombed, there was no country music, and instead of his usual position at the window, he'd adopted a posture between irritation and languor in one of the leather chairs.

Kestrel's confidence ebbed very quickly, not only because of the reception, but because Eagle's symptoms mirrored those of Hawk so closely that alarm bells rang. Kestrel was sexually naïve to the point of embarrassment, but he sensed this was an unholy alliance which would render any mere office politics on his part superfluous. His fears were confirmed when Eagle saw Hawk behind him and his features softened.

"Hullo, Jim," he said gently. "Any news?"

Hawk shook his head.

"I haven't had time to start on it yet. I'll deal with it today."

"Good, good. Priority remember," said Eagle.

Hawk remembered Kestrel's words in the corridor outside.

"What about these finches in the aviary though? Kestrel said something about a migration."

Kestrel felt a rush of alarm. Eagle, not surprisingly, had no idea what Hawk was talking about, but his own priorities were clear. Hawk had been told to find out where Bad Boy was and that came before everything.

"You deal with that, Kestrel," he said. "I want a full written report by this evening."

"Right, boss," gulped Kestrel, glad to have emerged from the situation with no greater punishment than a creative writing exercise.

The three of them waited; Hawk aware only of the oblivion that stalked at the edges of his vision and into which he intended to drop gratefully at the first opportunity; Eagle weighed down by the same weariness but aching with a greater need, that which had been awakened by Bad Boy Jackson; and Kestrel, wide awake but incapable of any initiative since he had first to discover exactly what had happened between Hawk and Eagle the previous evening.

The silence was eventually broken by Hawk, who actually fell asleep while standing there and only woke when he was on his way to the carpet. The thump as he reached it and his subsequent apologies shook them momentarily from their torpor.

"Well then. Let's get on with it," said Eagle, and waited.

No-one seemed to know what "it" was, so Eagle continued. "Haven't either of you anything to report?"

They both shook their heads.

"Hmmm," mused Eagle, trying to shake his preoccupations clear. And then he remembered it was he who'd summoned them.

"Right then," he said, forcing himself to stand and move over to his desk. He picked up a sheet of paper and was immediately reminded of why he'd sent for them.

"Bit of bad news, I'm afraid. Specially for you, Kestrel."

Kestrel's day was beginning to corrode even more rapidly round him, but he managed to squeeze out, "Oh? What's the problem?"

"That fledgling of yours, Grebe, up in Inverness. He's been

plucked."

Kestrel was alarmed. All new guys were his responsibility, and one lost meant a smaller empire for him as well as an implication of failure which made his position much more precarious.

"Any details?" he asked.

Eagle consulted the piece of paper.

"Not much. Haven't had a post-mortem yet. Stabbed."

Absent-mindedly, Eagle pushed a button on his computer. "Stand by your man" flooded the room, frightening the semi-conscious Hawk into attentiveness, reassuring Kestrel with its familiarity, and helping Eagle to concentrate on the business in hand.

"What the hell are they killing fledglings for?" he asked. "How much did this Grebe know?"

"Hardly anything, sir," answered Kestrel. "He started about the same time as Robin and Sparrow. They're all downy. No use to the opposition, alive or dead."

"Hmmm," said Eagle. "Somebody must have thought so. Who've we got up there?"

"Just the ringer who was working with him," said Kestrel.

"Not good enough," said Eagle. "I want a first-hand account. Better get up there yourself."

Kestrel was alarmed at having to spend time in Inverness leaving Hawk and Eagle together in their new liaison, but his protests were ignored by his boss, who simply pressed a button on the intercom on his desk and said, "Mary, get Kestrel on a train to Inverness. Book him into a hotel up there. Indefinite period."

He released the button. There was no reply. He looked back at the intercom and pressed the button again.

"Did you hear me, Mary?" he yelled, before releasing it once more.

This time, Mary answered.

"Sorry sir. I was just checking the reports from the Anstey field."

"The what?"

"You know, the Norwegian sector. Apparently the water's just 350 feet deep. The estimates for recoverable reserves look really good—more than 300 million barrels of oil, 53 billion cubic feet of natural gas. We're going to need diverless systems, rope access topsides and new thinking on a green-field infrastructure..."

"Yeah. Well..." said Eagle. "Next time, answer me. You're not indispensable, you know."

He released the button, then pressed it again to add the afterthought, "Bitch!"

Hawk was glad to be an outsider in all that had gone before, not even having the energy to rejoice over Kestrel's imminent departure, and his wandering mind resented the need to refocus when Eagle, back at his window, said, "And you, Jim, how about the next meet with Sparrow? That guy's got some explaining to do."

Hawk faltered.

"Er, why d'you want me to see him? I mean," he remembered hastily, "there is that other matter you wanted me to investigate."

Eagle's face clouded briefly as the private thoughts invaded the public person.

"Yes, of course. As I said, that's your priority. But afterwards you'd better get hold of this Sparrow dude and find out what the hell's going on. What's his M and C instruction, Kestrel?"

"Three-thirty, Marks and Spencer, tomorrow," said Kestrel. "I'd have to check it to confirm of course."

"We still using Marks and Spencer?" asked Eagle with a little surprise. "Used to be crawling with our guys, Belazzo's, Russians, God knows who else."

"Still is," said Kestrel, "but there are more shoppers too. Swings and roundabouts really."

"Is that so?" said Eagle. "Ah well then, that's it Jim. Three-thirty tomorrow. See if you can see what's happening."

Kestrel had had an idea and sought a little ingratiation.

"Er, excuse me, boss," he said.

"Well?" said Eagle as the tune from the computer changed.

"It's struck me," said Kestrel, "it's quite a coincidence that Grebe's death's happened so soon after the bomb went off at Sparrow's."

Eagle looked at him blankly. "So?" he said.

Kestrel swallowed and indicated the obvious.

"Well, two attempts on two fledglings. Maybe there's a connection."

Eagle's face lightened with comprehension.

"You may be right," he said. "What d'you suggest?"

"Well, protection for Robin down in Stonehaven for a start."

"Protection?" said Eagle. Then, "Yeah, sure." But as he spoke, he himself had an idea. "Unless," he went on slowly, allowing it to form, "we just leave him. Then if he gets blown away too, we'll know our theory's right."

Kestrel accepted the inevitable.

"Good idea, boss," he said, knowing it would be futile to point out that confirmation of a theory was of little value if the enemy operation about which one was theorising was meantime brought to a successful conclusion.

"That's it then," said Eagle.

The door opened quickly and Mary strode in. Eagle's eyes blazed.

"I didn't hear you bloody knock, Mary," he shouted, losing his temper instantly, as lovers do.

Mary pointedly ignored him and clumped to the desk. Once there, he slammed down the message he had brought in, turned on his heel and strode out again, heaving the door shut behind him with all the power of his arm and shoulder.

Even Kestrel, whom none of this concerned, was a little frightened by the display. Hawk, from guilt, and Eagle, with a frisson of remembrance of Mary's strength and disdain, both felt their fragility threatened by the noise and the passion the man had generated. To fill the silence Eagle went to pick up the piece of paper which was all that remained of Mary's violence. He read it and tutted.

"Goddam it!" he said. "More complications for you, Jim."

Hawk's head was already aching from weariness, noise and other people's passion, and it was without enthusiasm that he asked, "What's that?"

"Sparrow again," said Eagle. "Silly bastard's got himself arrested."

Since Kestrel was officially responsible for Sparrow, he felt obliged to ask, "What for?"

Eagle glanced again at the message.

"Er ... murdering a policeman," he read.

The enormity of the crime caused both Hawk and Kestrel to look startled.

"Bloody hell!" said Kestrel.

"Yeah," said Eagle, adding as he passed the message to Hawk, "See what you can make of it, will you Jim? Might have to get the

58

chief superintendent onto it."

"Right," said Hawk, anxious to leave the office. "Is that it?"

Eagle nodded and flapped his hand to indicate dismissal. Both were relieved that this particular session was over and made with disguised haste for the door. As they reached it, Eagle's voice stopped them.

"Jim," he said.

"Yes?" said Hawk.

"Don't forget," said Eagle, slumping back into his chair, "priorities."

****

She'd taken her time checking the contents of the suitcase since contact was still five minutes away. The shaving kit, towel and toilet bag were in the bottom beside the pyjamas. A paisley dressing gown separated them from the jeans, three shirts and a sweater. On top, the vests and underpants completed the purchases she'd made. Shoes would have to wait until Inverness.

She noticed that everything in the fireplace had been reduced to ashes except, unaccountably, the grey wig, which sat forlornly amongst the smouldering remains of the dress like an ageing hamster. Everything was set.

She screwed up some paper, pushed it under the wig in the grate and put a match to it just as her mobile started ringing. She flipped it open and listened.

"Hi there, Bird Watcher."

"Hey, Big Snake," said the woman.

"Sparrowhawk gone, is he?"

"Yep."

"You're getting ready to drive up to Inverness, right?"

"Right."

"Take Blackbird and White Whale with you. I've already briefed them."

"OK."

"Take it easy."

The Big Snake rang off. The woman closed the mobile and sank back into her chair. She liked the news that, when she went for Machin, she'd have two helpers. The old hamster in the grate had become a delicate blob of spun coal and she raked it along with the other cinders before beginning to pack her own case.

****

After the Machin arrest, Lodgedale had gone to a great deal of trouble to strengthen his case. Machin's prints were all over the syringe, fibres from his sweater had been shoved under the fingernails of the corpse, and Mhairi, the lady from number 26, had been persuaded to agree she'd seen Machin come out of his house in the early hours and conceal himself near the kitchen window. The fact that she'd been in custody at the police station at the relevant time was unimportant since there was no record of any charge having been brought against her and the station staff were firm believers in police solidarity.

Her husband posed no problem since he too was in custody and, if it came to a trial, the prosecution would make short work of a witness who beat up young policemen late at night.

Lodgedale had all but dismissed the murder from his mind and turned back to his primary concern, the implication of the postman in the bombing, when his chief superintendent, Donald McCoist, rang him. Lodgedale picked up the phone, recognised his superior's voice, and became marginally deferential.

"Ah, Arthur," said McCoist, "I understand you've got the chap who bumped off our lad last night?"

"That's right, sir," said Lodgedale. "Machin's his name. Christopher Machin."

He waited for approbation.

"Yes, that's the chap. Well, it's no go, I'm afraid."

Lodgedale didn't understand.

"I don't understand, sir," he said.

"You'll have to release him."

Lodgedale's deference vanished.

"Bugger off," he told his chief. "I've got a cast-iron case."

McCoist had anticipated his response. "Now calm down, Arthur," he pleaded. "I know how you've worked at this, and I'm sure you've been your usual efficient self. But I'm afraid it's no use. It's out of our hands."

"What d'you mean?" snapped Lodgedale.

"The usual business," his chief hurried on, anxious to deflect his subordinate's anger onto someone else, "I've got a coded note from the Home Secretary's office in front of me. He's personally ordering Machin's release."

"Who the bloody hell does he think he is?" stormed Lodgedale. "What's he know about the police force?"

"I don't know, Arthur, honestly," said McCoist, "but we can't ignore him, can we?"

"Bloody MPs. They're supposed to be the people's representatives, aren't they?" went on Lodgedale in full flow. "I've worked bloody hard to solve this case, and there was no motive, no evidence, nothing at all. But there is now, and our high and mighty bloody leaders want to undermine British justice by saying it's…"

"Arthur," shouted McCoist to halt the tirade, "there's nothing we can do about it. I've received my orders and now I'm passing them on to you."

Lodgedale began to splutter some fresh invective, but the chief superintendent hurried to end the conversation.

"Listen," he yelled, "I know this has upset you, and I'm on your side, but it's got to be done, and that's final. So I think the least our beloved masters can do is give you a few days off. Take some leave. That's another order. Go away and cool down a bit. Otherwise I dread to think what'll happen to any villains you arrest in the next few days."

He'd tried to make this parting shot a joke, but the terrible silence which greeted it indicated total failure, so he merely took advantage of it to add, "That's it then. Release him and then take a few days off. Cheers."

The line went dead, and Lodgedale was left gripping the phone and staring from purple features at a treacherous universe.

He knew himself well enough to recognise he must stay in his office until his temper subsided, otherwise there'd be more murdered policemen, and he'd be responsible. From his desk drawer he took an iron bar which he kept for such occasions and began to twist it into violent shapes and then straighten it again.

After ten minutes of snarling and heaving he was sweating profusely but the manic edge of his fury had been blunted. He could now begin to reorganise his world. First of all he phoned his wife to tell her he'd be late home. She knew his tone well enough to realise that his sexual antics that evening were likely to be excessive but thankfully brief, and she did her best to depressurise his mood. Her attempt was moderately successful and Lodgedale was soon able to begin to apply his version of rational thinking to the new set of circumstances which faced him.

Machin's release was inevitable, and re-arraignment for another offence was for the moment impossible but remained a clear priority for the future. This left the constable's murder unsolved, but thankfully he had the occupant of number 26 in custody, and since the man had after all wilfully assaulted two patrolmen shortly after the presumed time of Baxter's death, the basis of a case was already there. He would simply have to wipe the syringe and get the new set of prints on it, clean the fingernails of the corpse in preparation for new fibres, and reconfuse the man's wife so that her evidence incriminated her husband.

Working out the details of these forensic adjustments helped to calm him further and, before steeling himself to order Machin's release, he considered the chief constable's other instruction—that he should take some time off. Lodgedale never considered himself to be off duty. Arresting was his hobby. Even his dreams were peopled with felons, so the prospect of an actual holiday didn't appeal.

He cast his mind over his immediate preoccupations, and became gradually aware there was after all a police-loving God in heaven. Machin's real postman was on holiday. He looked at his notebook. Inverness, that was the place. The leave which had been forced upon him was obviously a sign.

CHAPTER SEVEN

That evening, Machin sat at home nursing bruises and a still aching groin. Thankfully he hadn't seen Lodgedale again, but when he was released by the station sergeant with sneering hints that his future was heavily mortgaged, he'd returned home, fully expecting to be dragged from the taxi and bludgeoned again by his tormentor. He hadn't been told why he'd been released and he suspected everything.

His mind tried to escape its recent experiences by moving to thoughts of The Cage, the contact at the wrestling, the individual in the kingfisher shirt, but none of them made any more sense or held any comfort. Briefly the image of long ago Tessa welled in his memory. If only she hadn't been sick that night, none of this would have happened. Instead, she might have got pregnant, he would have had to marry her.

His mind drifted to thoughts of a job in a small village school, a cottage, regular sex with Tessa, bits on the side, first with pupils, then with their parents, and an allotment. The phone cut short his idyll.

At first he decided to ignore it, but the desire for contact with something normal, one of his colleagues at school perhaps, or just a friend, forced him to lift the receiver. His hopes were instantly crushed by the now familiar tones which said, "Sparrow. From Eagle. Millet and Cuttlefish. Has decoding been effected? Acknowledge."

"Oh Christ!" groaned Machin, before adding quickly, "Acknowledge. All right?" And the slight delay before the click told him his response, although irregular, had been accepted.

So the pressure was still on then, and his involvement in all this incomprehensible nonsense was inescapable. He limped into the kitchen where the book still lay beside his half-eaten cornflakes. He retrieved it and his pencil, his empty stomach

63

convulsing briefly at the combined effects of memory and the smell of the morning's vomit which still coated the sink.

He hurried back to his couch as quickly as his swollen testicles would allow, went back over his instructions and began referring to the book and assembling the message. When completed, it read, "Prisoner's … execution… A strong cord was fastened round the head … till he expired… Intercourse with foreigners."

It sounded so much like a potted account of his recent experiences that he suspected a sinister joke, but since nothing else about The Cage suggested humour, he accepted the message at its face value. Which was precisely nil, until he applied the second decoding, which required him to be in front of Marks and Spencer at 3.30 the following day.

This was so absurd that he decided he must have made a mistake and he repeated the entire decoding exercise. The result was the same and Machin surrendered himself to the inevitable. He dragged himself wearily to bed but the dreamless oblivion of the previous night was replaced by a racked parody of sleep in which he was assailed by flocks of wrestling birds carrying copies of Gibbon's *Decline and Fall*. Each of them had the face of Lodgedale and, in place of a beak, a huge knee.

****

The pavement outside Marks and Spencer was again thronged with shoppers and bibliophiles. Gibbon's *Decline and Fall* had obviously done just that and on this particular day had been replaced by a spate of biographies. Toland's *Hitler* and Maurois' *Hugo* threaded among Longford's *Wellington* and Marchand's *Byron*. A wide berth was being given to one timid-looking individual carrying a hardback copy of a Jeffrey Archer novel, but otherwise *Mary Queen of Scots* and *John Lennon* mingled happily enough as their owners wandered about muttering obscure ornithological catch-phrases.

A haggard Machin, still bruised from his recent adventures, stood listlessly, feeling none of the exhilaration which had driven him here on the previous occasion. He carried no book and was therefore treated with mistrust by most of the others, and he had no idea what sequence was supposed to be followed to ensure contact.

Amongst all the other chatter about rooks and gannets, he was surprised to hear a voice quite close to him say, "Do you read a lot of Dickens?" When the question was repeated more loudly, he realised it was probably being addressed to him.

He glanced quickly at the speaker but, not feeling like a cosy literary chat, he simply shook his head. The man insisted, "Don't you find he's essential to any understanding of narrative objectivity in prose fiction?"

Machin sighed. He didn't have time for this. He was still scanning the people on the pavement. Remembering an article on Barbara Cartland in the previous week's *Sunday Times Colour Supplement*, he said, "The arbitrariness of phenomenological perceptions has superseded all *a priori* notions of affective control ever since Proust dispensed with linear causality and substituted temporal elasticity as a central image for the irradiating consciousness."

There was a brief pause in all the monologues and conversations around him. When they started up again, the man said, "What the bloody hell are you talking about?"

Machin looked up, and at last registered the fact that it was the same man he'd followed before. It wasn't surprising that he'd failed to recognise him at first; the receding gingery hair was hidden by a fez and he had a thick scarf over his mouth.

"Oh, I'm sorry," stammered Machin, "I didn't realise..."

"Don't you know the Dickens code?" asked Hawk.

"Er, no," replied Machin.

"Bloody hell. What's Kestrel been thinking of?" said Hawk as he began to walk away. Machin was uncertain as to how to proceed. Hawk stopped, looked back, and, controlling his anger, gave a slight twitch of his head to indicate that Machin should follow. As the two set off, a third man, in a black Barbour jacket, who was carrying a copy of *Mein Kampf*, fell into step behind them.

Their progress was less spectacular than on the previous occasion and they were unremarkable as, led by Hawk, they made their way up Union Street and along Carden Place. Eventually, they arrived at a bench under the trees and Hawk sat on it.

After only a slight hesitation, Machin joined him and both were alarmed when the man with the Barbour jacket sat between them. The stranger was clearly an inhibiting factor because none of them spoke for a long time. The patience of the man in the middle was the first to break.

"Well?" he whispered loudly, half turning towards Hawk.

"I beg your pardon," said Hawk.

"Well, here I am," said the man.

"I'm sorry, I don't understand," said Hawk.

The man's whisper was discarded as exasperation began to take over.

"Look, don't be bloody silly. The Dickens code. I heard you. Saw you nod your head at me to follow. Well, I've followed…"

Hawk again cursed the turmoil into which street contacts had fallen since his day. Disregarding the possibility that the man was a plant, he decided on directness.

"I wasn't signalling to you. It was him I meant." He nodded at Machin.

The man turned from one to the other. Exasperation was evolving into anger.

"What? You mean I've come all the way up here and… Oh bloody hell!"

He looked at his watch and back at Hawk.

"You stupid bugger," he said, and then got up and began running back towards Marks and Spencer, knowing full well he was already too late.

They watched him disappear and were embarrassed to find themselves alone together.

"I don't know where they find them nowadays," said Hawk.

"Who?" asked Machin.

"Criminals," said. Hawk. "More like Betterware men, most of them."

"It's certainly not like the telly," said Machin.

The awkwardness of the recent departure still hovered between them. Machin, who wanted nothing better than to revert to the role of passive viewer of programmes like *CSI* was the first to broach the subject of his relations with The Cage.

"Look," he said, "I'm as bad as that bloke who just went. Worse, probably. I don't know how I got into this, and I've no idea what to do. My garden's been blown up, somebody's killed a policeman outside my kitchen window, and God knows what else is going on that I haven't found out about yet. What am I supposed to do?"

"That's up to you," said Hawk, unsympathetically.

"But how? I mean, all I want is out. Simple as that."

"No it's not, I'm afraid," said Hawk. "You're in whether you like it or not. You should've thought of that when you were having it off with that nurse."

Machin racked his brain for memories of nurses, and realised Hawk was referring to his student days.

"Oh, come on. How was I to know where it'd lead?"

"Don't give me that," said Hawk, still irritated by the incident with the man in the Barbour jacket. "Most students get to have a normal sex life, and it doesn't get them into the Aberdeen mafia."

"You're a fine one to talk about normality," said Machin on the defensive.

"What d'you mean?" said Hawk quickly, anxious suddenly about the magazines in his bedroom cupboard.

"I saw you at the wrestling the other night."

Relief that his real secret was intact mingled with apprehension at the memory of the public display into which Eagle had forced him.

"That was an undercover job," he improvised.

"Undercover job?" laughed Machin. "Christ, I'd hate to be around when you're advertising yourself."

Hawk had allowed himself to be side-tracked once again. He felt the same frustration that gripped him when Kestrel outmanocuvred him in their jousting at The Cage. He was too sensitive, too vulnerable for this business. Even a fledgling was getting the better of him.

"All right Sparrow," he said, "Grebe's been plucked, Robin's probably oven-ready by now, and as for you..."

"Get stuffed," said Machin petulantly.

"Exactly," rejoined Hawk. "If you don't take a great deal of care, you'll be next. I suppose you think the explosion was a mistake, do you?"

Machin was sobered by the reminder.

"But surely you can get me out of it. I mean, I'm not being deliberately rude or anything, but I just want to get back to normal."

"Normal? You run drugs for Tony Belazzo, you chat up a few dealers in French for Joey McBride, and you think you can just say thank you very much and retire?"

"Why not?"

67

"D'you really think the Belazzos will allow that now they've got you? Forget it," snapped Hawk. "There's no way back."

"OK," said Machin. "Maybe you're right. But what do I have to do? I can't handle all this."

Hawk thought for a moment, then asked what had happened at the wrestling. When he heard about Bad Boy's message, he nodded.

"Right. You'll have to do as they say," he said. "They're contacting you, so they're probably not the ones who set up the explosion. I mean, there wouldn't be much point, would there?"

"Well, who did then?" asked Machin.

"I don't know yet, but if you keep in touch the section will give you all the protection you need," said Hawk, with a confidence he knew to be totally unfounded.

"And how am I supposed to do that when I'm hitch-hiking up north?" asked Machin reasonably.

"I thought of that," said Hawk, reaching into his pocket. He took out a small box from which dangled a short length of wire. He handed it to Machin.

"Wear a wire," he said. "This is the transmitter. The wire's the aerial. Carry it with you from now on."

He reached into his pocket again and this time produced a CND lapel badge.

"And this is the microphone. We'll be able to monitor where you are and listen in to any conversations you have."

For a moment Machin was not sure he entirely approved of such an idea, but the price of having them eavesdropping on all his private encounters was a small one to pay for the feeling of security that came with the little box.

"Do I turn it on and off?" he asked.

"Yes. It's a modulating frequency transceiver coupled with a dynamic synthesiser to compress oscillations within a modified spectroscopic compression ratio. All you have to do is vary the wavelength according to predetermined tonal values and suppress anomalous aural stimuli to…"

"What the fuck are you talking about?"

Hawk looked at him and sighed.

"OK, stick the bloody microphone on your lapel. This black button turns it on and off. The brown one controls the volume."

"What's its range?" asked Machin.

"Plenty," said Hawk.

"OK, what happens now?"

"Well, we'll just have to wait and see what they want. Until we know that, there's not much you can do."

"I suppose I'm a sort of decoy, then?" said Machin hesitantly, unwilling even now to admit he was anything other than a French teacher.

"I'll tell you what," said Hawk, rising from the seat and obviously preparing to leave. "If you don't start learning to use the codes properly, you'll be a bloody omelette as far as we're concerned."

He composed his face into a settled, heavy-lidded, enigmatic stare to underline the significance of what he considered to be a *bon mot*. He held the look for three seconds then turned and walked away, only just resisting the temptation to turn back as he heard a surly Machin mutter "Bloody poofter."

****

In Inverness, Lodgedale was out of sorts. He sat on a bench by the river looking out over the water and hating the open-ness of mountains and sky and the sweet, bracing air that was blowing over from the west. He hadn't even found a bench close enough to the road to enable him to get a decent whiff of the exhaust fumes of the cars which crawled by. Only the fact that the postman, whose whereabouts had tempted him away from Aberdeen, was sitting on the third bench along from his own enabled him to tolerate the oxygen which hurtled in off the mountains.

When he arrived at police headquarters in Inverness, the problem of finding this lone tourist needle in a holiday haystack had been compounded by the fact that he understood so little of what his Highland colleagues were saying. Lodgedale was from the central belt and this lot spoke in a long, slow, curly accent that simply made him too impatient to listen.

He'd eventually conveyed to them the nature of his business and they'd found a sergeant who was originally from Motherwell and whose accent was therefore much closer to what Lodgedale considered to be the norm. Together, he and the sergeant had organised enquiries at all the hotels and guest houses until they had a list of suspects short enough for Lodgedale himself to handle.

From force of habit he arrested the first two on the list after he'd questioned them. The second arrest was the more comprehensive (and more violent) of the two because the man concerned had said how nice it was to be in the Highlands and away from traffic fumes.

At police headquarters he was amazed to discover that they released both men shortly after their incarceration. He protested loudly to the desk sergeant that he thought Northern Constabulary were supposed to be enlightened. When the sergeant looked at him with an open, honest stare and replied "We are. We don't leave any marks. Ever," Lodgedale gave up all hope of getting any meaningful cooperation from them.

A telephone call to his own sergeant back in Aberdeen had helped, via the postman's employers, to pinpoint his man. The rest of the short list, unaware of how near their lives had been to devastation, were allowed to continue their holiday.

Lodgedale's surveillance had begun immediately. The postman was small and always wore a tartan donkey jacket. At first, the sight of this coat had quickened Lodgedale's already eager anticipation of the eventual arrest. If this guy was so proud of being a Scot, it'd be no bother getting him to fight. This in turn would lead to him resisting arrest and effectively giving Lodgedale permission to beat the shit out of him. And, of course, when it came to the crunch, he'd probably, by definition, be drunk and offer the easiest of targets for anything Lodgedale cared to perpetrate.

This momentary lifting of the inspector's spirits only served further to increase his dissatisfactions when he overheard the man in a pub, to which he'd followed him, order a vodka and tonic in an accent which had obviously been acquired many miles south of Aberdeen.

The only reason Lodgedale hadn't instantly arrested and charged the man was that he hadn't yet decided exactly what he was going to be guilty of and so hadn't yet telephoned his sergeant to prepare the relevant clues. He'd made up his mind to think about this as he watched the villain (he never used the word suspect) in the hope he might do something which would give him away.

Unfortunately, in the two days he'd been tailing him, the man had proved to be just a boring little shit. He spent most of his time in his hotel, coming out only to walk about and go for the occasional drink. This meant Lodgedale had to sit about in the hotel lobby reading, which he detested, or, even worse, wander about in the fresh Highland air which he was sure would do him no good at all in the long run.

The accumulation of all these negative effects was merely helping to ensure the eventual arrest would be even more bloody than Lodgedale's usual efforts.

Only one element in the whole situation seemed to offer any real interest. During the period of his surveillance he had now and again caught sight of another individual whose presence was evident too frequently to be coincidental. He was a stocky little man with horn-rimmed glasses who always carried a copy of the *Financial Times*.

From the occasions on which he'd observed the man in the hotel lobby, Lodgedale had noticed three things: it was always the same copy; the man was always reading something in the centre pages; and sometimes his reading required the paper to be held upside-down. The conclusion that the postman had an accomplice was instantaneous, and the myriad possibilities this entailed were deliciously confirmed when he discovered the man had taken a room at his own hotel, just along the road from that at which the postman was staying.

He glanced at the man, who was now sitting on one of the seats between himself and the postman, and noticed the havoc the wind was causing with the paper which he still held steadfastly before his face.

The man looked round the edge of the flailing newsprint and caught Lodgedale's eye. The inspector's jaw tightened into his parody of a grin as he noted that, guiltily, the man immediately resumed his close study of the paper.

Lodgedale had come out into the wilderness looking for one man; he would go back with two, and since Chief Superintendent McCoist knew nothing of life beyond the Aberdeen city limits, there'd be no interference in his enquiries until he'd made his case absolutely watertight.

Suddenly, the wind plucked a centre page from the *Financial Times* and flung it along the path. The stocky man leapt up and chased after it but the postman stopped its progress with a deftly placed foot. As its owner knelt before him to retrieve it, he looked up at the postman and Lodgedale knew, with the certainty of all his years of experience, that something significant had passed between them as they exchanged a few words.

He was tempted to descend on them there and then and haul them in for some questioning and grievous bodily harm, but as the man with the paper got up and walked on, he decided he'd let the intrigue develop a little before he pounced. Despite the river, the sun and the fresh air, he was beginning to enjoy his holiday.

CHAPTER EIGHT

Eagle's parents had sent their son to school in England at the earliest opportunity. It wasn't that they found the English educational system particularly commendable, but it was at least a long way away from where they lived.

They'd chosen a minor public school which ensured that the cultural shock to their offspring was comprehensive. He'd always been selective about sports, for example. The muscle and violence of gridiron attracted him but baseball seemed pointless.

In England, rugby, with its combination of the pain inflicted by boys much larger than himself and the delights of the subsequent communal bath or shower, was an obvious favourite. Cricket was a mystery, although it did have the attraction of requiring total immobility for long periods.

Then, one day, his captain had asked him to field at backward short leg and he had spent almost the whole morning with his gaze riveted on the back view of a succession of batsmen bending over only three yards in front of him. When all other participation in sport had been forgotten, he had kept this nostalgic memory of young men in cream flannels gratuitously displaying their most attractive features for his delectation.

Now, however, just one evening out with Hawk had changed his life. The sweat, the sadism, the gaudy eroticism of wrestling had converted him. This was indeed the sport of queens.

He sat now, on the fifth floor of The Cage, greedily riffling through the pages of the magazines Hawk had brought him, dwelling only momentarily on the photographs of shining torsos, extravagant costumes and exquisite brutalities, as his single burning passion drove him relentlessly in search of references to Bad Boy Jackson. Previously, his sleeping and his waking hours had been filled with thoughts which, at their purest, rose to the level of being only mildly unhealthy. But today, they bulged with visions of himself and the fighter locked in anatomically impossible contortions, with parts of Bad Boy crammed everywhere, and Eagle himself screaming symphonies of delirium in celebration of his reduction to abject object.

As the imagined agony of each penetration rose into his small skull, he would pause in his researches, shudder his eyes closed, and then move more hungrily back among the portraits of the minor titans who surrounded his god.

During one such pause, his eyes opened to a sensation of pulsating crimson which convinced him that the hot blood of his desire had at last exploded into the room. He dipped far enough off his cosmic peak, however, to realise it was in fact the red light above his door. With a convulsive clenching of his upper lip, he stared hard at the door, wishing the intruder into oblivion.

The light flashed on. Eagle, with a final glance at a photograph of "Nigel the Bayonet", bunched himself up and crabbed, half-stooping, to the door. He deactivated the fail-safe alarm, unfastened the catch, hurled the door open and leapt through it.

Hawk, waiting patiently on the mat, was terrified by the whirling bundle of arms and legs that fell on him. He felt himself grabbed at neck and groin and lifted excruciatingly before being released on a parabola which launched him headlong into the front of Eagle's desk. As he felt the flash of pain in his forehead at the point of impact and the warm spill of blood that followed it, he was grabbed again and his face was forced under the desk against the wastepaper basket while his arms and legs were dragged and bent behind him into positions he knew to be incompatible with his normal bone arrangement.

His mind refused to function. What had happened? An SAS putsch, perhaps? With one of their crack units, its insanity honed to a scream by training which would kill all other life-forms? A Belazzo infiltration, the preface to a wet-job to end all wet-jobs? A domestic quarrel between Eagle and Mary?

But even as these scenarios jostled to surface through the breakers of pain that crashed over him, a voice he knew babbled incomprehensible clues.

"Oh, Helen, Helen," slavered Eagle. "High priestess of my savage god. Oh, the torments you've opened up for me! Will all the perfumes of Arabia stop the rot? A Boston Crab and a Double Armlock. But none of it is enough. What use is submission?

Where is he? Where is he?"

By means of the system of levers which had been created out of his arms and shoulder blades, Hawk's head was jerked violently against the floor at each punctuation point in Eagle's rantings.

"Why me? (Thud.) Why me? (Thud.) Of all the people to whom you could have revealed the majesty of such ebony delights, why was I singled out as the unfortunate wretch who should glimpse the fruits of paradise only to have them snatched away? (Thud)."

The last sentence, wrung slowly by Eagle from his usually inarticulate psyche, had been long enough, and sufficiently devoid of punctuation points for Hawk to begin the orientation process he so badly needed.

It was indeed Eagle who held him, but a dominant Eagle, in the grip of his passion. Just in time, because Eagle was beginning a series of exclamations, he yelled, "Donna, I've found him. Bad Boy Jackson, I've found him!" And further explanation was rendered impossible as he passed out from the pain of a small bone in his wrist breaking under the convulsive heave which Bad Boy's name had provoked in his tormentor.

Eagle shuddered the last of his orgasm out in his accustomed whimpering and looked at the senseless shape tied in such intricate knots before him. The blood oozed from the forehead, the spindly hands and legs wove in and out along the spine and Eagle marvelled that such a shape could belong to the same species as Bad Boy Jackson. Nonetheless, if his crazed remembering could be trusted, this thing had intimated it knew the god's whereabouts.

That memory, together with a post-orgasmic lassitude, inspired him to untangle his minion and begin the face-slapping which always worked in films. After almost four minutes of slapping, indeed at about the time when Eagle's frustration was transforming large slaps into small punches, Hawk's eyes flickered open and Eagle felt able to stand up and walk over to the window for a rest.

"Well," he said. 'something to report?"

The apparent normality of his stance and the accompanying question confused Hawk even further as his consciousness began to tell him he was lying in a vat of pain half-way underneath the desk.

"What?" he said, the word and pieces of tooth issuing

simultaneously from between his lips.

"What's with you? Deaf?" said Eagle without turning. Hawk's confusion was impenetrable, but the good fortune which had prevented Eagle actually killing him came once more to his rescue as a knock on the still-open door signalled the arrival of Mary.

The ex-seaman stepped into the office and rapidly assessed the scene. He had been determined to monitor the affair between Hawk and Eagle, but none of his own experiences had ever led to the mayhem he now saw. Cannily, he opted for discretion.

"Mornin', Mr Hawk," he. said. "Feeling a bit under the weather, are we? There's a lot of flu about. You want to watch it."

"Never mind the social chat," snapped Eagle. "What do you want, you nasty little pervert?"

Mary was astonished. In all Eagle's rantings during the moments of ecstasy they'd shared he'd never descended to the commonplaces of morality. Eagle's definition of perversion was what other people did, and Mary now knew with certainty (and relief) that their affair was at an end. It was clearly time to move on to blackmail and all the other retributions he had always anticipated would be the real fruits of their relationship.

"Well?" insisted Eagle, spinning round and glaring at him.

"Two things, sir."

"Yes, yes, get on with it."

"The Anstey field. It's a single well tieback with pipelines, umbilical and dynamic risers. They're asking for seventy plus subsea spools, four Y-piece connections and tie-ins with retrofit risers."

"And?"

"Well, the Italian engineering firm's asking for two million. But there's an outfit in Grimsby will do it for three hundred and twelve thousand. What do you think?"

Eagle flapped a hand to indicate the question was unimportant.

"Second," went on Mary, "a message. From Mr Kestrel in Inverness."

"Oh shit," said Eagle, "is that all?"

"I think it's important. Otherwise I'd never have dreamed of interrupting your ... discussion with Mr Hawk."

As usual, Eagle missed the irony. He turned testily back to his window. "All right, what is it? Read it, pig, read it."

Mary's hands tightened on the paper he was holding but he

resisted the urge to physical violence, knowing full well Eagle would only enjoy it. Vowing instead to double his blackmail demands, he read Kestrel's communication.

"Consider identification Grebe-plucker possible. Probability to be confirmed after all other possibilities discarded. Subject possibly definite but certainty improbable. Possible confirmation probable soonest."

Eagle turned slowly to look once more at his secretary.

"Are you taking the piss, Mary?" he asked.

"No," replied Mary. "That's the message. Verbatim."

"Well, what in Christ's name is it s'posed to mean?" shouted Eagle, becoming more and more angry. On the floor by the desk, Hawk had heard it all and was anxious to get everything back on an even keel.

"Er... Excuse me, boss," he began, as he tried to get up.

"What?" snapped Eagle.

"Aaargh!" screamed Hawk as, in attempting to rise, he put his weight on the wrist which Eagle had broken.

"'Aaargh', Mr Hawk?" quizzed Mary, enjoying himself.

Eagle, momentarily fascinated by the appearance of pain in Hawk's features, stepped towards him to help or hinder.

His approach galvanised Hawk into co-ordinated effort. He stood quickly, his head spinning and buzzing, and said, "Er ... no. The message. From Kestrel. I think I know what he means." And, even in the extreme situation in which he found himself, his subliminal ambitions made him add, "Insofar as it's possible to understand anything that fool says. He's so unreliable."

"Never mind that. What's the silly bastard talking about?" asked Eagle.

"Well, it seems to me he's suggesting he's identified the man who murdered Grebe, but isn't a hundred per cent certain yet. He's doing some more investigating."

"Is that it?" asked his chief.

"I think so," said Hawk.

Eagle attempted to wither Mary with a look.

"And what's so goddam important about that which makes you come barging in here while a meeting's going on?" he sneered.

Mary opted for retreat, but his pride forced him to say as he turned back at the office door, "I would have thought that landing the biggest contract we've ever had and catching the murderer of a fledgling was more important than indulging geriatric fantasies."

Eagle went purple and ran to the door, screaming down the corridor after the retreating Mary, "Geriatric? Geriatric? You cheeky, insulting bitch. You wait till I see that stoker you're living with. I bet he doesn't know where that stain on your kitchen ceiling came from."

But Mary was on his way down the stairs and the last words were heard only by people in rooms further down the corridor. They wrote down Eagle's outbursts and filed them with all the others which they'd collected and which they too were eventually planning to arrange into the requisite blackmail sequence or sell to the Soaraway Scottish *Sun*.

Once back in his office, Eagle fumed away at the window, his train of thought shattered by the speed and variety of the changes which were overtaking him. He toyed with the idea of putting another arm-lock on Hawk, but he looked such a mess that not even Eagle could consider contact with him attractive. Hawk still sought, actually and figuratively, some stability.

"Will you be going up there?" he ventured.

"Where?" asked Eagle.

"Inverness," said Hawk.

"What the hell for?"

"Well, if he's up there … well, I thought you would."

"Who? Kestrel? What the hell would I want to see that four-eyed bastard for? See enough of him in here. Or d'you mean this supposed murderer he's found?"

"Neither, boss," said Hawk, feeling just about strong enough to play his trump card.

"Who then?" asked Eagle.

"Bad Boy Jackson. He's wrestling up there next week."

Eagle's heart leapt joyfully within him. He turned to Hawk with a smile of elation and rapture on his ghastly face, and his happiness overcame the previous disgust which his subordinate's appearance had caused. He almost ran across the room, but then decided, in deference to Bad Boy, for whom he was now saving his body, not to embrace Hawk and instead grabbed him by the hand and shook it in wild felicitations.

Hawk fainted again, the compound fracture having now been further compounded. Eagle dragged him to a chair, repeated the previous sequence of slaps and punches and when recovery still proved elusive, he took a bottle of whisky from his cabinet and began pouring it down Hawk's throat.

Between awakening to excruciating pain and drowning in whisky, Hawk's subconscious chose the former and he retched back into consciousness. A grateful Eagle pleaded, "Say it again, man," and the befuddled Hawk began uncomprehendingly to sing, "You must remember this, a kiss is just a kiss..." Eagle slapped his face hard and Hawk began to cry. Eagle decided to try psychology.

"Jim," he said gently, "if you don't pull yourself together, I'll cut your balls off."

Hawk knew Eagle was capable of far worse and so, through fogs of pain and misery, he forced himself to concentrate hard and managed to still his sobbing.

"That's better," said Eagle, patting his broken wrist attentively. "Now then, let's get it straight. Did you say..." He paused and took a deep, shuddering breath. "...Bad Boy is fighting in Inverness?"

Hawk nodded and his sore head sent throbs of pain down to meet the stabs that were on their way up from his wrist.

"I'll go there right away," said Eagle with enthusiasm, and then, with a rare association of ideas, "That's where Kestrel is, isn't it? I can kill two birds with one stone."

The callous disregard for Grebe's fate which his words betrayed went unnoticed in his new determination. Hawk, wishing his boss would leave at once, nonetheless felt obliged to convey the full story of what he'd learned from Sparrow.

"Er ... boss," he began. "There's something else you ought to know about Bad Boy. Something we didn't know when we first ... met him."

"Well? Well?" said Eagle, eager for news of his love.

"He works for Tony Belazzo."

Eagle's face froze as his brain absorbed the information and suddenly the hideous smile spread like a stain across his features.

"Great!" he shrilled, "we've got something else in common. Oh, Jim, you've no idea. I've been looking through those books you brought me, reading about wrestling, trying to get a handle on the things big bad Bad Boy enjoys. I've learned toe-holds and forearm smashes and backbreakers just so that when we meet again I'll be closer to him. And now you tell me he's into crime too. Oh Jim, we were made for each other. That has got to be a sign."

"Whatever," said a doubtful Hawk. "I'm sure you'll be very happy together. But he's with the Belazzos."

"Oh Jim," said Eagle, lyrically, "Belazzo, Eagle, The Cage, they're just names. Underneath we're all the same. That machete we found stuck in the guy from Leith who floated down the Dee, it was almost identical to the one Joey gave his daughter for her twenty-first. No, no. The modern world's moved on, Jim."

Hawk was unfamiliar with this new cosmopolitan version of an Eagle who recognised the right of others to exist. But love does strange things to a man, and whereas a garish new outfit had been sufficient to control a crazed Southern boy addicted to servility, nothing in Hawk's power could reach this incipient citizen of the world with his newly-acquired set of strangleholds. He was dangerous, and the further he was sent from the seat of power, the better for Hawk and everybody at The Cage.

There was, however, no need for Hawk to engineer any schemes for his removal; Eagle's passion was moving faster than Hawk's fears for the organisation's security.

"I'll get off to Inverness right away," he said briskly. "I want you to get me tickets, all that stuff. Fix it up now. I'll just go home and throw a leotard into a suitcase. I'll need a couple of hours."

Hawk offered a token protest in the certainty of its rejection.

"But what about The Cage? The Edinburgh contact's coming up tomorrow evening, and Billy Driscoll's… "

"First things first, Jim," interrupted Eagle. "You take care of all that. I'll leave a message with Mary … the bastard," he added, with a tiny flicker of memory, "telling her you're in charge."

A flush of power briefly swamped Hawk's aches and pains as he watched his boss begin gathering up the magazines which were spread over his desk. At last he was to have control. Eagle, it was true, would be with Kestrel, an alliance he didn't trust, but the greater claims of Bad Boy would muddy any plots Kestrel might initiate. Meantime he, Hawk, alone in Aberdeen, and in charge of The Cage, could consolidate his position and even establish some networks of his own about which Eagle would know nothing.

The Caesar whose decline he was plotting had bundled the magazines together and now looked around for other necessaries, but his mind raced ahead of him to a wrestling hall and, better, changing rooms in Inverness. He could wait no longer.

"Right Jim," he said, making for the door, "it's all yours. I'll be off. Pack these up ready for when I get back, will you?" And he threw the bundle of magazines to him as he rushed by.

His parting words, "Don't forget, now. You've got two hours," were shouted back over his shoulder as he ran down the corridor. They were religiously noted down by the listening people but unfortunately missed by Hawk who was unconscious on the floor by the desk, felled once again by the mallet of pain that hit him as he tried to catch the magazines and they landed on his broken wrist.

CHAPTER NINE

Machin stood at the edge of the road, out past Hazlehead near the crematorium turn-off, watching the mostly foreign machines squirting out of Aberdeen in batches and swishing by him. He looked at his watch. It was twelve o'clock and he was feeling twitchy. Very soon he'd be accosted by another creature from the new world he was being forced to inhabit. He looked along the approaching cars, scanning the unyielding windscreens for a glimpse of anything that looked remotely Italian.

Some sixty yards away, the left indicator of a white Mercedes began to flash. Machin saw it and his heart started thudding. It didn't look like the sort of car you went to a funeral in. It drew level with him, pulled in and stopped.

A reflex caused him to reach into his pocket and switch on the transmitter which he'd pre-set to the maximum range and volume. In The Cage, a computer channel opened, activated by his signal. His mind raced with images of Smith and Wessons, trilby hats and violin cases.

A woman got out and stood beside the car. She was stunning. His thoughts doubled back on themselves and lurched to satin sheets, orgies and whoever the current Lauren Bacall was. Almost immediately, the polarity of the lurch changed again as he acknowledged that death by orgasm was still death.

Then suddenly, with his mind heaving back and forth between all these threats and possibilities, he found himself saying a name, but with an inflexion that changed it into a question.

"Tessa?" he said. "Tessa?"

The fair-haired woman held out her hand and came towards him.

"Chris," she said. "How are you?"

Machin flooded with relief but for the moment was unable to articulate any further sounds. He took the outstretched hand, kissed the proffered cheek, and just looked at her. She was even more desirable than she had been as a student. He could only grin foolishly, shrug his shoulders and raise his hands in gestures of total bewilderment. Tessa smiled more broadly.

"Are you supposed to be hitching, Chris?"

He nodded.

"At your age?"

Her naturalness released the brake in his throat.

"What the hell are you doing here? I mean, this is ridiculous. How long is it since I've seen you?"

"Well, since we graduated, I suppose."

"God, yes. Years. It's absurd. Absurd."

The shock of the meeting had driven all other thoughts from his head. He didn't notice that a red Toyota had pulled in behind the Mercedes, he hardly heard Tessa's answers to his gabbled questions about herself and other mutual acquaintances who'd also graduated into oblivion at the same time. He still couldn't believe what was happening to him when she got back in the car and pushed open the passenger door for him to get in. He lay back in the low-slung leather and breathed in the opulence of the expensive machine.

"Christ, Tessa, whatever line you're in, you're doing well for yourself," he said, as she edged out onto the road.

"I don't complain," she said. Then, with a half-smile, "Well, Chris, where are you heading?"

Machin suddenly realised what he was doing.

"Oh shit," he said. "Er, I'm … I mean, I'm not going anywhere, really… I, er…"

"I see," she said. 'standing beside the road, hitch-hiking, but not wanting to go anywhere."

Machin interrupted her. "Look, Tessa, this is going to sound weird, but I've got to get out. I mean, I've … I've got to meet somebody… I… Oh Christ, I'm sorry, I can't explain it but I've got to get out."

"Oh?" said Tessa, sketching the question on her features as she turned her head to look briefly at him.

"Yes," he said. But the perfume from her and the line of her legs down to the pedals and the lovely skin struck memories in his head which he'd sought so desperately in the days since the Belazzos had re-established contact.

83

"Oh, Tessa, I wish I could tell you. I do really. You won't believe this but I've actually been thinking about you a lot recently. Honest, I wish I could stay with you now and just let you drive me anywhere. I don't care where. But I can't. I've got to get back to that lay-by. I'm supposed to be waiting for..."

As he hesitated, she prompted, "Armadillo?"

His surprise froze in his throat. He was afraid to say anything. On the one hand, a meeting with Tessa was infinitely preferable to an encounter with some Scottish extra out of Goodfellas, but on the other, the very normality of the whole thing implied a web of associations that stretched beyond his imaginings. He could never be the same again and there was indeed no escape.

Tessa's smile indicated her pleasure at the shock she'd delivered. As Machin continued to stare at her, she turned her head and mouthed a little kiss at him, deepening his confusion. As she turned back, still smiling, to concentrate on the road, her mobile began to ring.

She hit the button on the dashboard and said "Yo."

"BW," said the voice. "Where are you?"

"On my way, Big Snake," she said.

"With or without?"

Tessa looked across at Machin.

"With," she said.

"Blackbird and White Whale close?"

Tessa looked in her rear view mirror.

"Couldn't be closer."

"OK. Have a nice day."

Tessa hit the button again.

Machin had heard it all. When he spoke, his voice was quiet and tentative.

"Tessa, what the hell's going on?"

Tessa's reply was clipped.

"I'm taking you to Inverness."

"What for?"

"Your own good."

The see-saw of despair and elation still tilted back and forth in Machin's head. From a smiling, kiss-blowing Tessa he'd moved to a curt stranger seemingly unwilling to communicate. And yet, on reflection, he realised that, if he'd scripted the next advance in his criminal activities, he wouldn't have dared to include a white

Mercedes, a beautiful Tessa and a trip to the Highlands.

They had three or more hours ahead of them so he decided there was no point in making any waves and he began to talk about mutual acquaintances, forgotten places, and the trivia which had occupied so much of his undergraduate attention. Tessa contributed little to his reflections at first, but neither did she contradict, question, or even ignore them, and so he progressively talked himself into a more stable mood.

The comfort of the car was deceptively reassuring. Memories of university and times which preceded responsibility cradled them in their warm metal box and insulated them from the world of exploding rosebeds and manic policemen.

The fact, for example, that several innocents would be severely stung by pellets from a .22 air rifle just seconds after they'd driven past them at various points along their route would go happily unnoticed by them. The retired banker mowing his lawn, the farmer beside a tractor, the G.P. on his bicycle, and the car salesman on his way back to Edinburgh were all to suffer at the whim of the big man sitting in the passenger seat of the red Toyota.

It stayed some twenty yards behind the Mercedes as he continued to make fine adjustments to the sight of his very powerful air-rifle. Driving past targets at 60 mph gave him a great chance to test it. Reflexes and marksmanship were constantly at the limits. He was having a good time. The black man who was driving the car said nothing and just concentrated on the Mercedes up ahead.

By the time they'd driven past Huntly, Tessa was listening to Machin's reminiscences with a semblance of interest. She was even mildly touched to discover his long-standing interest in her hadn't altogether died.

He'd reached that state of intense private lyricism which frequently precedes self-abuse and Tessa felt a strange mixture of disgust, pity, anger, and very mild arousal when he at last accompanied one of his little shared memories with a gesture that brought his right hand across onto her left thigh.

Perhaps there would be time for some self-indulgence when they got to Inverness, but she knew the necessity of remaining in charge of both the situation and Machin, and sexual foreplay at sixty mph was only acceptable when no other preoccupations intervened.

She let his hand rest there for a few moments and then, gently, with even a touch of tenderness, she said, "You know, Chris, I'm glad we never actually made it in bed. Inge ... remember her? She told me ... well, about your penis." And, in order to make her point clear, she took her left hand from the wheel and held the thumb and forefinger about an inch apart.

The blush that pulsed immediately into Machin's face was as hot as a head of steam. He looked quickly out of the nearside window, concentrating hard on a man who was cycling up a lane some 200 yards away towards the pellet which had his name on it.

What the hell was he supposed to answer to such a crack? How could he possibly continue a conversation which had so effectively castrated him? He was thankful that only the two of them were involv... Oh God! The microphone! Transmitting it all to The Cage. A reflex action sent his hand up from Tessa's thigh to the CND badge in his lapel. Tessa noticed the movement, saw the badge and assessed the situation at once.

"Well, well, Chris," she said. "I didn't realise you were so far advanced with your aviary that they'd issued you with a bug. What sort is it?"

Machin, his personality in tatters as a result of the peremptory destruction of his sexual identity, was incapable of playing at subterfuge.

"I don't know," he muttered.

"Let's see," said Tessa, cheerily, conversationally.

Machin unpinned the badge, took out the transmitter, and handed them over to her.

"Don't suppose it makes any bloody difference now," he said.

Tessa looked quickly at the transmitter and failed to suppress a sneer.

"Bit out of date, isn't it? I notice they don't give you their expensive stuff. This is only worth about seven hundred quid."

Machin didn't answer. Tessa looked at him and, having firmly established her dominance, allowed pity to rise to the surface of her mood. She smiled again and went on, "Shame to waste it, though."

She laid the transmitter in her lap, brought the badge up close to her lips and spoke into it, low, breathy, incredibly sexy.

"My breasts are yours," she said. "Let me feel your tongue and

86

teeth on them and guide your fingers here, here to this soft dark sweetness between my thighs…"

Machin listened, aghast, as she transmitted at least five minutes of progressively more blatant pornography to The Cage. As she whispered on, Tessa looked at him now and then and smiled to indicate this was a joke for them to share and Machin was gently eased back from his condition of moral castrato by two facts: 1) Tessa was obviously including him in her escapade, and 2) her monologue had induced an erection.

The self-doubt her previous comment had inspired caused Machin, looking at the erection, to decide it was indeed barely perceptible, but at least the bloody thing worked.

Tessa was satisfied with her efforts and concluded her performance, her whisper becoming more urgent.

"All right, take me, take me," she moaned. "Please. Plunge that (pause) thing into me. I'll tell you anything. You want to know who controls my section? His name is…" and the sentence climbed into a sigh and then a shrill shudder of release before she threw the microphone and transmitter out of the window and under the wheels of a Roadline pantechnicon which was overtaking them. Tessa laughed and glanced across at Machin.

"Oh, come on, Chris," she said as she saw the expression on his face. "We'll have a good time. Maybe even get to use that if we can fix it," she added, patting the small bulge in his crotch.

Machin yelped with pain.

"Oh Christ," he said. "Please don't so that. It's a bit tender."

"Well, well," she smiled, "been busy have you?"

Machin only grinned weakly, preferring to let her believe the soreness came from sexual excess rather than from the residual effects of Lodgedale's knee. The erection was beginning to hurt and Machin forced himself to look out at the passing fields while he recited some irregular verbs to himself. He thought he saw a farmer fall against a tractor, but the spot was immediately hidden by some trees and the incident forgotten.

Now they were genuinely alone and soon his pluperfect subjunctives had succeeded in ridding him of his erection. The intrusion of sexuality into their contact had freed most other inhibitions and Machin was ready once more to try to fathom some of the events of recent days.

"Seriously, Tessa," he said. "What's going on? I mean, why

did they suddenly contact me after all this time? I've got nothing to offer them … to offer you, I mean. You're with them, aren't you? And why are we going to Inverness? I don't know where the hell I am recently. Can't you tell me anything?"

Tessa glanced at and accelerated away from a man in a Vauxhall Astra who was desperately gunning its engine to try to get past this woman in her Mercedes.

"It's fairly complicated," she said easily. "I don't think you'd understand much of the ins and outs of it all."

"Try me," replied Machin. "Or at least tell me the bits that concern me."

Tessa's reluctance was clear, but Machin had to know something if they were to get his co-operation and so she set her lips, gave a tight little nod and began.

"All right, Chris, I'll tell you what I can, but don't interrupt and don't ask silly bloody questions. Deal?"

"Deal," said Machin, delighted to be reminded of a little catch-phrase everyone had used at university.

"OK. We want to build up our potential. There's never been a shortage of cash in Aberdeen. We want a bigger share, more outlets."

"What the hell makes you think I'll be of any use? What outlets do I have?"

Tessa said nothing. Machin said he was sorry. It was eight minutes before she spoke again.

"As I was saying," she said pointedly, "we want outlets."

Machin put up his hand like a schoolboy. Tessa stopped and glanced at him.

"Sorry, Tessa," he said, "but I don't understand what you're talking about. I mean, who are you? And what do you do?"

Tessa's patience held.

"Look at this car. Where d'you think I got that? From being somebody's P.A.?"

She waited. Machin considered the question.

"It's possible. There are plenty of women running companies now."

"Not in Aberdeen. Come on, Chris, you know bloody well, the only way I could earn the sort of money I do is through being devious. The oil's still a bonanza. The days of sending helicopters out to platforms to deliver just a packet of screws are long gone.

But there's still millions to be made out there. My organisation's mopping up a lot of business in the services line—maintenance, refurbishment, operating assets."

"What about your principles. I thought you were a socialist."

Tessa forgave the interruption. "That was then. Today, I'm a realist. Your mates at The Cage are doing everything they can to shaft our lot so we've got to keep up with them. Each of us knows the other one's there. It's like a sort of tennis match, only with engineering contracts, HR provisions, and bums and tits when the guys come ashore too."

She stopped, then continued almost as if she were talking to herself.

"The trouble is that recently it's been getting out of hand. I mean, when people start getting killed, that's serious. It's undermining the whole bloody system. Someone's rocking the boat. There's somebody muscling in—Russians, Yardies, I don't know, maybe even the Chinese. They're trying to destabilise the whole thing. They're taking the fun out of it. That bomb in your garden, for instance; we'd never do that. Even dickhead Eagle wouldn't go that far."

"So who are they, then?"

Tessa shook her head. "Nobody really knows yet. Nobody's been able to put a finger on them. They seem to work more as individuals. But somebody's controlling them. It's not just random. Up till now there's just been us and The Cage. So we're calling them the Third Way. They're bloody sinister. We've been after them for a year, but there's never anything you can put your finger on with them. They always seem to be a step ahead. They've been picking up contracts all over the British sector, trying to move into the Norwegian one. And they're getting nastier."

"How?"

"Well, they're having a go at you and us both. They're destabilising the whole bloody set-up. That's where you come in."

Machin didn't need to frame the question; it was contained in his facial expression, his attitude, everything, as he turned towards her.

"They want people to think we've lost the place. Want to make us a laughing stock in the trade. So they hit the new guys. Like you."

"What for?"

"To show how far they've infiltrated us. Nobody's supposed to know about you and others like you. So when they eliminate you, that's pretty impressive."

"Not for me, it's not."

Tessa ignored him.

"God knows where they get their information, but it's absolutely accurate and they use it without stopping to think."

Fear curdled in Machin's chest.

"That's why you were contacted," said Tessa. "For your own protection. We had to get in touch with you and warn you things might be starting to happen."

"Like my garden blowing up?"

"Right," said Tessa. "You're not much use to us, but it makes us look bloody fools if you're eliminated."

"I'm touched by your concern."

"If you lot survive, we all survive," said Tessa unemotionally. "It's as simple as that. That's why we've set up Armadillo."

She paused to allow for the inevitable question. When it came, she went on, "It's an operation designed to protect our own guys, and at the same time identify and eliminate the Third Way lot."

"Why are we going to Inverness then?" asked Machin. "Some sort of hideout up there?"

"Not exactly," said Tessa. "My boss—that was him on the mobile, the Big Snake—he's identified one of them up there. Seems like he got rid of one of your colleagues … er … Grebe, I think. Silly bloody names."

"Bit like Bird Watcher and Big Snake then," muttered Machin, but so quietly that she didn't hear him.

"Pulled a piano wire so far into his neck he nearly decapitated him," she said.

Nausea washed through Machin and he immediately broke into a cold sweat. Tessa continued in the same tone of semi-banter.

"God knows why they're concentrating on your lot. I thought we were the main enemy. Looks like they're getting even more ambitious. Could be a total take-over."

Machin, being careful to maintain as steady a voice as he could, said, "But I don't see why you're taking me up there. You know there's a killer there looking for people like me. Seems a bit perverse."

"It's all right," said Tessa, "we won't be there long."

"But why are we going?" insisted Machin.

Tessa explained, a trifle impatiently, that they'd only stay there long enough to find and dispose of the Third Way man. As Machin lapsed into silence to consider the enormity of this new information that transformed his roses-round-the-door housewife into a matter-of-fact killer, it was as well he didn't know the real reason for his presence.

After Tessa had disposed of the Third Way guy in the hospital, her boss had told her there was another one operating in Inverness. She'd been told the name of the hotel in which he was staying and had a general description of his appearance, but the Big Snake had suggested that in order to make a positive identification the man had to be persuaded to break cover and a decoy would speed everything up.

As Tessa drove towards her quarry, the decoy sat beside her, trying once more to understand the world he lived in, and promising himself that if he got out of all this intact he'd devote himself to comprehensive mediocrity. Four hundred yards away a retired banker twisted away from his lawn mower as he felt a sharp pain in his shoulder.

CHAPTER TEN

As the Mercedes and the red Toyota reached the roundabout which separates the Inverness traffic from that heading for the Kessock Bridge and the north west, Hawk was beginning to experience some of the stresses that accompany power. As soon as Eagle had left the previous evening, he'd visited the Foresterhill casualty department where his wrist had been X-rayed and encased in plaster, which had made work very difficult for him. He knew obscurely that the benefits he hoped to reap from Eagle's absence must be established quickly. That meant a thorough reorganisation of the office so that, on his return, Eagle wouldn't be able to find his files and data and would be utterly dependent on Hawk for guidance.

His attempts to sift through consignment slips, contract notes, tender documents, directories of active operators in the oil and gas sector, and scores of files on police and local councillors were constantly frustrated by the lump of plaster and the uselessness of his right hand. On top of that, as the evidence of his tampering lay blatantly about him, a smirking Mary stood before him speaking in tones so deferential that Hawk knew something sinister was afoot.

"I thought you'd want to know, boss," said the ex-sailor, lingering over the "boss" just long enough to turn it into an unqualified insult. "It's about the Anstey field."

Hawk, caught *in flagrante delicto*, was anxious to get rid of him.

"All right," he said, "let's get it over with."

"Certainly, boss. It's the subsea infrastructure. There's a manifold and a manifold extension. It's enough to serve three wells but with the risers under pressure, we'll need a shutdown of the..."

"I can't be bothered with that shit," said Hawk. "Deal with it. It's what you're paid for."

"Very good, boss," said Mary. "But there's something else."

"What? What?" said Hawk.

"Something I thought you'd want to hear for yourself."

He pointedly shifted some of the incriminating documents along the desk to make room for the micro-cassette player he was carrying.

"This," he said.

"What is it?"

"It's Sparrow. You'll see I've wound it on a bit," said Mary. "There's a lot of dross at the beginning. This is the bit that concerns us though, I think."

Still staring hard at Hawk, he pressed the switch. The machine was surprisingly powerful. Out of it came slow, heavy breathing into which small female whimpers intruded. Hawk looked sharply at Mary, whose eyes were still fixed on him, and Tessa's voice said, "Yes, yes. Oh my God. Oooh."

Hawk listened in astonishment for a few moments more as Tessa told someone how powerful erectile tissues could be in the right hands, and then, in total confusion and hot embarrassment, he signalled for Mary to switch the tape off. In the silence which ensued and which sounded louder than the tape, he said, "What the bloody hell's that all about? I thought you said it was from Sparrow?"

"It is, boss," said Mary, enjoying himself. "That's his contact. And that's the nature of the meet he had with her, if you'll pardon the pun."

Hawk needed a respite. This was all too much.

"All right Mary," he managed to say. "That'll be all."

"Huh. Will it, I wonder?" said Mary. "I mean, once they've had a taste of it, if you'll pardon my crudity, once they get into the old D. H. Lawrence routines, well…"

"Piss off, Mary," said Hawk, losing control in face of such obvious provocation.

"Certainly, boss," said Mary, with too much alacrity and too wide a smile. "You're the boss."

Hawk, shaking, watched him cross the room and go out, closing the door behind him. He jumped as it reopened immediately and Mary's face, with the same smile fixed in among the beard, looked back into the office.

"I said piss off," screamed Hawk.

"Yes, boss. Right away, boss," said Mary. "Just one more bit of news I forgot to give you. Mr Robin, sir, down in Stonehaven. He's been plucked."

Hawk was stunned. "Robin? Dead?"

"Yes, boss," grinned Mary. "Right, I'll piss off now then, boss."

And before Hawk had the chance to ask for details he closed the door once more.

Hawk's temples hammered as the combined effects of his embarrassment at Tessa's tape, his anger at Mary's insolence and his panic at this latest information crowded into his skull. Something was very obviously wrong. First, Eagle had heard that things were happening in Dundee, then fledglings had begun to be plucked, and now, just as he had a chance to supplant his chief, these problems began to press and require a response from him before he had time to familiarise himself with them.

He went to Eagle's drinks cabinet and poured a small measure of sweet sherry into a tumbler. He topped the glass up with soda and took a swig at the pale fizzy liquid as he tried to tease the strands of his predicament apart. He looked at the tape recorder which still lay among Eagle's private papers and, now he was alone, a little thrill of anticipation went through him as he thought he must listen to it in its entirety and in shameless privacy.

He was, of course, unaware that several hundred copies of the monologue were already circulating in pubs around Aberdeen. The technician who'd downloaded the file had taken the precaution of listening to the tape first and immediately noted the commercial possibilities which were opened up by Tessa's performance. Already the five minute tape was fetching thirty pounds and it would no doubt become one of the many collectors' items which had originated in The Cage.

As far as Hawk was concerned, however, the tape was exclusively his and in time might find its way into his bedroom cupboard with the magazines. He decided that, at the moment, he was too overwrought to consider the implications of Robin's death, and a leisurely spell with the tape recorder would be both informative and therapeutic.

As he sat down behind the desk, however, the telephone suddenly gave out its strident warble and flooded him with guilt. He snatched it up and, his voice cracking, said, "Hawk here."

"Who?" said the voice on the line.

"Hawk. Who's that?"

"This is Kestrel. What the bloody hell are you playing at, Hawk? Where's Eagle?"

Even through the clickings on the line Hawk could hear Kestrel's discomfiture and it helped to settle him.

"Eagle's soaring," he said, quickly inventing some fresh terminology.

"Soaring!" shouted Kestrel. "What d'you mean, soaring?"

"Just what I said, Kestrel."

"Oh, don't talk bloody rubbish, Hawk," said the distant Kestrel. "Why the bloody hell would Eagle want to take maternity leave?"

Hawk was briefly flustered. Had he boobed? Did soaring mean taking maternity leave? Or had Kestrel guessed he'd invented the term and was he double-bluffing? He mustn't lose the initiative for so little.

"Look, never mind that. It's classified anyway," he improvised. "He's left me in charge. And I'm busy, so what do you want?"

There was silence on the line. Hawk knew the information had hurt and was being absorbed and evaluated.

"Crafty bugger," said Kestrel at last.

Hawk replied quickly.

"If you've anything to report, do so. If not, get back to some work."

That made Kestrel angry.

"Oh, don't worry, sunshine," he said. "I've been working all right. And I've been getting results. Have you? Boss?"

Hawk rose to the sarcasm.

"I'm afraid so, underling," he countered. "For example, there's been another of your cock-ups in Stonehaven. Robin's been plucked."

"That was predictable," came back the immediate reply. "And I bet you've done bugger-all about it."

"Why should I clear up after you?" said Hawk, unaware that the conversation was beginning to resemble a fairly typical exchange between third-graders working out a pecking order.

"You don't need to, pal," snapped Kestrel. "I'm doing the dirty work."

"Oh yeah?" said Hawk.

"Yeah."

"Prove it."

"Easy."

"Oh yeah?"

"Yeah."

"How then?"

"I've found the bloke who rubbed out Grebe for a start."

"Oh yeah?"

"Yeah."

"Big deal," said Hawk, and slammed the phone down triumphantly.

The triumph came only from the fact that he'd thought of slamming down the phone before Kestrel did, and underneath it lay a real concern at the danger to his ambitions which Kestrel represented. He must speed up the reorganisation and Kestrel must be the first to go.

Angrily, he drained the sherry and soda from his glass and, careless of its effects, went for a refill. He'd deliberately not told Kestrel Eagle was on his way to Inverness. With any luck, they wouldn't even meet. Eagle would, after all, be far too busy with Bad Boy. And anyway, Kestrel must be kept in ignorance until Hawk could make some definitive move to dispose of him.

The adrenaline was still flowing fast as he sipped at the fresh drink and his eagerness to listen to Tessa on the tape had been increased by the passion in his exchange with Kestrel. He put the glass on the desk and, awkwardly, because of his plaster, rewound the tape and switched on. Sparrow's voice came out of the machine.

"I really wish I could stay with you now and just have you drive me anywhere. I don't care where. But I can't..."

Hawk didn't want to hear this. He snapped the switch down, wound forward and turned it on again. This time, it was a snatch of conversation between a man and a woman.

"Where are you?"

"On my way, Big Snake."

"With or without?"

"With."

Big snakes? With or without? What sort of depravities was Sparrow up to in that bloody car? It was obviously very important for Hawk to rewind and listen to the whole encounter. As he settled back to do so and to find out who the other man in this travelling bordello was, however, he was surprised to find himself thinking his voice sounded familiar. The accent and the words were wrong, but not the voice. He couldn't identify it, but it was certainly one he knew.

****

In Inverness, Kestrel fumed. Leaving Aberdeen had been bad enough with the evidence of a shared late night experience scarred across the features of Eagle and Hawk. All the way up, it had worried him and their talk of priorities at the last meeting began to take on alarming connotations.

The anxiety he felt explained his fanatical determination to expedite his business in Inverness and scuttle home at the earliest opportunity. He was determined to solve the murder of Grebe instantly in order both to demonstrate his competence and to allow him to return to the machinations in The Cage.

The ringer who'd been working with Grebe had been helpful in directing him towards a particular hotel in which a suspicious-looking individual had been hanging around for a couple of days, apparently keeping him, the ringer, under surveillance. Kestrel's suspicions about this individual were deliciously confirmed on the second evening of his visit when he went to meet the ringer and found him lying on the floor of his room in the guest house with the point of a golf umbrella forced into his chest and a large mahogany sideboard on top of him.

Kestrel reasoned that, given the circumstances of such a death, suicide was unlikely. Also, the odds against being impaled by a golf umbrella and simultaneously crushed by a sideboard were too great to make it accidental. The probability was murder, and since the ringer had indicated he was being watched, it was a reasonable enough assumption that the person who'd been watching him knew something of the crime.

Kestrel's ambition to succeed being even greater than his fear for his own safety at the hands of someone strong enough to push umbrellas into rib-cages, he determined to watch and incriminate the man towards whom the ringer had directed him.

It was indeed a Third Way operative, the postman, who had

disposed of first Grebe and then the ringer. Unfortunately, however, the ringer had given Kestrel no description of the postman other than the vague "suspicious-looking individual" and so Kestrel had identified the wrong person.

Although the postman did indeed hang around the hotel indicated, the continuity of his presence there was obscured by the much more ostentatious hanging around that was carried out by Lodgedale, who also had him under surveillance.

Kestrel, seeking to identify his prey, had bought a copy of the *Financial Times* for cover and sat in a corner of the lobby. He'd looked around, noted those present, including the small man with the incongruous tartan donkey-jacket, but before any of them impinged properly on his awareness, his attention was caught by a scuffle near the lift doors.

A woman in a fur coat and carrying a poodle had just emerged from the lift. The dog had been frightened by the noises of the doors and yapped loudly, causing the large man in the trilby standing nearby to jump. The man had taken one pace across to the woman, snatched the dog from her arms and drop-kicked it across the lobby. Lodgedale (for it was he), had then leaned forward before the woman had recovered her wits and said quietly to her, "If you don't piss off right away, you'll get the same treatment."

The woman backed off quickly, scooped up her whining poodle, unknowingly causing it serious internal injuries as she did so since Lodgedale's kick had splintered its ribs and they were now piercing its lungs, and ran out to find a policeman. Kestrel, for his part, naturally assumed that a man with such a penchant for casual violence must be the prime suspect.

Since that noteworthy event, Lodgedale had duly obliged by hanging around the lobby and acting so suspiciously that Kestrel had no doubt at all that he had identified the killer he was searching for. And so he watched Lodgedale and Lodgedale watched the postman and the postman waited for further orders before returning to his round in Aberdeen.

The triumph of Kestrel's detection was supposed to have reached a peak in his report to The Cage, but glory had quickly soured as Hawk's news had come down the line. The thought of that weedy ginger bastard sitting at Eagle's desk playing Tammy Wynette numbers, and probably studying Texan culture to impress Eagle, was intolerable.

Why was he there? What the hell had they been up to the night before their last meeting? What were the priorities? And where the hell was Eagle?

He walked to and fro in his hotel room trying to fathom these mysteries but succeeded only in confirming his own feeling of impotence. He must get back to The Cage. But to do that he needed proof. He needed to be able to identify his suspect.

His imagination convinced him that, when he did return and enter Eagle's office, he would find Eagle and Hawk married or at least locked in an unimaginably obscene embrace, and so he needed to arm himself with a shock equally powerful. Nothing less than a cast-iron case of proven murder wrapped in irrefutable evidence would do.

As his mind ceased clattering around and settled on this sole fact, he began to consider it more rationally. The man had a room in his own hotel. If any evidence were to be found, clearly it would be there. He would therefore have to search it. The prospect was unattractive; the fate of the poodle sneaked into his mind, followed hugely by the memory of the golf umbrella and the mahogany sideboard, and he knew any search must be planned carefully and surrounded with meticulous alibis.

His habit was to write his problems on scraps of paper and after twenty minutes the only one he had not discarded said, "Legitimise presence in room." Since the only people whose presence in the suspect's room would not be questioned were the manager and the chambermaid, he had no option but to masquerade as one of them.

Reluctantly, he realised his choice was pre-empted by the fact that the manager was six feet eight inches tall and had only one arm as a result of a road accident. Kestrel was a stocky five foot six and although he bore even less resemblance to a chambermaid than he did to the manager, the upper limb deficiency left only the one option.

He would need the black dress and white apron they all still wore and so he rang at once for room service. Luckily, it was a dull-witted chambermaid who arrived. Even more luckily, she was about Kestrel's height, thickly-built and startlingly ugly. And even more luckily still, Kestrel, being completely asexual, was unaware of the potential problems which crowded around the question he put to her.

"Look," he said, "this is rather important. I work for a big oil company. Would you mind taking your clothes off so that…"

He had no need to continue. The chambermaid, who had endured for years the lonely shame of hearing her fellow-workers relate the intricate accounts of their escapades in the rooms of male guests and seeing them bank the huge tips that were consequent upon such service, had never herself been on the receiving end.

Kestrel was amazed at the speed with which the apron, dress and bra fell from her. In the shortest possible time, she was lying stark naked on his bed. Kestrel was delighted. He began to undress.

"Thanks very much," he said. "It won't take long."

This last remark caused her to lift her head from the pillow rather anxiously, and her embryonic fear matured instantly as she saw him pulling on the dress she'd just discarded.

"Would you mind zipping up the back?" said Kestrel, completely oblivious to the mound of receptive female wobbling on his sheets.

The mound moved.

"Oh shit!" it said. "Just my luck."

"I beg your pardon?" said Kestrel.

"You're not going to fuck me, then?" asked the mound.

"No thanks," said Kestrel, too busy with the zip to consider the enormity of the suggestion she was making.

The maid, after all her disappointing years, was a stoic. As quickly as her interest and readiness had grown, so they diminished. She sat on the edge of the bed.

"How long d'you want the dress for?" she asked.

"Oh, ten minutes should do," said Kestrel. "I'll pay for it, you know."

"Yes, I know," said the maid.

"One other thing," said Kestrel. "Have you got a set of keys?"

The maid pointed to a table beside the door; she'd put her keys on it when she came in.

"Good. Look, I know it's a strange request," said Kestrel, "but, as I said, I work for a big oil company and there's a man staying here I've got to investigate, so I'll need to get into his room. You'll be well paid, but you'll have to keep quiet about it."

His anxiety concerning her silence was wasted. She'd already decided she would fabricate a story about her encounter with Kestrel. His money would help to verify it, and at last she'd be able to take her place with the others and counter their gibes with at least one apparently legitimate service. She simply nodded, showed him the sub-masters on the key-ring, and lay back on the bed as Kestrel, badly disguised as a chambermaid, opened his door quietly, peered out, found the corridor to be empty, left the room and closed the door behind him.

With the curious irony that fate always reserves for itself, just as Kestrel turned right to make his way along the corridor, a figure appeared from the stairwell to his left, saw the retreating chambermaid and began to creep after her. The two figures, hunted and hunter, moved along the corridor towards the service stairs. Kestrel's reasoning was that these stairs were the proper location for a chambermaid and that anyway, their relative darkness would help to cloak the inadequacies of his disguise.

For different reasons, his hunter was also glad of the darkness. Kestrel disappeared through the door onto the darkened landing. His follower, smiling grimly, quickly pushed through the door behind him and, seeing Kestrel's pale legs disappearing up the stairs, let out a low, hissing growl. Kestrel heard it and stopped. He turned, and warily came back down the steps he'd climbed. His blood banged in his head as he saw the shape in the gloom, but he had to go through with his charade. On the landing he approached the figure and his fear splintered into incomprehension as the man also moved towards him.

"Good God!" said Kestrel. "What are you doing here?"

CHAPTER ELEVEN

Two hundred and seventy-eight yards away, Machin stood trembling before two huge Belazzo boys with tears beginning to overflow onto his cheeks and a craven whimper waiting for release at the back of his throat.

He and Tessa had arrived in Inverness the previous evening and the unpleasantness of the drive had reached a peak at the receptionist's desk downstairs when Tessa had said, "We want a double room, please. On the second floor, overlooking the street. Mr and Mrs Bird."

As with everything about her, each element of her request was calculated. Unknown to Machin, the specific location and outlook of the room was chosen because, thanks to the Big Snake, Tessa knew that from this window she could look directly across the street and through that of the postman.

Machin's assumptions about their sudden accession to marital status were also false since her sole object was to keep a permanent eye on him. They'd arrived in the bedroom and Machin had eventually made to kiss her. She'd responded with a gentle, remonstrative tap of her hand on his crotch, knowing exactly how firm it should be to remind him of his soreness and temporarily unsex him.

Just to underline the position, she'd insisted that, for the first night at least, she should have the bed to herself while he slept on the floor. A night of draughts, thinly-covered floorboards and alternations between wakefulness and nightmares had not prepared him for the meeting with Tessa's back-up.

She'd decided, since Machin already knew them for what they were and since they were supposed to provide protection, there was no point in them maintaining the separation that had kept their Toyota behind her Mercedes all the way to Inverness. She'd therefore asked them to come to her room to meet Machin.

The formal introductions were almost over. All that remained was for a smiling Eric the Emancipator to release Machin's hand from his grip. Machin, unaware of the fact that one of Eric's hobbies was to reduce to powder any metacarpals placed in his hand, had said, "How do you do?" and thereafter been incapable of uttering a sound as the pain squeezed the tears from him. The whimper that was stuck in his throat at last broke out through a sob, causing Tessa to turn back from the window out of which she looked constantly and say, "Release him, Eric."

Regretfully, Eric did so and looked idly round for something to break as Machin hugged his hand, fought to hold back his weeping and wished he'd gone to a monastery instead of a university.

Bad Boy stood near Tessa at the window.

"So, what do we do now we're here?" he asked.

Tessa turned to gaze back at the hotel across the street.

"Nothing yet. Assess things. Wait for instructions."

"No initiatives allowed?" asked Bad Boy.

Tessa glanced quickly at him.

"About what?" she asked, genuinely unsure.

Before answering, Bad Boy jerked his head questioningly in the direction of Machin. The gesture was useless since Tessa was once more looking away.

"Is it OK to talk with him here?" Bad Boy was forced to ask.

"Probably," said Tessa. "I'll stop you if it's not. What's on your mind?"

"Phone calls," said Bad Boy.

"Who from?"

"Some kind of nut."

"Did he give a name?"

"Several. The main one was Donna."

Tessa looked round again.

"Donna?" she said.

"Yeah. But he also called himself Eagle."

"The Eagle?" asked Tessa.

"Seems like it from the things he said," replied Bad Boy.

"Well, what did he want?"

There was a silence. Bad Boy looked at his feet.

"Well?" insisted Tessa.

"Me," said Bad Boy quietly.

"You mean he wants to turn you?" said Tessa, suddenly serious.

"No, he wants to fuck me," said Bad Boy even more quietly.

Eric gave a blast of laughter and, to mark his delight, delivered a forearm smash to the wall which cracked the plaster.

Even Machin was listening, his astonishment at the revelation about his boss temporarily banishing his pain.

"Explain," said Tessa, still serious.

Bad Boy was clearly embarrassed by the whole episode but equally grateful to offload it. He spoke quickly.

"He phoned me again and again last night. I told him to push off at first. Then I found out who he was, and I just listened to him. He's given me the ex-directory numbers of all his line managers, I know which trawler skippers to use for offshore runs, whose warehouses are secure, the engineering contracts due for renewal, a list of teachers in schools from..."

"Wait a minute, wait a minute," Tessa interrupted him. "He told you all this on the phone last night?"

"Yes. To show his good faith, he said. In the end I had to leave the phone off the hook just to get some sleep."

"Christ," said Tessa. "Have you told the Big Snake about it?"

"Not yet," said Bad Boy, "I thought I'd check with you."

Tessa was reflective for a while, even her scrutiny of the hotel opposite forgotten. She'd read profiles on everyone in The Cage so Eagle's particular preferences came as no surprise. The new element was his infatuation for Bad Boy. Suddenly she looked at Machin.

"D'you know this Eagle?" she said.

Machin was unsure as to what ethics, protocol, or discretion required him to answer to such a question, but Eric's presence was an instant education.

"Yes, he's the boss in The Cage," he said.

"I know that," snapped Tessa. "Did you know he was bent?"

"I don't know anything about him really," Machin replied.

Tessa thought some more.

"You have a way of contacting him, don't you?" she asked suddenly.

Machin hesitated.

"Yes, I think so," he said. "I think there's a code I can phone to get him."

104

"Right," said Tessa, "that's what we'll do then. You ring him and Bad Boy listens in to check it's the same man."

Machin's unwillingness to get involved evaporated as Eric put the bedside phone on his lap and accompanied the movement with a friendly pat on his cheek which loosened the crown on his incisor. He took out and consulted his diary, lifted the receiver, and when the receptionist answered, gave her the number of Benton Exporting.

The line clicked and buzzed. Machin no longer felt excitement or even fear at his predicament. He'd recognised what should have been a self-evident truth from the outset—he was not even a pawn in the game, but merely an object being subjected to forces over which no-one seemed to have any control. At last came the inevitable female firing icicles down the line.

"Benton Exporting. Can I help you?"

He still had no idea how to ensure contact, but was beginning to learn from previous errors. He kept his sentences elliptical.

"Sparrow. For Eagle. Imperative contact. Emergency."

"What?" asked the voice, recognising no familiar structure in the terms Machin had chosen, but hesitating because they did have the halting inarticulacy which characterised the genuine article.

"Oh, hurry up, woman," said the desperate Machin. "This is Sparrow requesting permission to speak to Eagle."

These words lost him the momentary initiative, first because Eric began whooping with laughter at Machin's confessing to the name Sparrow, and more importantly because the operator at The Cage recognised them to be semantically and syntactically legitimate and therefore outside the normal pattern of contact phrases.

With the usual suggestion that he'd dialed the wrong number, she rang off.

Tessa was angry. After a sharp word to Eric, who tried hard to compose himself, she dialed the hotel receptionist and asked to be reconnected with the Aberdeen number. While connection was being re-established she scribbled some notes on the back of an envelope and thrust them at Machin.

"Try that," she said, and her words were almost simultaneous with those of the operator at The Cage offering once more the help of Benton Exporting. Machin read the scribbles.

"Er ... M and C enquiry. Ratify canary. Seed nature uncertain.

Eagle to consider."

There was a longish pause. Unknown to Machin, the operator was searching rapidly through the notes on her desk. His words had made no sense, but they sounded so authentic that they must be legitimate. As the pause endured, Tessa scribbled again and an amazed Machin read, "Who's a pretty boy then? Emergency status."

The operator gave up her search. With codes this esoteric, this must obviously be a top man. Her decision was helped by the fact that Eagle was absent and Hawk would have to take the call. If there were any repercussions, they could quickly be directed towards the acting chief's inexperience. She said, "Eagle in flight. Hawk on roost. Wait one," and plugged the line through to Hawk in Eagle's office.

There, the sudden noise of the phone made Hawk jump guiltily once again and switch off the microcassette player just at the point where Tessa was talking about secretions. Quickly he composed himself and lifted the receiver.

"Hawk here."

"Oh, thank God for that," said Machin. "Look, it's Sparrow here." (Eric clutched himself.) "I want to speak to Eagle."

Hawk's residual guilt feelings at being caught yet again listening to the tape were rekindled by the fact that he was actually speaking to one of the participants in the orgy. He felt jealous of Machin, angry at being interrupted, and keen to establish his own superiority.

"Oh, charming," he said. "Are you sure you can spare the time?"

"Eh?" said Machin, giving Tessa a puzzled shrug.

"I thought you might be too busy driving about with your degenerate friends, indulging in sexual acrobatics in some snazzy automobile. Felt any good Big Snakes recently?"

Tessa, whose mind worked more quickly than those of the others, remembered Hawk's personality profile. She motioned for Machin to keep Hawk talking while she scribbled more instructions. As she handed them to Machin, Hawk had just worked himself round to the details about what happens to static electricity when nylon underwear is rubbed for any length of time against the perspex facings of a dashboard. Tessa urged Machin to interrupt.

"I've got just one question for you," Machin read, uncomprehendingly. "What about elbows?"

The sudden silence was unearthly.

"What?" said a barely audible Hawk.

"You heard. Elbows," said Machin.

The remnants of Hawk's strained wits had been scattered by this evidence that his secret passion for elbows, especially those on young boys and girls, was somehow the property of one of the newest recruits to the organisation. He needed time to orientate himself, but first he needed to find out how accurate Machin's information was and how widespread its circulation. As he began to speak, his voice came out as that of an alto, which he coughed back down to his normal tremulous tenor.

"Of course I have no idea what you're talking about, but if I did, who else would?"

Tessa shook her head. Machin said nothing.

After a pause, Hawk went on, "Er… It's just for professional reasons, of course. Just sort of theory really. Purely anatomical. Because it's obviously a subject I know nothing about. Nothing at all…"

Eventually, his voice trailed helplessly off. Tessa whispered instructions to Machin.

"All right, Hawk," he said in obedience to her demands. "Let's just say I know. Now, where's Eagle? I want to talk to him."

"He's … er … not here. I'm in charge."

"Where is he then?"

"Inverness," answered the now thoroughly miserable Hawk. And Tessa was satisfied when, in response to further questions, Hawk revealed that he didn't know exactly where Eagle was, only that he was looking for Bad Boy. She motioned Machin to ring off and he, in an attempt to salvage something for himself from it all, asked by way of saying good-bye whether Hawk, being the boss, had any instructions for him. From the pit of his despair Hawk tried to rescue some scraps of his function and resorted once more to the ploy of arcane invention.

"Oh yes," he said, "of course. Er … Millet and Cuttlefish 0171-999-9999. Now, about my bedroom cupboard…"

But before his faltering explanations could begin, Tessa, angry that Machin had taken an initiative, took the receiver from him and replaced it with a bang.

107

"What's that mean?" she asked.

"It's one of their codes," replied Machin.

"I know that," Tessa snapped, "but what's it mean?"

"I don't know. I'd have to work it out. It takes ages."

"Right," said Tessa, "that's your little job for today while we have a look for dickhead Eagle."

Briskly she issued instructions to her two companions and in a very short time had left the hotel with Bad Boy to begin the search.

In Aberdeen, a twitching ginger string of insecurity that was the temporary acting head of The Cage sat beside a silent tape recorder in the desolation of his now public fantasies while in Inverness his minion was left in the care of Eric the Emancipator trying to decode his acting chief's instruction. This time, Hawk's invention was particularly unfortunate. He'd just ordered Machin to assassinate the Lord Provost of Edinburgh.

****

In the darkened service stairway of the hotel just along the road, Kestrel stood face to face with the man who had followed him and was now studying him and his outfit with careful attention. Eagle, for it was he, hadn't bothered to answer his subordinate's brusque enquiry as to why he was there since first, it was none of his business, second, he was certainly not obliged to answer such questions, and third, he was preoccupied by the pleasant discovery that both of his deputies shared at least one of his sexual deviations.

First, there was Hawk in his kingfisher silk and suede, and now the frankly transvestite Kestrel wearing not only female attire but also a uniform of subservience. Had his mind not been so thoroughly conditioned by his greed for Bad Boy's derision, he would there and then have initiated the sexually naïve Kestrel into ceremonies and attitudes which that service staircase hadn't witnessed since the days of Victorian stability.

In his increasing desperation to be spurned by Bad Boy, however, it was mildly antidotal to see that, should his wooing of the wrestler fail, there was at least the promise that life back at The Cage might be enlivened by these new discoveries. At least some parts of his troubled existence might blossom.

On his arrival in Inverness, he'd booked into his hotel and

immediately begun his quest. His familiarity with Freemasonry had enabled him to discover Bad Boy's hotel, and the whole evening had been spent in repeated phone calls offering to betray the entire Cage hierarchy if Bad Boy would only deign to reject him.

The fact that Bad Boy's phone had become permanently engaged around midnight hadn't entirely diminished the exaltation Eagle had felt simply from talking to his god. He'd slept through blissful dreams of submission and, on waking and telephoning once more only to discover Bad Boy had gone out, he'd decided to enlist Kestrel's aid in his search.

The elation of a man past fifty in the throes of his first love made him indulgent to almost everything, and particularly receptive to the discovery of his subordinate's perversion. He stood fingering the coarse material of Kestrel's dress.

"Paul, my man," he said, "Why didn't you tell me you liked dressing up like this? Life in The Cage could've been so much more pleasant."

Hawk, burdened with his own deviance, had been quick to understand that of his chief and recognised its potential for exploitation. Kestrel, on the other hand, having himself no sexual peculiarities, or even normalities, was unaware of their full potency.

In an otherwise relatively quick-witted mind, the role of sexuality was uncharted. His mother had been a self-employed prostitute in Leith and, as a child, he'd witnessed her various encounters from infancy into puberty. This regular transformation of his mother into a contorted, heaving lump of noise, coupled with the necessity of having to turn off the television set several times every evening, since they lived in one room and the customers didn't want it on while they performed, left him with two interpretations of sex; first, it was a job, and second, it meant deprivation and was therefore to be avoided.

He began patiently to explain to Eagle the reason why he'd put the dress on, but Eagle, grown canny after years of closeted innuendo, smiled understandingly and kissed him on the cheek. Still the fullness of Eagle's misconceptions failed to dawn on Kestrel and he was about to elaborate further on his need to gain untroubled access to Lodgedale's room when Eagle said, "When we get back to Aberdeen, you, Jim and I must compare wardrobes.

Share frocks, panties. Exchange recipes maybe." Then, with a wink, "And equipment too."

Despite his ignorance, Kestrel sensed the game he played with Hawk was about to change. He must learn the rules and make sure his stakes had been placed when the hands were dealt. Since Eagle's arm was now tightly round his waist, he decided to enlist his help in searching Lodgedale's room.

Through Eagle's caresses (which remained half-hearted since he was still determined to save himself for Bad Boy), he explained his suspicions about Lodgedale and his determination to acquire corroborative evidence. Eagle was charmed by the way in which his settled life was suddenly taking off in so many exciting directions. The danger of the enterprise thrilled him, as did the descriptions of the degree of violence which their suspect was capable of unleashing. He decided to treat the whole thing as a small entertainment which would occupy his mind briefly before he set about his main task.

So the two men, each feeling a closeness that had never before been part of their relationship, set off together up the service stairs towards Lodgedale's empty room.

CHAPTER TWELVE

Machin was glad of the need to concentrate on decoding the M and C which Hawk had blurted out to him. Tessa and Bad Boy had left. Eric was dividing his attention between the postman's room across the street and Machin. He'd quickly run out of jokes about sparrows, but continued to repeat the three he knew in an endless cycle.

Machin, summoning up all his courage, had decided to tell Eric that he needed silence in order to decipher the message and as Eric moved to batter him for such insolence, he pointed out that he was doing it on Tessa's instructions and she'd be angry if he hadn't completed it before her return. Eric had contented himself with tearing the duvet cover into strips and sulkily looking out of the window hoping the postman would do something to provoke him.

The M and C absorbed Machin entirely. He hadn't brought his exercise books with him, but his previous decoding had been so thorough that the techniques involved were still fresh in his mind. As the message began to form however, his disbelief increased and a new terror grew in parallel with it. After two hours, the last part of the pattern was complete.

He sat back, looked at Eric, and envied him the simplicity of his role. It seemed Eric had only to destroy or protect; his own functions were so much more confused.

According to his new instruction he was to buy a copy of John Fowles' *Daniel Martin*, underline the seventh word in alternately the third and ninth lines on the fourteenth page of each chapter. He was to be outside the Public Library at noon on the 17th. There, a contact, using the Lewis Crassic Gibbon code, would supply him with a rail ticket, some Scottish money and instructions, all of which would be necessary for the trip he was to take to Edinburgh to assassinate the Lord Provost with either a rope or a baseball bat, whichever was more convenient.

None of it made any sort of sense. He was glad of the thought that Tessa would interpret and provide guidance for him. He jumped as Eric, at the window, suddenly swore loudly.

"Shit. He's leaving."

In the hotel room opposite, the postman was clearing things from drawers and the wardrobe and folding them into a suitcase. Eric watched and his agitation increased. Everything the man did provided further evidence of his intention to check out, and Eric knew he must not do so until Tessa returned and decided on the best way to cover his movements. The man must be detained, and Eric's mind knew only one form of detention. He would have to leave Machin alone in the hotel for a few moments, but there he foresaw no problems.

Other minders might have tied up their captive, but Eric's method was quicker. He moved to Machin's chair, said, "Stand up," and when his fearful captive did so, knocked him out with a forearm smash. It was all so much quicker than fumbling with ropes and knots.

He stretched Machin on the bed, took the keys and went quickly down and across the street then up the stairs to the postman's room. There, he resisted a temptation to kick the door down and instead knocked as gently as he could.

The postman, who had no reason to suspect anything, was nonetheless startled at the loud banging. He opened the door, however, whereupon Eric moved swiftly into the room, executed a cursory forearm smash and followed it with a jab to the throat since the postman, being infinitely tougher than Machin, was still conscious after the first blow.

Eric completed the demolition with a chop to the man's neck and was pleased at his own efficiency as he stood with the postman senseless at his feet. With a rare flash of insight, Eric reasoned that the man might regain consciousness before Tessa returned, in which case his efforts would have been wasted.

He took the postman's left shin and left foot, one in each hand, and twisted them in opposite directions until he heard little snapping sounds which suggested some parts of the mechanism had been displaced. Having thus effectively immobilised his man, he suppressed an urge to do the same thing to the other leg, both arms and the neck, left the room, and returned to where Machin was beginning to come round.

Eric's training as a wrestler had endowed him with anaesthetic skills as finely tuned as those of hospital consultants. He knew exactly how long the effects of a forearm smash would last and the one he'd delivered to Machin had been clinically judged. He grinned as his captive surfaced into consciousness.

Across the street, the postman lay still, unaware of the pain that awaited him when his turn came to follow the route up from oblivion.

****

Pain and distress were fairly common phenomena at that particular time in that area of Inverness. In Lodgedale's room, Eagle and Kestrel had given up trying to heave the combination of double-bed and wardrobe off them and were content to use what remained of their breath to scream. They had had no difficulty in entering the room but, after closing the door behind them, they had taken only one step before all hell was let loose. Wires twanged, pieces of furniture fell and they were pinned to the floor by the two heaviest items in the room.

Lodgedale, in one of his enforced bouts of reading, had tried part of a James Bond novel. He hadn't bothered to complete it because the violence it contained seemed tame, contrived and literary. One of the book's passages, however, revealed that the master-spy always set certain traps whenever he left a room so that on his return he'd know whether he'd had any visitors.

To Lodgedale the idea seemed sound but undeveloped. Sticking hairs across the edges of doors was fine; it told you the door had been opened, but not who'd opened it. Lodgedale's variation on this basic Bond technique was to substitute a strong elastic trip-wire just a yard inside the door, attach it to the most lethal objects in the room, and arrange it all in a series of pulleys that brought everything crashing down in front of the door at the slightest pressure on the elastic. That way, on returning, you not only discovered the room had been entered, but invariably those who had done the entering were still there.

The relative lack of progress in this case was depressing Lodgedale. No arrests in four days, no interrogations, not even a spot of recreational riot control, and the relative lack of black skins in Inverness meant there was never any occasion for a bit of harmless racism. Thus deprived of all the normal parameters of police work, he felt he was losing his edge.

When he'd woken up that morning, his whole metabolism was wrong. He felt fresh, his cheeks glowed, and his appetite was enormous. It was awful, and so, knowing he needed some sort of pick-me-up, he'd spent a few hours at the bus depot wandering among the exhaust fumes.

The treatment had had the desired effect for, on his way back to the hotel, he felt mean and ugly once more. His ear, tuned to the discords of violence, picked up the screaming at the bottom of the stairs and, his pulse racing from the combined effects of carbon monoxide and the new input of adrenaline, he rushed up, praying the screamers would be his.

Eagle and Kestrel heard the door bang open and their screams became babbles of relief and pleas for help. The relief, of course, was short-lived. Lodgedale had come in, noted with satisfaction the heap of bed and wardrobe and with glee the four legs sticking out from under it.

One pair of legs was trousered but the other was bare and seemed to belong to a maid. Lodgedale, ever alert, bent to look at the maid's crotch and was surprised at how pronounced her mons pubis was. Surprise quickly became suspicion however, and he decided the maid's gender must be checked.

There were various methods available to him but he stayed in character and aimed a kick at her crotch. Kestrel, whose scrotum was, of course, the target, exploded in areas of pain he'd never before suspected. Like all experimenters, Lodgedale repeated his test in order to verify his first set of results, was equally pleased at the outcome and turned his attention to the trousered crotch which he decided to use as a control group. Eagle's previous delights had been derived from masochistic fantasies but no stretch of his distorted imagination could interpret the present experiences as pleasurable and the volume of his screaming matched that of Kestrel.

After only a brief period of such gratuitous violence both men fainted and Lodgedale, deprived of the satisfaction of hearing their screams, reluctantly decided to stop and try to discover who they were and why they'd entered his room. His system of pulleys enabled the collapsed furniture to be rearranged fairly quickly and soon he was sitting on the edge of his bed enjoying the moans that came from the two men as they regained their senses and delighting in the fact that the one dressed as a maid was the postman's accomplice.

"All right then," he said at last. "What's the game then?"

It was a rhetorical question, since his long experience in the force had taught him that all suspects, whether guilty or innocent, responded in the same manner to the opening questions of an interrogation. It was many years since he'd actually listened to such responses and nowadays he automatically used the question as a mere prelude to more punching and kicking. When he'd finished, he sat down on the bed again and repeated, "I said what's the game?"

Eagle, despite as well as because of the agony that had been dispensed, was beginning to feel a certain regard for Lodgedale. If he hadn't promised to save himself for Bad Boy, the sheer brutality of this man might have attracted him enough to overlook his ugliness. He smiled at him, and Lodgedale, gratefully assuming the smile to indicate defiance, stood up to continue the assault. Kestrel, however, was ignorant of all these refinements.

"Stop, stop," he whined and whistled, having not enough breath or muscular control to form coherent and consecutive sounds. "I'll tell you everything."

Lodgedale, disappointed, stood on Eagle's left hand and then sat down.

"Right, get on with it," he said. "And if just one syllable turns out to be a lie, I'll stop the good cop routine."

Kestrel was terrified to think that the beating to which they'd been subjected was an example of restraint on Lodgedale's part and made up his mind to give him a full, unadulterated account of the events which had brought them to this disastrous encounter.

Lodgedale listened to the whole thing, interrupting only once, at the point where Kestrel revealed it was they who had asked that Machin be released from custody, to call them both bastards and have a little display of temper which coincidentally broke a bone in Kestrel's right forearm and most of those in Eagle's right hand.

Eventually, the story was continued and concluded and Lodgedale sat digesting the information. Kestrel and Eagle lay in their separate crucibles of pain waiting for their tormentor to pronounce judgement.

115

"Right," he said at last. "You're under arrest."

Kestrel thought of protesting and the thought provoked a final half-hearted assault from Lodgedale before he telephoned reception and asked to be connected with the police station. There, the desk sergeant could make little sense of Lodgedale's story but agreed to send a squad car.

Only one incident troubled the transfer of Eagle and Kestrel from the hotel to the detention cells. As they were bustled across the pavement, Eagle looked across the street and saw Utopia. He shouted, "Oh my God. It's him," and the surge of power that gushed through him amazed the two constables who were holding him. It was only Lodgedale's knee in his kidneys that prevented him breaking free and making his escape.

Across the road, Bad Boy and Tessa looked, along with all the other passers-by, at the grey little man resisting arrest and the strange maid who was limping meekly to the car. Bad Boy, remembering both the voice and the face from their previous meeting at the Exhibition and Conference Centre, quickly told Tessa they'd found their man. It was difficult to believe the Cage's top man was being arrested so publicly, and Tessa suspected his indiscretions while telephoning Bad Boy might already have been discovered.

As the car drove away she and Bad Boy continued back along the street to their hotel while in Kestrel's room, the naked maid had fallen asleep and was impregnating his sheets with her unmistakable odour.

****

Events seemed to be rushing on rather too quickly for Tessa's liking. On her arrival back at her hotel, armed already with the knowledge that Eagle had been arrested, she learned that her naïve little sleeper, Machin, had instructions to assassinate the main man in Edinburgh and the Third Way guy she had under surveillance was preparing to move on.

She didn't entirely approve of Eric's decision to immobilise their man, but, on the other hand, it did give them time to align their priorities, contact the Big Snake and retain control of developments. Of all her tasks, the continued surveillance of the postman was the easiest to arrange. She sent Eric to sit in the lobby of the hotel opposite with instructions to time and monitor every outgoing call from residents via the receptionist, and Bad Boy was posted at the window to keep an eye on the postman's body which hadn't moved since Eric's visit.

The new factor which made less sense than all the others was the order which had been issued to Machin. Being totally unaware of the fact that Hawk had transmitted what he thought to be a random M and C to preserve a semblance of his authority, she was unable to fathom why an untried, untrained, unwilling and inept fledgling should be sent on a seriously difficult assignment. Although logic seemed to have little place in the running of The Cage, she decided the first priority should be to check the validity of the order.

She instructed the hapless Machin to ring The Cage once more, first briefing him on the manner to adopt and the information she required. Machin, whose head was still throbbing from the after-effects of Eric's anaesthetic, had entered a world of utter unreality.

His previous existence, spent in classrooms and pubs, illuminated only infrequently by flashes of awareness and, consequently, frustration at its mediocrity, seemed to have been lived by someone else. Now, it glowed as an unattainable cocoon of central-heating, welfare state, breast-feeding, and all the other narcotics that stripped away the painful curse of individual identity.

He listened to her instructions, dutifully dialed The Cage and duly got the metallic reward.

"Benton Exporting. Can I help you?"

Machin switched dully into gear. No excitement, not even fear, just efficiency.

"Eagle. From Sparrow. Millet and Cuttlefish. Decoding acknowledged. Verification requested."

"Acknowledge, Sparrow. Wait one."

There was a pause, then, "Sparrow. Millet and Cuttlefish unrecorded. Verification impossible. Request source identification."

"M and C source, Eagle's egg. Nomenclature, Hawk," said Machin, reading from Tessa's script.

"Wait one."

Another pause. Some clicks on the line. Then a male voice,

thick with bonhomie.

"Sparrow, my old love. Nice to talk to you. We haven't had the pleasure before. Eagle's secretary here. Now what's all this M and C stuff you're on about?"

Machin was momentarily thrown by the shift from guttural ellipsis to standard colloquial.

"Er, hullo. Well … er, when I last phoned, a chap called Hawk gave me an M and C, and it seemed a bit … well, extreme."

Mary laughed.

"Typical of him. What exactly was it?"

"0171-999-9999," said Machin, and his words triggered an explosion of joy on the other end of the line.

"What? Knock off old Hamish? What the hell for? Harmless old bugger. Must be a mistake. I reckon he meant 0181-999-9999. Try that for size, eh? Now then, how're you getting on up there with the sheep-shaggers? And how's that lassie who picked you up? Tell her I loved the tape. Looking forward to the next instalment. Take care. Bye."

Machin had supposed The Cage held no more surprises for him but this chatty, apparently normal little contact left him as stunned as the previous attempts. Tessa had caught the occasional snatch of the conversation too, and something about it bothered her. It refused to come into focus and her present preoccupations were too numerous for her to devote any time to it now.

She took the receiver from Machin and said, "OK, we need to know what the new signal means. Get working."

Wearily, Machin started his calculations once more. He hoped it wouldn't take long since the second set of digits were identical and therefore the contact outside the library with the John Fowles book would be unchanged.

As he began to break down the other two sequences, Bad Boy called Tessa to the window. Across the road, the postman had dragged himself to his bed. He was obviously unable to stand and had succeeded only in flopping across the coverlet. He lay for a while and then, clearly in considerable pain, turned over and reached for the bedside phone. Tessa said urgently, "Quick. Get across to Eric. This is the call we want. Get it from him and bring it back here right away."

Bad Boy left and Tessa watched as the man spoke into the receiver, replaced it and lay back on the pillow, his features clenched tight with pain. She went to her case, took out a tape recorder, amplifier and speaker and laid them on the window sill. Clipped to the amplifier was a small button microphone. She took it off and slipped it into the pocket of her jacket.

Bad Boy was away for less than five minutes and returned with the news that the postman had asked the receptionist to get him a doctor. She'd phoned a Dr Princely who'd promised to come as soon as he could.

"Right," said Tessa. She pointed to the equipment on the window sill. "I'm going over there. I'll be leaving a mic there. Listen in and check that it's working."

Bad Boy nodded. Tessa left him to keep watch on both the postman and Machin and hurried to the pay-phone in an alcove off the hotel lobby.

She was grateful that the doctor's name was Princely and not McKenzie or Smith because there was only one relevant listing in the directory. She dialed the number and his receptionist answered. Tessa explained how the recent call from the hotel had been a mistake and the patient was already being treated in A and E, so the doctor needn't bother. The receptionist was glad because Dr Princely had lots of calls to make and Tessa was glad she was glad and rang off amid mutual well-wishing.

She then went to a pharmacy she'd noticed on her morning's outing with Bad Boy, bought the items she needed, and returned to the postman's hotel. On her way through the lobby, she gave a quick shake of her head to Eric to discourage him from showing any recognition and took the lift to the second floor. She quickly found the postman's room and knocked.

"Come in," said the postman feebly, and Tessa was able to do so because Eric had thoughtfully left the catch off when his own earlier visit was over.

Tessa gave the man on the bed a big smile and said, "Hullo, there. I'm Dr Princely. Been getting into a bit of trouble, I hear."

Across the road, Bad Boy watched her tear the seam of the man's trouser leg, examine his ankle, then produce bandages and proceed to bind up the swollen joint. The whole thing took only a short while. As she finished winding the last roll of bandages, bad Boy heard a hum from the speaker on the sill and Tessa's voice saying "There, that should do it." She got up and walked to the window. Bad Boy waved and gave her the thumbs-up sign.

He listened as she walked to the door, smiled broadly and said, "That should help for the time being, but rest, that's the most important thing. Try to keep off it for a day or two. I'll look back and see how you're getting on as soon as I can, eh?"

"What about the pain, doctor?" said the man.

"Aye. Good question," said Tessa.

She went out and closed the door behind her.

Downstairs in the lobby, she motioned to Eric that his vigil was over and he followed her, at an appropriate distance, back to their own hotel and up to her room. She checked the postman's room with a quick glance, asked room service to bring up some coffee, and then concentrated on Machin.

"Any luck, Chris?" she asked.

Machin had come to believe that the moorings of his rational mind had snapped and that he was condemned to drift permanently in a world of illusions.

"Yes," he said. "I've still got to take *Daniel Martin* to the library, with the same underlinings. I've still got to use the Lewis Crassic Gibbon code, whatever that is, but this time my contact will be a woman, and I've got to go to bed with her."

"What for?" said Tessa.

"Sex," said Machin.

****

A fact which might have helped Machin to stabilise his reasoning faculty but which unfortunately remained inaccessible to him, was that the amended M and C was almost as much of a whim as the first. Mary, to whom Machin's phone call had been routed, had quickly realised that the instruction to assassinate a prominent Scot was a mistake. Sparrow would never be entrusted with such a mission, and Hawk was neither devious nor courageous enough to be involved in anything that required so drastic a measure.

The only reasonable assumption, therefore, was that Hawk had made another cock-up. The temptation to let the whole thing take its course was very strong, but the possible repercussions in the remote eventuality of such a mission proving to be successful might complicate matters just at a time when Eagle and Kestrel were away.

Mary decided to override the previous M and C with one very similar but potentially less disastrous. Hawk would engineer other cock-ups for which he would be dismissed; that was a certainty. And as Mary began to work out other areas of his strategy, his telephone rang once again.

Upstairs, Hawk had had time to recover from the initial shock which Sparrow's veiled threats had caused. From cringing elbow-fetishist pinned hotly on the frame of guilt he'd cooled to defiant outsider determined to be first and final with his retaliation. Sparrow must, quite simply, be eliminated before he had the chance to tell Kestrel or anyone else of Hawk's deviation.

Already, the rapid sequence of events which had occurred since he'd been left in charge had made him lose track of his intended reorganisation of Eagle's codes and networks. He was looking through them to find the list of thugs who could be called upon to perform wet-jobs. He knew they were to be found under "budgies" but he'd broken up that file yesterday for reclassification and was now faced with the problem of looking for a murderer among the wood-pigeons.

He jumped again (an occupational hazard, it seemed), as the door opened and Mary's smiling face peered around it. A basic instinct made Hawk flick on the fail-safe alarm in the hope of electrocuting the secretary, but nothing happened and Hawk tightened his lips in anger and hatred as he saw the boots and rubber gloves Mary was wearing as he came in.

"What the bloody hell is it now Mary?" he shouted.

"I'm really very sorry to disturb you, boss," said Mary, in a tone with the consistency of soft margarine. "I know how busy you are, but I've just had a message through and I think you're the only person here with a status sufficiently elevated to respond to it."

Hawk's sensitivity was raw from the succession of abrasive shocks. He responded hotly to Mary's sneering.

"All right, all right, you sarcastic bugger," he said. "What is it?"

"Grave news, I'm afraid," said an unrepentant Mary. "From Inverness."

Hawk stiffened. All his troubles seemed to emanate from that bloody place. He'd never given it a second thought, and suddenly Eagle and Kestrel were there, and the wrestling Belazzo boys, and a dead fledgling. And bloody Sparrow with his guilty information.

"What the hell is it now?" he said guardedly.

"It's our dear head of section, boss," said Mary. "And Mr Kestrel."

He paused, looking for effect, and got it.

"Well?" shouted Hawk, whose purpling complexion made the pause worthwhile.

"They've been arrested."

"What?"

"They were found by a police inspector in a hotel bedroom. Together. Mr Kestrel was apparently dressed as a woman, too."

Hawk saw it all.

"The crafty bastard," he yelled. "Well, it serves the hypocritical bugger right. And as for that dirty old sod who calls himself boss, well…"

He stopped. Mary's smile told him that his indiscretion had not gone unnoticed.

"Yes, well … what are we supposed to do about it?" he asked, trying to haul his blood-pressure back down.

"They'll have to be released. The policeman who made the arrest is the same one who got Sparrow."

"What's he doing in Inverness?" asked Hawk.

"No idea. Looks fishy, though, doesn't it?"

"Can't we phone somebody? Get them released?"

"I don't think so, boss. I mean, with respect, I think as acting head, it's something you should deal with personally. I've contacted the chief superintendent. He says there's nothing he can do up there. He can give you a letter on headed paper but it'll be up to you to convince them it's legit. It's all a bit … delicate really, isn't it?"

As Mary talked, Hawk's dull mind was working. The personal link with the chief superintendent gave him a little pulse of power, and it was a power he wanted to retain. In Inverness at present, Kestrel, dressed as a woman, was sharing experiences with Eagle while Sparrow was walking about carrying a secret that could destroy his ambitions.

The opportunity to eliminate Sparrow and to confound Kestrel's schemes was being offered by Mary. Sitting in this office would solve nothing; ambition required action. He stood up.

"Fix me up with train tickets."

"Already done, boss," said a straight-faced Mary. "I'm afraid first class was crowded, so I've bought you a second-class ticket for the next available. It's a stopping train. Takes a while to get there. But I reckoned it was urgent, and in the interests of security, we should all be prepared to sacrifice some of our personal comforts."

"You'll be sacrificing bugger-all, you cheeky sod," shouted Hawk, all pretence at control discarded. "You'll be sitting here on your arse while I'm stuck in that bloody train all the way up there."

"Alas yes, boss," said Mary as he smiled, left the office and closed the door.

Hawk rushed after him, ready to shout obscenities that people would take down and file in a new folder dedicated to Hawk. The folder would have to wait for another occasion, however, because Hawk, in his fury, had forgotten he'd activated the fail-safe alarm and was now sitting under Eagle's desk, the plaster on his right wrist smoking.

CHAPTER THIRTEEN

Much later that day, shortly after Hawk's train had laboured into Inverness, Lodgedale was being dragged from the detention cells for the fourth time. On each occasion, it had taken three young and very fit constables to perform the exercise since Lodgedale was in full interrogatory flow. But the wise old sergeant in charge of the station had his priorities right. He knew that the case of the man who'd been murdered with an umbrella was already causing difficulties. It would stretch his fairly liberal chief's patience if he added to those difficulties by having to report the deaths of two prisoners in custody.

With a bravery befitting his calling, he'd ordered his men to remove Lodgedale from the area which housed Eagle and Kestrel. They were both bruised and bleeding, and after Lodgedale's second interrogation, X-rays had revealed the broken bones in their arms so that, like the approaching Hawk, each had his right wrist in plaster. They lay now in a sludge of pain and disbelief, dreaming of idyllic jobs as gardeners. Outside, Lodgedale's invective poured in the direction of the sergeant.

"You stupid, stupid sod," he was saying. "They're in the middle of their confession."

"I know, sir," said the sergeant patiently, "but there hasn't been a train robbery, or an assassination, or any of the sex crimes they've confessed to so far."

"Trivia," yelled Lodgedale. "Too bloody small-minded, today's force. What about the one in the frock? He's admitted to running an IRA cell in Pittenweim in the 80s."

"Oh, come on, sir. The Good Friday agreement, remember? And what would the IRA do in Pittenweim, anyway? When my lads asked him one or two things, just to check his story, like, he thought Pittenweim was in Cheshire."

"Where's Cheshire?" asked Lodgedale irrelevantly.

"I don't know," said the sergeant.

Lodgedale shook his head, annoyed that this barely comprehensible oaf was confusing him and leading him away from the main issue.

"OK, OK," he said, trying to calm down. "What about the cannabis they were carrying?"

"What cannabis?" said the surprised sergeant.

"In the briefcase back in my hotel room," said Lodgedale.

"Ah, now there you've got something," said the sergeant, deciding it would be politic to charge the two men with something.

"Right, we'll start with that then," said Lodgedale, eager to begin incriminating somebody for something. "I'll just nip back and get it."

"No need, sir," said the sergeant, reaching under his desk, "I've got some here, all ready, made up into one ounce packets. We issue it automatically to our men with every search warrant."

"Are you still allowed to use ounces? Thought it all had to be grams and kilos nowadays."

"We like the old ways up here," replied the sergeant.

"Well, at least you've got the stuff," said Lodgedale. "I was beginning to wonder whether you lot did any normal police work here. I should think about two or three pounds for each of them would do it..."

As he and the sergeant, in their uneasy truce, began to organise the evidence on the station counter, however, Hawk's taxi drew up outside. He paid off the driver and loped up the steps and into the station. Lodgedale and the sergeant looked up. The first thing the former noticed was the plaster on Hawk's wrist.

"He's taking the piss out of me," he said to the sergeant and stood up to assault Hawk. The threatening stance made Hawk reach quickly into his pocket for the letter he'd brought.

"I've come from Chief Superintendent McCoist," he said.

Lodgedale stopped, looked at the sergeant and said, "There you are, what did I say? He's taking the piss," and he clutched Hawk's lapel. The sergeant picked up the paper which had fallen from Hawk's hand and noticed the Grampian Police crest just in time to make him shout, "Hang on. He's telling the truth," and thereby save Hawk a large bill for dental work.

Lodgedale flung Hawk onto a bench and pointed a vicious finger to indicate he should stay put. He then read through the directive which the sergeant was holding.

"Bloody marvellous," he said at last. "Release 'em, it says. Just like that. That's the second time recently that bugger's stuck his nose into police affairs. Last week I had an open and shut case. Bloke called Machin. He'd only knocked off one of my lads, hadn't he? And what's he get for it? A pat on the head and off you go."

As Lodgedale's righteous indignation suffused his face with shades of mauve, Hawk listened more intently, noting the distaste, disgust, and manic hatred the policeman felt for Machin. Since part of Hawk's own mission in Inverness was to silence the same man, there stirred under the crust of his fear a small thrill of gratitude that fate had provided him with an instrument as lethal as this psychopathic inspector. Timidly, he waved his hand like a supplicant, and instantly regretted it.

"I told you to sit still," shouted Lodgedale as he leapt at him and delivered two punches and three kicks which took the edge off his anger.

"But I know where Machin is. He's here in Inverness," screamed Hawk as Lodgedale wound himself up for the next phase.

Eagle and Kestrel, back in the cells, recognised Hawk's voice and began to call for help. Lodgedale was torn between a conditioned reflex which prodded him towards the prisoners and the fascinating titbit Hawk had offered. The sergeant resolved his dilemma.

"I'll go and let them out," he said, adding as he flapped the piece of paper at Lodgedale, "I mean, we've got no choice really, have we?"

Lodgedale nodded and concentrated on Hawk.

"Now then, you snivelling git," he said, as kindly as he could. "What's all this you're on about?

Hawk responded to the kindness.

"That Machin you were talking about," he said, "he's one of our lot."

"Whose lot?"

"Ours. The Cage. Code name Sparrow, we arranged his release."

"What cage? What sparrow? I'm not interested in fucking aviaries. What're you on about?"

"You know. The Cage. Aberdeen. The oil. Crime."

Lodgedale had heard of The Cage but left it to others. He had little time for crime of the organised variety. Investigating that called for the slow, patient accumulation of evidence, painstaking forensic procedures and the like. He preferred direct action, *mano a mano*. Hawk hurried on.

"But it was all a mistake. He's, er, a bit of an embarrassment to us. The top men want him ... eliminated..."

"What d'you mean, eliminated?" asked Lodgedale, his interest aroused.

"Exactly what I say. He's got to disappear. We can't afford any arrests or enquiries. He'll just have to be ... disposed of. You might be just the man for the job. Especially as he's here in Inverness at the moment. What d'you think?"

Lodgedale was delighted at this positive turn his holiday was taking.

"No bother squire," he said, getting up. "Where is he?"

"Well, er, just a minute. There are one or two things to settle first. I mean, this must be a complete undercover job. That's to say ... it's not police work, you know."

"Who gives a shit? Where is he?"

"That's the other thing," said Hawk. "I don't know his exact location, but I've arranged for him to meet somebody on the 17th. You could, er, catch up with him then."

Lodgedale's expressions of frustration were choked by Hawk's warning "Sssh", which terminated the exchange just as the sergeant led the battered Eagle and Kestrel out from their detention.

The three men from The Cage stood looking at one another. Each was totally confused. Eagle had no idea why he'd been arrested, and Hawk's presence reminded him only of Bad Boy. Kestrel's "murderer", the man he'd thought responsible for the plucking of Grebe and his ringer, had turned out to be a police inspector. And Hawk had to fathom the relationship between Eagle and the defrocked Kestrel and at the same time conceal the information about his own idiosyncrasies. Each noticed the plaster on the right wrist of the other two and each suspected some obscure conspiracy which was directed against him personally.

The station sergeant, the only normal man in the place, tried to sort things out. He produced tea, talked of the fortunes of

Inverness Caledonian Thistle and asked their opinion of the best time for pricking out leeks. Kestrel's mistake in identifying Lodgedale as the prime suspect for the murders was explained and examined, and reawakened Lodgedale's own interest in their discussion. It was quickly realised that the man he'd been following, the postman, was indeed the one whom Kestrel should have identified.

Kestrel kept a discreet silence as his error was revealed. He wasn't anxious to point out that the inspector was by far the most obvious criminal he'd ever encountered and behaved in a way that made all other suspects seem like Jesus. The fact they were all agreed on the object of their pursuit brought a measure of relief to the three Cage men since it did alter the probability of being attacked by Lodgedale to a mere possibility.

"What's this postman chap doing here now, then?" asked the sergeant. "I mean, if he's finished off your two blokes, why has he no packed up and gone home?"

They thought about this until Kestrel, seeking to retrieve some of the ground lost by his mistake, said, "Perhaps he's heard Sparrow's here. Maybe he's going to kill him, too."

"Sparrow?" said the surprised sergeant, who was already very wary of Kestrel because of the maid's outfit.

"Yes, another of our fledglings, I mean, employees. Chap called Machin."

There was a strange noise from Lodgedale. The word Sparrow had caught his attention and the confirmation supplied by the surname had forced an intake of breath which he'd tried to control. Reflexively, Eagle and Kestrel had ducked, but Lodgedale looked meaningfully at Hawk, willing him to understand. Hawk smiled but revealed nothing. Lodgedale, however, gloried in the continuing good favours fate was reserving for him.

He'd come to this vile town of breezes and fresh air to arrest a postman and invent a crime for him. Then a police spokesperson no less had commissioned him to murder a criminal, who'd been dragged unjustly from the clutches of the law. And now here he was, being told the postman would commit his murder for him and he need only wait and watch to catch the culprit red-handed. No evidence need be fabricated, the two missions would be accomplished, and he could return to Aberdeen in triumph to complete vindication in the eyes of his chief constable.

Another bonus waited also. He wasn't yet aware of the fact, of course, but since his departure, his wife had been building up an explosive charge of suppressed sexuality by her nightly contemplation of the piece of intestine. She'd preserved it in a pickle jar and it now stood proudly on their bedside table.

****

Eric sat biting large pieces of teak out of the dressing-table, Bad Boy concentrated on his knitting, Machin sat in his miserable notoriety, and Tessa, her eyes fixed on the postman in his bed across the street, just waited. Since Eagle had been arrested and Machin's contact was not due until the 17th, they could do nothing but wait for the next call from the Big Snake.

There was an air of rather stagnant depression in the room. Tessa and her two friends were active criminals and yet their present role was that of mere counter-punchers. They were helpless, closeted in this hotel until other people made the moves that would unleash them.

Only Bad Boy, whose passion for knitting had grown in the hours he'd had to while away in dressing rooms waiting to fight, was able to ignore the tension. Unfortunately, his method of relaxing only served to increase the irritation of the others. The specially strengthened steel needles he used clicked and twanged infuriatingly together as he sped through a fairly simple section of the Arran sweater he was making for an SNP friend back in Aberdeen.

Into this high-tensile atmosphere the ringing of Tessa's mobile came as a massive relief.

Tessa grabbed it.

"Hi, Big Snake. What you got?"

"Eagle's been arrested."

"I know. We saw him."

"Yes. Did you know they were releasing him, too?"

"Really? What's going on?"

"Who knows?"

Tessa sighed deeply.

"Well, BS," she said, "it may not be so bad. He's been trying to get in touch with Blackbird, told him all sorts of stuff."

There was silence for a moment.

"Useful stuff?" said Big Snake at last.

"I think so."

Another silence gave Tessa a small stab of pleasure. The Big Snake seemed to know so much about everything, sometimes even before it happened. It was a tiny victory to surprise him. He was apparently unaware of Eagle's revelations to Bad Boy, and the slightly altered pitch of the voice when it eventually came back at her confirmed the opinion. His response was longer and slightly more explicit than usual.

"OK. We can't have that. It'll set them all flapping about in their bloody nests, making our job harder. Get rid of him. He's in Hotel Bay View, room seven two."

"Got it."

"OK. What's the story with the postman? Still under surveillance?"

"Yep. He was getting ready to leave. We ... delayed him."

"Good. He's got to go, too. Take him out. Use your decoy."

"OK."

Tessa rang off. She was puzzled. How did the Big Snake know so much about the activities of Eagle and the others? And why did he suddenly want Eagle and the postman killed? Her years with the Belazzos had taught her never to articulate such questions but she was too intelligent for them not to form in her mind. But here she was, being used very much as a pawn in some game whose moves seemed almost predestined. The Big Snake's assertion that too free a flow of information from any source (in this case from Eagle via Bad Boy), would unbalance the relationship between them and The Cage was logical. But their prime function was to accumulate such information, so why the hell was he turning off such a rich fountain of it?

She realised the others were looking at her, waiting for orders. Even Machin's sad eyes were turned in her direction. Poor Chris. The Big Snake had suggested that the decoy ploy, an ugly title which Eric had given to the scheme when it was first mooted, be initiated, and that Chris be used to set the postman up for the hit. She didn't quite have the heart to spell it out just yet, and so decided to maintain a little individuality in the methods she employed to dispose of her two targets.

"OK," she said quietly. "First of all, we discourage Eagle, disorientate him, make him vulnerable."

"What for?" asked Eric between mouthfuls.

"So that he'll lay a few nice little eggs for us before he's plucked."

Eric's grin told Machin what plucked meant. Tessa continued.

"Bad Boy, I want you to ring him."

"Oh shit," said Bad Boy. "He'll give me all that crap about ebony and exquisite disdain and stuff."

"It goes with the job," said Tessa, with a brief smile. "But look, all you've got to tell him is you're already promised."

"What?" said Bad Boy.

"That's right," went on Tessa. "Your favours have already been bestowed, fully and frequently, on his two assistants, Hawk and … what's the other one Chris?"

Machin looked up, uncertain of what he was being asked.

"What's the name of the guy who's supposed to be your boss?" asked Tessa.

"Eagle."

"No, the other one."

"Er … Kestrel."

"That's it. OK Bad Boy, listen up. Hawk and Kestrel are your boy-friends. You love them, no, adore them and…"

She elaborated further on her theme, indulging once more the creative imagination she'd put to such good use via the bug Machin had carried in the car.

Bad Boy and even Eric were astonished that such a beautiful creature as Tessa could contain such degenerate insights. They were almost glad when she was suddenly interrupted by noises from the speaker on the window sill.

They all listened intently. There were two voices choking out some incomprehensible phrases. It was a conversation between the postman and, presumably, his boss. Tessa couldn't crack the code that was being used but once more, as she listened, she had an uneasy feeling something was not quite right. It was slightly muffled by the bandages but some of the words were clear enough to disturb her.

There was obviously some urgency about the topic they were discussing, but it wasn't merely the content which caused her brows to furrow as she began to understand it, it was that voice, the voice of the postman's boss. She recognised it and didn't understand.

CHAPTER FOURTEEN

Later that evening, Hawk and Kestrel also had cause to ponder something conveyed to them by a transmitted voice. There was no enigma attaching to the voice, it was Mary's, but its message gave cause for reflection. The fact that they were all away from The Cage had to be exploited and so he'd telephoned each of them separately.

First it was Hawk's turn. He was lying back on top of his bed looking at the illustrations in his much-loved copy of *Little Women* when the phone's ring made him slam the book quickly under his pillow. He took a deep breath and picked up the receiver. He gave his room number and felt a little peeved when he recognised Mary's voice.

"Hullo, Hawk. Is that you?"

"Oh Christ, Mary. What do you want?"

"Very sorry to disturb you so late, boss, but it's rather urgent. Can I speak freely?"

"Seems to me you do too much of that already," stammered a sweating Hawk.

"Thank you," oiled Mary. "Well, word is … Eagle's finished. Been shooting his mouth off, apparently. Gave some black bastard the addresses of some of our engineering contacts. Strange, I didn't think he knew any of them. Anyway, I mean … a black guy … you can understand people getting upset, can't you?"

"Mary, I can't even understand you. What the hell are you talking about?"

"Eagle, Mr Hawk, boss. He's through. The boot, the elbow, the sack, redundant, superfluous to requirements, outsourced, downsized…"

"All right," interrupted Hawk, his nerves strained even further by the mention of elbow. "So why are you telling me this?"

"Oh, just a favour," said Mary. "Thought you might like to be the first to know. I mean, it's common knowledge that when the top spot's up for grabs it'll be between you and Mr Kestrel, so I thought you might like to ... well ... have a go at discrediting him a bit, maybe. Ease yourself into a lead in the home straight, as it were."

"I see," said Hawk as the realisation dawned. "Yes, I see. Er ... look, I appreciate this Mary. Thanks for the information. I won't forget it."

"My pleasure, boss," said Mary and, as he was replacing the receiver, he muttered, seemingly to himself "Mr Eagle, the elbow, who'd have thought it?" just loud enough for Hawk to hear it and tremble.

Mary then dialed Kestrel, who was wakened from an aching sleep in which sharp memories of Lodgedale's attentions kept vying with the residual odours of the maid to torment him. He put the receiver to a sleepy ear.

"Hullo."

"Mr Kestrel? Urgent business," said Mary. "Sorry to disturb you."

"It'd better be good, Mary," spluttered Kestrel.

"It is," answered Mary. "Juicy even. It's Eagle. He's finished. Turned out to be a bit of a grass. You know, the usual."

"Thank God for that," said Kestrel, immediately regretting the reflex that had produced the words. But Mary seemed not to be concerned by his little outburst.

"Exactly," he continued. "And I just thought you'd probably want to be the first to know. I mean, you'll need to do something about Mr Hawk, won't you?"

"What?" said Kestrel, knowing full well what Mary was implying.

"You know full well what I'm implying," said Mary. "He'll have to be put aside, won't he? So he's not in your way."

"Ah yes," admitted Kestrel. "Quite right. Yes. Well, look here, thanks, Mary. I appreciate it. I'll make it worth your while, too. Keep me informed, eh?"

"Right. My pleasure," said Mary and rang off, very pleased with his evening's work.

The two rivals were now wide awake, their former preoccupations banished as each began to ponder his hatred of the other and formulate from it a method of disposal.

****

Lodgedale, normally so refreshingly direct with his solutions and his activities, was indulging in a little unaccustomed thinking. The beauty of the scheme which would encourage the postman to kill Machin, only to be immediately apprehended by himself, was still a source of delight. But if some parts of the jigsaw could fall so nicely into their allotted places, why not others?

He bore a huge grudge against Eagle and Kestrel. He had, after all, arrested them and they, like Machin, had been prised from his grasp. They shouldn't get away with that. And they were after the postman too, and they were responsible for Machin. He was concerned that they might get in his way again. The only logical conclusion was that he must dispose of them first, and since his chief superintendent wouldn't allow him to do so officially, then he must contrive something unofficial on their behalf.

His first impulse was simply to push them into the river when it was dark, but they'd have to be decoyed to the water's edge, held under, and so on. And they'd no doubt be stupid enough to shout and cause a commotion that might bring others to their rescue, in which case he'd have to push them in, too.

The thought of the river Ness filling up with splashing people, all of whom he was trying to hold under, persuaded him to consider alternative solutions. His mind worked through its usual chamber of horrors but nothing surfaced and so he was forced at last to look beyond his normal pastures of pain. The only feature that contained any promise was the fact that they were both supposed to be working under cover. If he could in some way compromise them, force them into a glare of embarrassing publicity, perhaps they'd be obliged to retreat, at least long enough for the murder to take place.

The effort to follow his thought through taxed his brain, which had had so little practice. He succeeded in fixing once more on Machin, however. Hawk had told him Machin was due to meet somebody outside the library on the 17th. If Lodgedale made sure he was there, witnessed the contact, identified the two as villains and somehow caused some sort of public fuss, then surely Eagle and Kestrel would have to stay well away for fear of being compromised. Simultaneously, Machin would be placed in fully illuminated public view so that the postman could easily find and get rid of his victim.

The details of the plan refused to clarify themselves, but there seemed a justness about it which pleased him, and so Lodgedale added his hostilities to those which were already being formulated and which were all designed to embroil, confuse, and variously destroy Machin, the postman, Eagle, Kestrel, and Hawk.

****

Machin sat on an upturned bucket in a corner of a gymnasium filled with grunting, sweating, skipping and punching hulks. Tessa needed peace and quiet to assess her new instructions and the enigma of the postman's contact and so she'd sent Bad Boy and Eric off to get in some training. Although Machin was no trouble, she found his mute, ignorant stare something of a distraction and felt a twinge of guilt at having involved him in the first place. If she was going to use him to bait a murder trap, it would be better if he weren't sitting there watching her do it. So she'd told the others to take him with them and, as they hurled one another about a ring and rehearsed the choreography of their coming contest, he sat on his bucket.

In the hotel, Tessa, sitting near the window and still watching the postman, was comparing her various instructions and intuitions and trying to work out the pattern behind them. The Big Snake had told her to eliminate Eagle, because he was talking too much, and the postman, because he was killing people. And she was to use the expendable Sparrow as the bait.

She'd eventually cracked the code which the postman and his boss had used and learned that they knew all about Sparrow's projected meeting outside the library. The postman now had instructions to be there on the 17th and to identify and eliminate Sparrow.

None of these facts was in any way surprising. Ever since the Third Way's people had been active, murders and disappearances had been part of the job. The riddle that continued to perplex Tessa concerned the contact who'd given the postman his orders. It was a voice she recognised. She'd listened to the tape of their conversation over and over again. The throttled verbal acrobatics that the code sequences required couldn't entirely hide the fact that the postman was talking to the Big Snake.

She was well versed in the causes and effects of unethical activities, but she was finding this hard to fathom. Big Snake was controlling both the Belazzo organisation and the Third Way. It made no sense at all.

The Cage would probably soon disappear, the Belazzos and the Third Way rivalry would continue, and having a foot in both camps was one way of making sure that you were in touch. But since the Third Way's principal aim seemed to be to overturn the present balance in Aberdeen, connection with it seemed positively perverse, since whichever of the two won, it would have to wipe out the other.

To belong to both sides in a fight to the death was suicidal. The conclusion was awesome. Big Snake was fully aware of the risks he was running and didn't give a shit. He wanted to get rid of both and take over everything with his Third Way, or maybe just on his own.

The fascinating perplexity of these thoughts was increased in Tessa's mind by a certainty that there was an extra dimension to it which she hadn't yet penetrated. She knew that somewhere just beyond her present powers of recall there lurked another factor which had a bearing on the Big Snake's duplicity. When it did come to her it might provide a clue, but for the moment it lay tantalisingly amongst her more recent experiences. At some time, somewhere, she'd noted a discrepancy or perhaps a similarity, but its nature continued to elude her.

She wasted no more of the present on it, but turned her attention instead to the pleasurable contemplation of the scheming with which she must fill the next few days. Machin was her trump card. The Big Snake wanted her to use him as a decoy, and wanted his postman to kill him. Such an asset must be preserved, and all threats to his security must be abolished. It was perhaps through him that the truth about the Big Snake's split loyalties might emerge, and so she decided the first priority should be to set limits on their field of activity over which she alone, even to the exclusion of the Big Snake, would have authority.

At present, with Eagle wandering loose, Hawk and Kestrel as unknown quantities, the postman confined but primed to kill, and the Big Snake looking over everyone's shoulder, the paths they all trod were too random. She must know, at all times, where everyone was, what they were doing and what their intentions were. Their horizons must be restricted and controlled. In the north east of Scotland, the means of achieving such constriction was ready-made.

She made a phone call, agreed terms with the person at the other end and promised payment on completion. She confessed to the man she was talking to that there might be an element of illegality in the transaction, but the only effect of this was one she'd anticipated; the price went up. Otherwise all was fixed for the evening of the 17th.

That meant the following day and so she had to start at once. She picked up the phone once more and got the receptionist to connect her with the gymnasium in which Bad Boy and Eric were training. When the janitor answered, she simply said, "Hullo, this is Mrs Thompson. Is my Eric still there?"

"Who's your Eric?" said the janitor.

"Eric the Emancipator," said Tessa. "He's fighting with a black man."

"Dunno," said the janitor.

"Well, you just tell him," continued the shrill Tessa, "his dinner's been on the table ten minutes already and it's freezing."

She put down the receiver quickly, knowing the call would have the desired effect. Eric and Bad Boy had told her the only messages that ever seemed to get through to wrestlers and boxers in the gymnasia in which they trained were threatening calls from wives. Janitors ignored the press, promoters, agents or the police, but domestic affairs, especially when they seemed precarious, were sacrosanct.

The message was duly passed to Eric, who took his thumb out of Bad Boy's eye and twitched a gesture which indicated that they had to leave. On the way out they collected Machin, who'd been called into service as a sparring partner for a middleweight since there was nobody else available to do the job.

When they arrived back at the hotel, Tessa was a little concerned at the state of Machin's face, which had reddened and blotched during the sparring. She quickly established that no permanent damage had been done and transferred her attention to Bad Boy.

He was to masquerade as a Dundee contact and pay the

postman a visit. From the tape, Tessa had worked out the recognition sequence and Bad Boy would have no difficulty in being accepted as a Third Way operative. He must then cancel the postman's instructions to attend the meet outside the library and substitute instead the new instructions which Tessa based on the telephone transaction she'd made earlier.

Bad Boy understood little of what he was doing, but had faith in Tessa and set off at once for the room across the road. After he'd gone, she checked the amplifier, speaker and tape recorder to make sure she could monitor the encounter between them.

Soon, she heard Bad Boy's knock at the door. She looked across the street. The postman hauled himself up and struggled across the room to open it. He stood looking at Bad Boy, whose muffled voice came over the speaker, delivering a long sentence about salted cod. The postman listened politely and then told Bad Boy about shoals of herring in the Black Sea. Bad Boy listened in turn, spoke for a while about turbot, plaice and whiting, and, after another session from the postman on gurnards and skate, moved smoothly into a short paragraph on Dover sole, an aside on mackerel, and a final, curt dismissal of the coelacanth.

Tessa's work on the coding system had obviously been accurate because, barely pausing to mention haddock, the postman held the door wide and Bad Boy came into the room.

The worst was over. Now that Bad Boy's credentials had been authenticated he could convey his information in the knowledge that it would be accepted without question. The postman listened as the wrestler cancelled the library trip and made an alternative appointment for him to meet Machin on the evening of the 17th in the seclusion of the place Tessa had selected. He nodded his understanding and, in reply to Bad Boy's "shrimp", said "lugworm" and opened the door for him to leave.

Tessa was just sitting back in satisfaction at having organised the first part of her scheme successfully when a still muffled, but very loud crash came from the speaker, followed by a variety of thuds, bumps and yells. She looked across the street. The postman was at his door and appeared to have locked it, but he, too, was listening to the violent noises that were being made in the corridor outside his room.

Whatever was causing the din, Bad Boy was part of it, and the postman had obviously no intention of getting involved. Tessa jumped to her feet, knew there was no time to waste, so reluctantly looked at Eric and pointed her thumb at Machin. Eric, delighted, lifted him up and concussed him with a half-power forearm smash, then laid him on the bed and followed Tessa, who had already left the room.

****

Lodgedale, although delighted at the cards fate was dealing to him, was concerned that he hadn't seen his suspect for a while. He'd patrolled the postman's usual haunts, established that his quarry had gone to ground and, at the man's hotel, asked the receptionist, with stentorian discretion, where he'd got to. She told him he'd had an accident and had to stay in his room and Lodgedale, happy to have relocated him, decided to keep watch at the end of his corridor so that he could stay abreast of any new developments.

He'd been there less than two hours when the first development arrived, in the shape of Bad Boy. The conversation about fish which had preceded Bad Boy's disappearance into the room was taken by Lodgedale as a personal insult. At first he'd been tempted to burst into the room and interrogate the two of them. But the tangle of connections which tied the postman to Machin and the others had made him marginally more circumspect and he decided instead to listen at the door.

At the first muffled mention of Sparrow, he'd congratulated himself on his restraint and his features had split into that vile grin which had preceded glimpses of purgatory for most of his suspects. He listened carefully to the arrangements which Bad Boy made with the postman and rejoiced that everything was going so well. And then suddenly the conversation was over. He heard "shrimp" then "lugworm", the door opened and closed, and he was face to face with Bad Boy.

To the inspector, the confrontation was that of Klemperer with the score of Beethoven's ninth. Before him was a criminal, newly-emerged from a confession of complicity with a man whose guilt was already proven. They stood, far from any witnesses, in a dark, deserted corridor. And, on top of everything else, the man was black. From all these ingredients, the policeman, in his elation, would produce the ultimate symphony of splintered bone, and proclaim the triumph of justice, the law and white skin.

With Messianic delight, he applied his toecap to Bad Boy's shin and his knuckles to his mouth. Bad Boy, who'd been unaware of his presence, was taken by surprise and knocked back against the door of the postman's room, but the reflexes of his profession caused him to stab stiffened fingers out towards where he knew his assailant's throat would be. The pain Lodgedale felt as they made contact punched into his brain and mingled with the happy realisation that, on top of everything else, his prisoner was resisting arrest. Previously he'd intended to bar no holds, but now he could be positively self-indulgent and looked forward to an absorbing twenty minutes or so in the pursuit of his main interest.

CHAPTER FIFTEEN

It was, of course, the opening chords of this symphony of violence that Tessa had heard over her speaker. By the time she and Eric arrived, both of the main themes had been stated and the two antagonists were developing their variations on them, Bad Boy with the skills of the professional wrestler, Lodgedale with the ruthless efficiency of the vocational police officer.

Tessa quickly signalled to Eric that he should try to stop them. Gleefully he piled in and for a moment allowed himself the luxury of mere involvement. But the fight was now too one-sided to be enjoyable or of any significant duration, so he and Bad Boy soon had Lodgedale pinned to the wall, spitting and swearing and vowing a vengeance which made *Daily Mail* editorials sound weedy.

Tessa indicated that they should shut him up. Bad Boy was reluctant to put his hand anywhere near Lodgedale's snapping incisors, so he gripped his throat and squeezed hard. Lodgedale could still breathe and hiss but, thankfully, his yells were silenced.

Tessa quickly searched him, anxious to find out which side he was on in this increasingly complex struggle. She was surprised to find his warrant card and the information that he was a detective inspector. Even in the semi-darkness of the corridor Lodgedale's colour could be seen to be changing. His eyes popped and veins crawled over his neck and temples.

Tessa thought quickly. The man was dangerous but, as a policeman, he was the law and would take no notice of anyone. And immediately she realised there was one exception to this rule. She stuffed his card back into his jacket and snapped a sudden order at Bad Boy and Eric.

"Jackson, Jones, leave him!"

Her expression told them she was serious. They relaxed their grip. In the split second before Lodgedale could renew his attack on them she said, "Cool it, Lodgedale. We're Special Branch."

The magic formula made Lodgedale hesitate long enough for her to press her point home more forcibly.

"Now stop pissing us about. What's your game here?"

Lodgedale was disorientated. Given his character and his record, it was obvious that he himself aspired to the Special Branch and he didn't wish to do anything which might diminish his chances of selection. On the other hand, he had violence to perpetrate. He stalled by jerking his head towards the postman's door.

"Him," he said. "I've got him under surveillance."

"Oh Christ," said Tessa, her voice razored with spite. "What are you pricks doing messing around on our patch? Come on. You'd better tell us everything."

She walked away along the corridor and down the stairs.

Lodgedale, encouraged by looks and prods from Eric and Bad Boy, followed and eventually they all sat in a corner of the residents' lounge. Tessa's sneering obscenities quickly convinced Lodgedale they must indeed be what they claimed. His immediate impulse was to ingratiate himself with members of the branch of his own force he admired most, and he gladly told her of his intentions with regard to the postman. He even mentioned his involvement with Eagle and the others.

Tessa was quietly astonished as the meshes of coincidence closed them all so neatly together in their pursuits and grateful that chance had brought Lodgedale to her attention. All the while she'd been making her own careful plans, this homicidal buffoon had been stalking his own fancies. At any time, he might have thrown his clumsy spanner into her delicate works. Luckily, she could now call the shots. She'd have to include him in the plans she'd been making. His anxiety to please the Special Branch was obvious and it was through that that she'd control him.

"All right," she said, as he was recapitulating on his treatment of Eagle and Kestrel before their release. "Shut your mouth. Christ, working prisoners over like that went out with hanging. You should see what Eric here does to female prisoners with the mark III vibrator."

Lodgedale was enthralled.

"What?" he asked, with genuine intellectual curiosity.

"Wait till you've joined. Then you might find out. Meantime, stick with your lollipop duties and parking tickets."

Eric, who still had no idea what was going on but deduced from Tessa's aggressive tone that they were moving onto the attack, said, "Here, guv, can I show him a body-slam?"

Tessa's eyes flashed alarm.

"Shut your mouth, you stupid git, or you'll be back with his lot."

Eric still didn't understand but recognised Tessa's signal. Lodgedale, on the other hand, assuming a body-slam to be the latest in police equipment, was childishly eager to be friends.

"Oh, go on," he said, "let him show me his body-slam."

Tessa bent towards him, a pointing finger just below the bridge of his nose.

"If you don't shut it," she said, "you'll get my knee in your balls and my report on your super's desk simultaneous-like. Got it?"

The authentic mixture of brutishness and formality did the trick.

"OK," said Lodgedale, and with a last attempt at ingratiation and a rare excursion into humour, added, "You're a fair cop."

Tessa looked witheringly at him, turned away and appeared to be considering things.

"All right," she said after a while. "Tell you what, we'll give you a chance. You can help us."

Lodgedale was overjoyed.

"Anything you like."

"Right. How much did you hear of what Jackson was saying to the other bloke?"

"Nearly all of it."

"So you know about tomorrow night's meeting, where, when, all that stuff?"

"Aye."

"OK. Be there."

"You're on," said Lodgedale enthusiastically, and added, "Should I bring any special equipment?"

"Just be there," said Tessa with a show of tired patience.

Lodgedale was anxious to know more about his new Special Branch contacts and the nature of their mission but Tessa had other ideas. She'd arranged for the postman to be at her chosen rendezvous the following evening and now, this unexpected complication of the inspector had been dealt with in the same way. Bad Boy would invite Eagle, and Machin would do as he was told.

That left Kestrel and Hawk and, with Lodgedale already being involved with both of them, she could use him as leverage. She spoke quickly, determined to end the exchange before he had time to get suspicious.

"Now then," she said, "your role in this is a bit special. We were looking for a way to get those silly sods who call themselves Hawk and Kestrel to be at the rendezvous. Think you could do it for us?"

Lodgedale opened his mouth to reply, but Tessa went on quickly, "You'd bloody well better, pal. We don't want any cock-ups, right? Now, our information suggests they're not too fond of each other. Hate each other's guts, in fact." (Tessa was remembering more of the profiles she'd read.) "All you have to do is whisper to each of them that the other's meeting up with a Belazzo boy and they could get some photos or something. You know, to incriminate them. See what I mean?"

"No," said Lodgedale, honestly.

"Christ," said Tessa, and then spelt it out painstakingly for him. Eventually he understood and nodded eagerly. The world was becoming such a pleasant place since that far-off morning when Machin's crater had seemed to offer him so little. He was sorry to see his colleagues standing up and preparing to leave. As he made to stand also, Tessa pushed him back into his seat.

"Now remember, prick," she said quietly, "not a word to anybody, and if I find you've fucked this up for us I'll have your balls in a mincer."

Lodgedale beamed at her admiringly.

"Christ," he said. "You're not just a pretty face."

****

Tessa and her boys had been away longer than they'd anticipated and, when they arrived back in their own room, Machin had already regained consciousness. He was sitting on the edge of the bed, with slow tears moving on his cheeks as he recalled his lost innocence. He'd accepted the fact that his existence from now on would alternate between periods of perception in which he understood nothing of what he perceived and periods of unconsciousness induced by Eric's forearm. The arrival of his three colleagues evoked no response from him and Tessa was moved by the state to which he'd been reduced. She sat beside him.

"Chris, look. I'm sorry about the violence, and you're going to find this hard to believe, but it was for your own good."

Machin nodded. Tessa ran her fingers down his cheeks, collecting the tears.

"The day after tomorrow, it'll all be over, or at least this part of it. You'll be able to go home. But you'll have to trust me."

Machin nodded again with neither more nor less conviction. Tessa saw he was in no condition to listen to reason. Quicker than most, he'd succumbed to the combined effects of the deprivation of his will and liberty, the physical assaults and the intervals of kindness; he'd be a pushover for brain-washing.

Her arm went round his shoulder. Her other hand cupped his chin and raised his face, and she concentrated all her technique on applying to his loose mouth a warm enveloping kiss of the sort that make your eyes water. She supposed that it had at least part of the desired effect, for his eyes opened briefly, looked in some surprise at her, then clenched shut again and released an even more copious flow of tears.

Through the kiss she felt him sobbing and so decided to postpone the second instalment until later. She drew her lips from him and cradled his head in her shoulder, rocking him gently as Eric and Bad Boy stood by shuffling their feet in embarrassment.

After a while Machin's sobs became drier and more intermittent and the therapy of the crying had been so effective that he apologised to all three of them for his shameful display. Eric was about to relieve his own embarrassment by clumsy jokes about effeminate schoolteachers when Tessa, anticipating the gaucheries, silenced him with a glance. She smiled at Machin, kissed him again, this time maternally on the cheek, and said, "Don't worry about it. You've had a helluva lot to put up with."

Machin continued to protest his shame but Tessa was anxious to speed up the momentum of her final arrangements.

"Listen, Chris," she said. "D'you feel fit enough to go through with tomorrow's meet?"

Memories of his scheduled encounter came back to him: the library, the Lewis Crassic Gibbon code, the woman, sex. Tessa's perfumed presence made the sexual content of the package appealing, and together with a certain desire genuinely to atone for the shame of his recent fit of sobbing, was sufficient to make him nod an answer.

"Great," said Tessa. "I thought you would. Well look, all you have to do is follow your instructions. I'll be there keeping an eye on things so you'll have plenty of protection. And once that's over, I've arranged for most of these guys who are making your life such a misery to … let's say, vanish."

Machin didn't dare point out that most of his recent misery had come from Eric, and the carefully chosen "vanish" caused a slight shiver, but Tessa, after all, was an old friend, and he had absolutely no alternatives.

Tessa was glad that particular die had been cast and grateful to Machin for the speed of his recovery. The only unplaced piece of the design was Eagle. Events had been moving so quickly that Bad Boy hadn't yet had time to telephone him and plant the notion that Hawk and Kestrel were rivals for his love. Tessa was confident that once he'd done so the final touches would have been applied to a well-baited trap.

She jotted some notes on a pad, read over them and handed them to Bad Boy, who'd meantime taken refuge in his knitting. He read them in turn, punctuating the process by the occasional pleading look at her and the beginnings of protest. But she was firm and when his attitude of helpless disgust indicated to her that he'd absorbed and understood her jottings, she leaned over, picked up the phone and waited for the receptionist's voice. When she heard it, she said, "Hotel Bay View, please."

Bad Boy slumped further into his chair, the consolation of his knitting forgotten. The Bay View receptionist answered the call, Tessa asked for room 72 and handed the telephone to Bad Boy.

In Bay View 72, Eagle was leaning on his window sill looking up at the stars that seemed to him unusually bright. Behind him his hotel room was a mess. The brief excitement of his meeting with the supposedly transvestite Kestrel and the potentially fulfilling session with Lodgedale had never fully taken his mind away from its hunger for Bad Boy.

On his return to his room he'd tried phoning his love but received no reply and so he'd whiled the time away by practising some more of the holds he'd learned from the wrestling manuals.

The plaster on his wrist had, however, posed serious problems as he'd grappled with his pillow, chairs, and the wash-basin. The results were now spread over the carpet in a pattern of feathers, splinters and lumps of earthenware.

At last, frustration and weariness had driven him in his longing to adopt the archetypal pose of unrequited lovers, poised on the edge of the abyss of night, staring Juliet-like into the velvet of infinity, and whispering the gentle sounds of his lover's name into the soft darkness.

"Bad Boy, Bad Boy, where the fuck are you, Bad Boy?" he sighed.

He wasn't to know that the ringing of his telephone was an answer to his question and at first he cursed violently, assuming that Hawk and Kestrel were plaguing him once more with their trivialities. As the ringing continued, he knew cursing wouldn't stop it and he stamped angrily through the wreckage to the phone, picked it up and shouted, "Look here, Hawk or Kestrel, I don't care which of you buggers it is, but this had better be bloody important..."

Under Tessa's urgent prompting, Bad Boy cut in.

"Be quiet, white trash," he said. "If I want any words from you, I'll say so, right?"

There was a fathomless silence. Eagle had found the road to Damascus. Out of a constricted throat, he managed only to say, "Is that really you?"

"I said shut it, scum," thundered Bad Boy. "Just listen."

Eagle, delirious with joy, flicked off his slipper and pressed his bare foot down onto a jagged piece of wash-basin.

"I'm going to tell you this just once, so pay close attention," continued Bad Boy's harsh and threatening voice. "The very notion that I'm talking to you, even at this distance, makes my flesh creep and my stomach turn. You aren't fit to suck my armpits."

He broke off as he was interrupted by a trilling whimper of delight which Eagle had failed to control.

"I'm warning you," yelled Bad Boy.

"Sorry. I'm sorry. Oh, my love, so sorry," whispered Eagle.

"Not as much as you will be," went on the wrestler. "You consider yourself worthless, don't you?"

"Oh, yes, yes," said the ecstatic Eagle.

"Well, you're crap right enough, but you're not in the same league as those two guys you hang out with. They really are the pits. So don't get ideas."

Like the first pangs of love, the sharp stab of jealousy took Eagle by surprise. Did Bad Boy really mean it?

"Who … who do you mean?" he asked, teetering on the edge of tragedy.

"You know bloody well. Those pricks, Hawk and Kestrel. Maggots. Unfit to be called men."

Paradoxically, Eagle agreed with this assessment, but to hear it from the lips of his own idol, whose scorn he needed for himself alone, caused an unbearable wrench.

"Oh no, my love," he begged, "it's me you hate. I'm the most detestable person you've ever met. I was made for you to loathe."

"Everything was made for me to loathe," countered Bad Boy, "but I've taken a liking to loathing Hawk and Kestrel. And I want you to watch me loathing them. So listen to this. I've invited them to a party on board a little boat in Peterhead harbour tomorrow night. Make sure you're there. It's the Katherine Jo Ross and she'll be alongside at eight-thirty. And remember, if you're not there I'll be all alone with Hawk and Kestrel. Now, lie down on the floor and stick your fingers down your throat."

Numbly, Eagle did as he was bid. He paid no attention to the loud giggle that followed Bad Boy's last instruction. He wasn't to know that Eric had found the whole thing hilarious and his silent laughter could no longer be contained. Eagle lay retching among the debris and the click in the receiver told him his love had left him bleakly alone once more.

As the bile flowed from him, he thrilled at the idea that, once again, his passion had uncovered areas of experience he'd never before entered. The euphoria at the fact that Bad Boy had actually sought him out and made contact was more than offset by the information that he must share those attentions with Hawk and Kestrel.

He was blitzed by jealousy. The egoism of the true masochist had never before permitted him to consider the feelings even of those who were persecuting him. But this inky scorn was so precious that he needed its exclusivity. Each time his mind veered across an image of Bad Boy standing over a cowering Hawk or a wheedling Kestrel, there was a clutch of pain in his stomach and a pressure in his head he knew he couldn't tolerate.

Their unholy usurpation of his rightful place must be punished. Lately, lots of The Cage's birds had been disappearing. If Hawk and Kestrel were on board this boat, he'd make sure he found them and he'd push the buggers overboard before they caused him any more trouble.

But not even this casual resolution to commit a double murder quieted the troubled Eagle's spirits. They were still alive tonight, and would be tomorrow, until he traced them on board the boat. And until that time they would continue to occupy a corner of Bad Boy's thoughts.

He tried hard to conceive of a plan to dispose of them immediately but what would Bad Boy say if he found out Eagle had broken his toys? No, he must force himself to wait. He decided, however, that even if they continued to exist in Bad Boy's mind, they would certainly not get near his body. He would issue instructions that would confine them to their rooms. With shaking hands, he picked up the telephone once more and asked to be put through to Hawk.

When Hawk answered, Eagle had great difficulty in refraining from screaming obscenities at him and crying in despair. His voice came out in clubbed rather than clipped syllables under the strain.

"Hawk," he stabbed.

"Is that you, boss?" said the guilty Hawk, who had been caught once again thumbing through a mail order catalogue looking at the pictures of little girls in short sleeves.

"Hawk, you sod… I know what you've been up to," continued the staccato Eagle.

Hawk, uselessly, put the catalogue behind his back. When he spoke, his guilt was clear.

"Er, what do you mean? I need a new monkey-wrench … and I heard they were cheaper by mail order…"

Eagle couldn't bear it. His subordinate's words, especially the insolent "monkey-wrench", were designed to be cruel. They ignored the depth of his love. He began to cry.

"Oh, Hawk, Hawk," he said in broken tones. "How could you? I trusted you. You were working for me and now … now I find out … this. Oh my God, it's too much for a man to bear."

Hawk, although thoroughly defeated by the thought that his secret was out, nonetheless considered Eagle was over-reacting somewhat.

"Oh, surely it's not that bad?" he said. "I mean, there have been other…"

He'd intended to list other Cage personnel whose private predilections had been uncovered without causing the boss to break down so completely, but Eagle anticipated a list of Bad Boy's other affairs and screamed through Hawk's words.

"Stop! Stop! How dare you, you Jezebel. Well, you're not getting it all your own way. You wait. I'll be there tomorrow night, on board. Oh yes, I've been invited too and by God you'll know I'm there all right. Just wait, that's all. Just wait." And he slammed the receiver down in fine Wagnerian fury.

Hawk was stunned. Lodgedale hadn't yet been in touch with him to suggest the visit to the boat which Tessa had arranged for them all, so nothing of what Eagle said made any sense. Towards the end of Eagle's strange final outburst, he'd realised it wasn't his own bizarre sexual predilections that were at stake. In his relief, his rational mind had resurfaced to remind him that, according to Mary, Eagle was on his way out.

This hysteria must be a sign of the dementia they'd all known about. Eagle was on the skids. Hawk must swiftly find a way to nullify any claims Kestrel might have to the perch. It was some twenty minutes later, while he was still deeply involved in his plotting but had advanced little, that the enigmatic phone call from Lodgedale provided the opportunity he was seeking.

The inspector was a stranger to subtlety or discretion; all his diplomacy was carried out at close quarters with blunt instruments. Had his suggestions not fallen so neatly into Hawk's requirements, Hawk would undoubtedly have been more suspicious, but he was desperate for a gift horse and its mouth was invisible at the other end of a telephone line.

"Hullo Hawk," said Lodgedale when Hawk answered the phone.

"Yes," said Hawk. "Who's that?"

"D. I. Lodgedale. Listen, if you want to incriminate Kestrel, he'll be on board the Katherine Jo Ross at eight-thirty tomorrow night with a black guy. Cheers."

And that was that.

Years of esoteric ornithology whose meaning he only occasionally grasped had made Hawk believe everyone spoke in a code no-one else understood. Lodgedale's words were mysterious but seemed to be right on the button. Eagle too, he remembered, had mentioned a rendezvous on a boat the following evening. It must be some sort of cipher and the chance to brand Kestrel as a traitor convinced him that at all costs he must be on the Katherine Jo Ross at eight-thirty.

Eagle had meanwhile recovered some of his control after the catharsis of his outburst on the line to Hawk but, like all jealousies, his sought further fuel for the flames that must lick at him until his rivals had gone. Although he had no need to, and although he now knew himself to be incapable of issuing the simple order which would confine his assistants to their quarters, he rang Kestrel. Again, as with Hawk, he managed at first to maintain his equilibrium.

"Right Kestrel," he said. "About tomorrow night…"

Kestrel, of course, had no idea what was coming, since he'd not yet heard from Lodgedale either, but his thoughts had very recently been on the policeman as he'd been bathing the cuts and bruises his interrogation had left all over him.

"Yes sir," he said. "Well, whatever happens I hope *he* isn't there again."

Eagle plunged back into his grief. Kestrel was actually confessing, flaunting his contact with Bad Boy.

"Why not?" asked the hopeless Eagle, as the now-dry sobs queued up in his diaphragm.

"You should see the marks he's left on me," said Kestrel.

Eagle groaned.

"All over," went on Kestrel. "I don't think there's a part of me he didn't…"

"Oh, my God! My God!" screamed Eagle again. "The whole world is in a conspiracy against me. Where are the pains of yesteryear?"

And again he rang off bitterly, leaving Kestrel to ponder and draw the same conclusions Hawk had reached only a short time before. The subsequent phone call from Lodgedale to Kestrel warning him of Hawk's supposed date with a black guy fell just as appropriately into his own scheming and he, too, was determined to be on the boat the following evening. One final telephone call strengthened his resolve. He decided to attempt a little sparring with Hawk, in the hope the latter might reveal something of his proposed treachery. He rang through to his room.

"Hullo, Hawk. Kestrel here. How's tricks?"

"Oh, you know. How about you?"

"Yes. Just the same."

"Good, good."

"Er … doing anything tomorrow night?"

(Pause).

"Maybe. Thought I might stone a curlew."

(Pause).

"Really?"

"Yes. How about you?"

(Pause).

"Er, not sure… I'll probably see if any ducks are limping."

(Pause).

"Oh. OK then. See you some time."

"Yeah. Bye."

As each man replaced the receiver, he was confident the other would be on board the following evening. Never had such semantic emptiness been so resonant with meaning.

CHAPTER SIXTEEN

Machin had spent a large part of the morning of the 17th preparing his edition of *Daniel Martin*. He was grateful for such an automatic task; it demanded his full concentration and pushed thoughts of the imminent meeting well into the background. Tessa's tenderness had continued and that, too, had helped to maintain his calm. When his mind did flick towards the coming events, the thought that this time the object of it all was sex held less terror than the previous unknowns or the enthusiastic protective impulses of Eric.

He couldn't know, of course, that Hawk's original M and C had been meaningless and Mary's revision of it was designed only to protect the Edinburgh official. No-one connected with The Cage would be at the library and the whole exercise would simply serve to fill in time before the real encounter which Tessa had arranged for the boat in Peterhead that evening.

When he'd finished and double-checked his work, Machin found himself with a little unwanted time for reflection. All the violence, all the off-handed chat about murders and eliminations, all the grandiose instructions about assassinating council officials could do nothing to shake him from the feeling that with his involvement in crime the world had shrunk. He knew that university had taught him to think about life rather than live it, and if he could recapture that faculty then perhaps he could get back to reciting "je m'appelle Christophe" to schoolkids and retreat into untroubled uselessness again.

Tessa, beautiful Tessa, had promised that tomorrow he might be freed. He was therefore determined to remain as cool as possible in front of the library, take the sex when it came, and thereafter apply for the first teaching post that was advertised on the tip of the Cornish peninsula.

The silence which surrounded his thinking was broken only by the twang of Bad Boy's knitting needles and small crunchings from Eric's teeth as he chewed pieces of glass. Tessa was watching the postman across the road as he made tentative journeys back and forth across his room with the aid of a stick he'd made from some wood stripped from his bed head.

Unseen, in a hotel a little further along the street, Lodgedale was staring intently at the hands on his watch, willing them to move more quickly towards noon. He was determined to be at the meeting in order to wreak as much havoc as possible. It wasn't that he had no faith in Tessa and her Special Branch schemes. This meeting offered him a preliminary bite at the cherry, that was all, and he saw no harm in following his own original plan. He'd use the event to create so much embarrassment that Eagle and the others would be forced to keep out of his way.

At last, at eleven o'clock, he wandered over to the library, reconnoitred the space in front of it, and concealed himself in a doorway to wait for Machin and the person he was supposed to meet.

Thirty minutes later, Tessa and Machin took a taxi to a street near the library where they got out, made sure of their bearings and checked on the final details. Machin had the book. Tessa promised she wouldn't be far away at any time and showed Machin the Beretta she'd brought for insurance purposes. The effect of the gun on Machin was ambivalent; he was glad it was intended as protection for him, but chastened to be reminded their activities might include corpses. A final reassuring kiss from Tessa sent him on his way, however, and he walked, as bravely as he could, to stand in front of the main entrance.

Unlike the afternoon at Marks and Spencer, there were no crowds of shoppers to conceal his presence. People did come and go in and out of the library, and most of them carried books. But no-one lingered and he felt himself to be utterly exposed and imagined hundreds of telescopic sights trained on him from all directions.

There'd been no sign of Tessa for a long time. He looked at his watch. Seven minutes past twelve. They'd agreed to give it fifteen minutes. Only eight more and he could scuttle back to the hotel unscathed and retire from crime for ever.

A seagull startled him as it flew up over the library's front. Another look at the watch. Eight minutes past. Surely no-one would come now. The pavement was deserted. He moved into the final stages of relaxed tension, and then suddenly spun round as he heard a step behind him. Coming out of the library was a woman. But he was reassured. This couldn't possibly be his contact. As she stepped arthritically into the light, he saw she was at least eighty years old.

He continued to watch her, even gave her a smile, and a high note of panic began to shrill in his head as she smiled back and moved towards him. She was going to speak to him. They had to be joking. Sex with an octogenarian was the key to his initiation? It wasn't fair that his whole future should depend upon his hormones responding to lubricious senility. He knew he could never make it. He must be mistaken. But the old woman continued her creaking progress towards him. As she reached him, she stopped, smiled again and spoke.

Machin was horrified as he heard her words. He had no idea what they meant, but they were delivered in such a strong Aberdeenshire accent that it could only be the Lewis Crassic Gibbon code. He hadn't ever spent much time with people in the country and was therefore unable to recognise that, through the tangle of her accent, all the woman wanted to know was the time. Helplessly, he handed her the book he was carrying. She looked at it, then up at him, and stretched out a bewildered hand to take it.

The gesture froze, as did every corpuscle in Machin's body, as the pavement filled with a raucous Banshee scream. Neither of them had time to identify its source before the charging Lodgedale was upon them and setting about the old woman with a fury that would have been the envy of the most consummate mugger.

Machin stood transfixed, witnessing the assault and dumbly registering the fact that this was the imbecile who'd invaded his own kitchen all those centuries ago. His thoughts, which he'd so painstakingly reassembled that morning, exploded once more into the hysteria which had become his natural state recently. He was aware of the arrival of Tessa, of her intervention in the assault, and of Lodgedale's scream of pain as the butt of the Beretta smashed the wrist of the hand that was holding the old woman's throat.

He heard Tessa shout, "Leave her alone, you silly bugger. She's Special Branch, too," and Lodgedale reply, "How was I to know, you silly bitch? Look what you've done to my hand."

Then Tessa was dragging him away down the street at a run

while Lodgedale ran away in the opposite direction and people hurried out of the library to the old woman who was lying on the pavement. By the time the police arrived, Tessa and Machin were in one taxi on their way home and Lodgedale was in another on his way to the hospital to have his wrist X-rayed. The police, deprived of any suspects, were determined to get all the mileage they could out of the old woman. Consequently, they were delighted when, remembering only Tessa's words from the whole harrowing episode, she kept repeating in answer to their questions, "I'm Special Branch, too."

Bewilderingly, at exactly the same time, in front of Marks and Spencer in Aberdeen, a nun carrying a crate and a loudhailer stopped, put down the crate, stood on it, raised the loudhailer to her lips and repeated several times, "Immediate avian migration." Thereupon, two thirds of the people circling about on the pavement threw down the books they were carrying and scurried away to lose themselves amongst the few genuine shoppers. There had obviously been a major change of direction at The Cage.

****

It took Tessa a long time to reassemble Machin's nerves. All the way back in the taxi he'd trembled and twitched as she held him tight and soothed him with the perennial "there, there" of the comforting female. He'd kept shaking his head to dismiss the truth of what he'd seen, but its suddenness and aggression had recalled all the other impossibilities of the past few days and he would need time to recover.

Once back in the hotel, Tessa decided she owed him a thorough debriefing. He'd never be any use as a Belazzo boy. She'd even be unhappy about using him as an expendable decoy. So all that remained was to counter the recent disorientating experiences with an alternative set whose effects would be equally devastating but remedial rather than destructive. She sent Bad Boy and Eric to keep watch in the lobby of the postman's hotel and set about devoting herself to restoring some of Machin's psyche.

While continuing to soothe and mother him, she coaxed him out of his clothes and began gently to wash him all over. Machin wasn't so far gone that he failed to recognise the depraved ambivalence of their contact. Here he was being coddled like a child, being rocked and shushed with lullabies, while at the same time, the gentle, stroking mother's hands found areas and evoked sensations of which his own mother had obviously been ignorant.

His wonder at the transitions that were being effected in him began to collect the fragments of his self together once more and he was unashamedly aware that Tessa the mother had been replaced by Tessa the woman. The soothing tenderness had melted into caressing provocation and such was her skill that the most persistent of Machin's traumas were at last stampeded away by the insistence of his Oedipal desire.

When she'd dealt with his initial impotence, she followed well-worn paths of titillation which were intended to provide sufficient input into his system to displace all the unpleasantness he'd witnessed. Eventually, she even derived some pleasure herself from the process. But more important than that was the gratification she felt when Machin at last fell back on the sheet, the sweat in drops on his forehead, and looked at her with a smile expressing smug, secure masculinity.

"OK?" he asked, as if he'd just done her a huge favour.

"Yes, thanks Chris," she said, in character.

"Light me a fag, will you?" he said, and Tessa, immediately dismissing the desire to deliver a karate chop to his crotch to remind him of the true balance of their relationship, meekly obeyed.

She took cigarettes from the pocket of Eric's coat and smoked one with him, although in truth she hated it. But Machin (himself a non-smoker), obviously thought it was the done thing, and his subsequent coughing prohibited conversation and allowed her to think. She was confident Machin was no longer part of the reckoning. Tomorrow, she'd take him back to Aberdeen and her report to the Big Snake would ensure he'd be allowed to retire without fear of being disturbed again.

The thought of the Big Snake quickly dispelled the last languid drifts of post-coital musing. The game he was playing remained the greatest mystery and at present there weren't enough clues to enable her to speculate. Her plans for that evening would meet his requirements; she'd get rid of the postman and Eagle, and two other top members of The Cage into the bargain. But what was the eventual aim? Who was Big Snake? And what could he gain from this progressive elimination of every baddie with whom he came into contact? And (the thought chilled her momentarily), why had she been allowed to survive? She hoped it was her efficiency, but knew better than to set any store by it. No, she must continue to work well for her control but at the same time be very wary of any instructions he gave her.

She was startled by the ringing of her mobile again. Eerily, it was the Big Snake.

"Hi," she said. "I was just thinking about you."

"Good. I hear you saved the Sparrow."

Tessa was immediately alert. Once again, he knew everything that was happening.

"That's right," she said. "That stupid bloody policeman turned up."

"I know. Forget him, though. Now, where are you going on the boat tonight?"

She should have known better. When she'd contacted the skipper of the trawler, her intention had simply been to gather all her problems into one convenient environment. Then, in an isolation she'd selected, they'd be dealt with according to their deserts. No-one knew about it except the individuals concerned and Bad Boy and Eric. So where the hell did Big Snake get his information? Boldness was her natural response.

"How d'you know about that?" she said.

"I'm asking the questions, BW. Trust me."

It was the last thing she wanted to do, but there was little choice.

"Now, just let me check, you'll be with Hawk, Kestrel, Eagle, the postman and that cop, right?"

"Right."

"Good, good. Well, just one thing. Make sure they're all there but get ashore yourself by nine, OK?"

"OK," said Tessa.

The whole exchange was an instant commentary on the Big Snake enigma which she'd been pondering as she lay beside Machin. Luckily, Machin was revelling so thoroughly in his virility that the interruption had done nothing to dismantle the good their sex had done him. He smiled at her now, the same sickly male smile, and flapped a languorous arm at her for her to return to him.

She realised she needed to be free of him in order to be ready for whatever the evening demanded. The fact that the Big Snake had taken over her arrangements meant her wits needed to be even clearer since whatever happened would be unexpected. She moved back to the bed, regretting the fact that Machin's fragility denied her the use of Eric's forearm smash or her own set of nerve-stunning specialities. Machin put his arms out to her and she knew there was only one real option.

She leaned over him allowing her beautiful breasts to hang against his lips as she spread her thighs across his stomach. She wasn't surprised to discover that his loins didn't stir. It was fine for pornographers to invent anatomical absurdities for their books, but bitter experience told her that in reality poor old Priapus was very much a loner. Nonetheless, she set to work once more, and Machin, now convinced that the past week had been a purgatory necessary for his accession to this heaven, matched her caresses and responded surprisingly quickly to her encouraging fingers and tongue.

On this occasion Tessa's intention was even more mechanically functional than it had been on the therapeutic first. She had no time to derive personal pleasure from it and she worked at him with determined application. The result was that, after an extra hour and twenty minutes in which, astonishingly, he'd managed three more orgasms, Machin lay on the bed soaked in sweat. As Tessa eased her nipple between his lips once more, his eyelids flickered briefly, his hand moved once in a clutching conditioned reflex, his mouth sucked twice then hung open, and his long breathing indicated the heavy coma of a man deep in exhaustion.

Tessa herself felt a slight weariness but it was induced by boredom rather than effort, and a quick shower soon restored her sharpness. When she was dressed, she checked Machin's breathing and was confident he'd be out at least until she returned sometime after nine, according to the Big Snake's instructions.

She left the room, locking the door behind her. It was nearly four-thirty. In five hours it would all be over.

CHAPTER SEVENTEEN

The other players in the drama had had varied days as usual. Lodgedale, after his abortive attempt to cause an international scandal, had spent the whole afternoon in the waiting room of A and E. Only by literally twisting the arm of a nurse and threatening an Indian doctor with repatriation had he managed eventually to jump the queue. His wrist was X-rayed and, as a result of the subsequent diagnosis, set in plaster.

He checked out of his hotel room and set off for Peterhead, vowing that tomorrow would see him safely in Aberdeen, whatever the evening brought. His plan was to get to the boat early and conceal himself on board.

Thanks to all the arrangements, something was bound to come out of it. At best, he would see the postman killing Sparrow and then he could arrest him and get back around midnight. At worst, he'd have the pleasure of watching Hawk and Kestrel dispose of one another, or rather, of watching one of them succeed and then personally supplying the vengeance the loser would have wished for. One way or another, the evening would hold some definite crimes and this knowledge helped him to tolerate the pain of his smashed wrist as he jolted along.

Eagle hadn't slept a wink. His tumbling thoughts were haunted by images of Kestrel and Hawk billowing through the dawn to a sleeping Bad Boy and kneeling by his bed eagerly waiting for his eyes to open and despise them. At five-thirty that morning he'd phoned his two subordinates and barked at each one of them, "Get over here. Now."

They'd had no time to query the order. Indeed, given the time, they only just managed to hear and register it, and it was two pale wrecks who met in the corridor outside his room at five-thirty-three. Each tried, without success, to appear alert. At the same time, anxious not to reveal that they knew of the other's plans for

160

that evening, each affected a casual insouciance. The spectacle of these two nearly middle-aged, sleep-befuddled individuals standing in a hotel corridor miming such contrary attitudes at one another did nothing to allay Eagle's suspicions as he flung open the door to let them in.

They in turn were shocked at the ravages which love and jealousy had clawed into their chief's features. He'd always been ugly, but this morning he was like a badly-weathered gargoyle. He didn't trust himself to speak and simply gestured them into the room and pointed at two chairs. Obediently, they sat and waited. They'd been used to this sort of thing back at The Cage, sitting silently while Eagle looked at the harbour and listened to country music. Often he'd turned back from his window and been surprised to find them in the room. And always on such occasions Hawk and Kestrel had silently charted one another's supposed activities, plotting and scheming the downfall which would leave the steps to Eagle's perch uncluttered.

So the present experience was a familiar one. But there were two things which made it different. First, the plotting of Hawk and Kestrel respectively had a clear focus, a direction, a location, a duration and a terminus. And second, there was the new element formed by Eagle's own determination to dispose of both of them at the same time and in the same place. The electricity of all these suppressed intentions was almost tangible in the air of the small room, and beneath its warning crackles there rumbled silently the explosive pressure of Eagle's jealousy.

They sat on and by eight o'clock still not a word had been spoken. All of them felt how far from normality they were on this special occasion and none of them trusted words or any of the usual formulae behind which they'd hidden their real meanings for so many years.

The first eruption came at eight-thirty. The room was becoming unbearably hot and their nervousness was filling the air with sharp unpleasant smells. Kestrel, marginally less constrained than the other two since his own tension contained no sexual component, decided to risk a suggestion that the window be opened. He spoke.

"Boss, d'you mind if we open the..."

"What? What? Don't give me that crap, you dirty little bastard," screamed Eagle, whirling on him and slapping his face before he could think to duck.

The silence returned, heavier still, with the fuse the exchange had lit burning through it towards the next charge.

Hawk and Kestrel both assumed that Eagle's weird behaviour was proof he knew he was on the way out. They guessed he was simply having a final fling, determined to make them suffer before his power was stripped from him and one of them took over his room on the fifth floor.

Towards noon, the pressure in Hawk's bladder had become too great to bear. He knew the risks of speaking but he must run them.

"Sorry, boss, but d'you mind if..."

Eagle exploded again.

"Mind? Mind? You foul bastard. Mind? Mind? What do you think? Sweet Jesus, you make me throw up, d'you know that? You make me puke."

Once again, the silence returned and Kestrel inwardly said "fifteen-all." But Nature proved greater than discretion. Hawk drew a breath and shouted quickly, "I have to pee."

Eagle shouted back, equally loudly. "So what? We all do, prick."

Hawk was launched and so continued shouting, "I mean now."

"Pee, then. Pee. Who's stopping you?" yelled Eagle.

"Thank you," shouted Hawk, and he made for the door.

"Where the hell d'you think you're going?" screamed his chief.

"Lavatory," shouted Hawk, even more desperate now that the possibility of relieving the pressure was so close.

"No you're not," said Eagle. "You do it here, in the sink."

Hawk, careless of his audience, glad even because the remnants of the washbasin were closer to him than the lavatory, rushed across, unzipped and leaned forward against the mirror in ecstasy as the urine began to flow. His relief was so total that he was unaffected by the proximity of the razor-sharp edge of the shattered sink to his genitals. He was also able to ignore the commentary his chief had launched into about the vile "thing" he held in his hand.

The sound of the jet into the basin and Hawk's idiotic smile quickly overcame all other sensations, and Kestrel and Eagle, who themselves were desperate for an identical relief, were forced to succumb to the same temptation. For a few precious moments the three of them stood in a little semi-circle around the broken washbasin, sharing for the first and last time in their lives a unique communion.

As they re-zipped and returned to their places, they all felt the slight relaxation of tension which the moment had produced. Maybe it was something to do with running water and static electricity, but whatever the reason, the. atmosphere was lighter, all pressures had been eased.

Still no-one spoke, but Eagle's close surveillance lapsed temporarily and allowed him to think beyond the confines of his jealous misery. If Hawk and Kestrel were to disappear tonight, he must prepare the ground. He didn't want questions when he took Bad Boy back to Aberdeen with him. The seed must be sown now. It was a pity that Hawk and Kestrel would hear it, but it mattered little in the end because in (he looked at his watch) just over eight hours they'd be dead anyway. He'd made up his mind and he picked up the telephone and asked the operator for a number. He was connected and, fairly quickly, a voice answered.

"Benton Exporting. Can I help you?"

"Eagle. Priority. Eggshell," he said.

Hawk and Kestrel looked up. Eagle ignored them and waited. Almost immediately he heard Mary's voice.

"Eagle, sir. What can I do for you?"

"Nothing, Mary. Nothing," said Eagle. "I'm just phoning to keep you abreast of our movements, just in case anything happens. The three of us, that's Hawk, Kestrel and I, are having a bit of a meeting at the moment, but tonight we've all been invited aboard a boat."

Hawk and Kestrel, alerted already by Eagle's expression "just in case anything happens", were thrown into total confusion by the rest of his news. As Eagle continued to give details of the evening ahead, each tried to find the part of the puzzle that was missing in order to make sense of the conflicting pieces of information they'd been given.

Eagle replaced the receiver and the three men sat in a silence even more profound than those which had preceded it during the morning. Each was now fully aware that the evening ahead was to be in some way terminal and no-one was prepared to speak in case he divulged some piece of information which might prove useful to the others.

They sat on through the afternoon. At four-forty they once more enjoyed the relief if not the previous fraternity of a communal pee, and it was not until seven in the evening that Eagle eventually said, "OK, you two. Get lost," adding heavily, "and have a nice evening."

CHAPTER EIGHTEEN

The Katherine Jo Ross, lying alongside the quay, was a medium-sized trawler. Her foredeck was littered with fish boxes, coils of rope and hawser, trawl boards and huge mounds of nets. Her wheelhouse started amidships and led back aft, occupying about a quarter of the deck's surface. In the stern, more ropes, boxes and nets completed a dark and smelly confusion around which the fishermen who crewed her could pick their unerring way with ease. To those unaccustomed to such items, it was a small but intricate and potentially perilous maze.

Her skipper, Rab Gordon, was well pleased with the rates he'd been offered for an evening's charter. It wasn't very often that anyone was stupid enough to want to pay to have the use of a working boat like his. Sometimes he was approached by a TV or film company, or, very occasionally, an angling club from the Midlands with pretensions, but today seemed like Christmas.

First the woman had been in touch and agreed a figure he'd simply quoted as a try-on, then, late in the afternoon, the other bloke had offered him the same again just to make certain arrangements regarding the accommodation of his passengers and the course he should steer with them. Normally, it would take them a good fortnight to earn the sort of money involved and he'd been very careful in briefing his crew.

"Mouse" Laurence, Ronnie George and Bobby Nicholas would be on the quay on stand-by from six in case any of them arrived early. The woman had said that one or two of them probably would, and they'd probably ask to be hidden somewhere. The lads had been told to humour them and see them safely aboard where the skipper would see to their accommodation.

The other man he'd spoken to had been a bit more explicit about what he wanted and asked that, once clear of the harbour, the skipper should stay on a bearing of 21 degrees, somewhere along which he'd be contacted with further instructions.

Predictably, the first of the passengers to arrive was Lodgedale. He'd reasoned that, since his job was to watch not only the postman and Sparrow but also Hawk and Kestrel, he should get there first to ensure that he got the choice of locations from which to observe the goings-on. The new white plaster cast on his right wrist gleamed in the gathering murk as he walked across the quay. It was seven-thirty.

Although he was indeed the first to arrive, the manner he adopted with the crew members and the fact that he was a policeman ensured they gave him the filthiest place on the deck. He was assured by the skipper as he piled fishing nets on top of him that there was no better vantage-point, but when the man had finished and gone away, he found he could only see out over the port side, the side facing away from the quay. He could hardly move because of the nets and the overpowering stench of fish made breathing uncomfortable and nausea imminent.

Lodgedale wasn't to know that this foul hideaway was to be his final niche in Britain. His career in the force would go no further and he would never collect the erotic profits generated in his wife by the piece of intestine. He began working away at his position in order to gain a little more freedom and improve his field of sight and he was so busy with his efforts that he heard nothing when Hawk arrived only five minutes after him.

When Eagle had eventually released them, Hawk and Kestrel had immediately indulged in a totally pointless charade in which each attempted to outwit and outmanoeuvre the other. Kestrel, for example, had leapt into a taxi which had sped away, whereupon Hawk had hurtled from the doorway of the hotel, grabbed the next cab and shouted "Follow that taxi" to an at first disbelieving driver.

Five minutes later, the two cabs had pulled up, one immediately behind the other, back at the same hotel and Hawk and Kestrel had got out again, each furious with the other but neither wishing to show it. As the first cab pulled away, however, Hawk suddenly leapt back into the second and said, "Quick. Peterhead." The driver shrugged, shook his head, but drove off all the same, and Hawk smiled in satisfaction as they left Kestrel on the pavement looking desperately for another cab.

On the quay, the fishermen saw the glow of another plaster

cast and knew their second passenger had arrived. He, too, wanted to be given a privileged viewpoint and they tangled him in cordage at the opposite end of the deck from Lodgedale, providing a hideaway that was equally rancid and would prove equally terminal.

The skipper had barely finished concealing him when Kestrel's glowing plaster announced the third arrival. He was furious that Hawk was nowhere to be seen and wondered why he hadn't come straight to the boat. His request to the skipper that he should be well concealed was as earnest as those of Lodgedale and Hawk. It was satisfied with the same thorough efficiency as he was knotted into a little nook on the port side of the wheelhouse to await, like the others, his final exit.

Eagle didn't arrive until eight-fifteen. He'd seen Hawk and Kestrel leave and then return and he'd assumed, naturally, that each was as jealous of the other as he was of the pair of them. He felt he could safely leave them to inhibit one another's progress for a while, confident that Bad Boy would be late for the rendezvous anyway. To him, their early departure was a waste of time and simply indicated how inexperienced they were in the intricacies of sado-masochistic relationships. He tried to gauge his arrival so that there'd be plenty of time for him to hide before the god materialised.

His plaster cast glowed his arrival to the skipper on deck, and Eagle, looking down across the mess of nets and tackle, was surprised Hawk and Kestrel weren't there. But then, again remembering their inexperience, he supposed they'd gone below into the relative hygiene of a cabin whereas he knew Bad Boy's preference would be to revile them superbly amongst the smell and clutter of tar and nets, boxes encrusted with dried scales, and all the other evidence of misuse and decay which littered the ghastly deck.

Gladly, he clambered down onto the stage that was to witness the next phase of his total commitment to his love, and he in turn asked the skipper to put him where he might invisibly survey the goings-on of his fellow passengers when they eventually emerged on deck.

The skipper had reserved him a spot amongst the nets on the starboard side of the wheelhouse, and when he was thoroughly bunched into the snare that would relieve The Cage of him for

167

good, the time was just coming up to eight-thirty.

The men on the quay knew there was only one more to come and, as they peered into the darkness, they were surprised to see that this one was apparently arriving on all fours. The plaster cast on the right wrist of each of the others had flashed their arrival long before anything else had been visible. This time, however, the white flash was at ground level and the approach was accompanied by a bumping sound. They failed to realise their mistake until the man was quite close. The plaster casts had conditioned them into believing these men were all members of a weird club involving broken wrists and they were slightly thrown when the bandages turned out to be wound round his ankle.

He walked with difficulty, supporting himself as much as possible on a piece of bed he carried under his left arm. Unknown to the fishermen, he carried in his right pocket a hypodermic needle identical to that which had been dropped in Machin's garden and which had despatched Detective Constable Baxter. The postman's intention was simple; identify Sparrow, inject, and then, if possible, clear out. Unknown to him, it was his own control, alias the Big Snake, who'd earlier been in touch with the skipper of the trawler and his instructions were about to be superseded by an entirely new plan of which he was ignorant.

The skipper helped him onto the deck, settled him on a heap of nets amidships, and arranged them around him, ostensibly to make him comfortable but actually to tie him in place. Never had a snare been so evilly contrived; he could see nothing, and retained only a minimal amount of movement in his right arm. Otherwise he was as secure as all the others.

Now that all his charges were safely aboard, the skipper climbed up into the wheelhouse, operated the engine-room telegraph, and started shouting orders to Bobby, Ronnie and Mouse, who'd already begun to loosen off the moorings and were standing by to let go.

Up on the quay, Tessa had watched everything and was looking now through night glasses as the trawler nosed out from the quayside and, getting way on fairly quickly, cut through the water towards the open sea. Four of the five separate bundles of nets had become very animated as their occupants had become aware of the changed motion, but the skipper, used to dragging cod and other species from the meshes, had found it simple to reverse the process and secure his charges without them even knowing he'd done so.

Tessa heard faint shouts and replies as Eagle, Kestrel, Hawk and Lodgedale recognised one another's voices. Obscurely aware that the Big Snake was up to something else of which she had no knowledge, she put away the glasses, and began to walk slowly up and down the quay, waiting for the trawler's return.

By the time the relatively sharp chop of the water near the shore had been augmented by the longer, more devious rolling of the open sea, the passengers on the Katherine Jo Ross had been driven one by one to give up their shouting and concentrate on disentanglement. The boat's motion combined with the stench to inject an urgency into their efforts which made speculation about what was going on an unaffordable luxury.

Kestrel was most sorely afflicted. A product of Stirling, he hadn't seen the sea until he was in his teens and sometimes he even felt queasy sitting in his bath. The certainty that all his internal organs had liquefied provoked desperate thrashings whose results were both welcome and unwelcome in that his upper torso convulsed itself free while his legs simultaneously locked themselves inextricably in the black meshes. The final heaves he made to drag himself up from their grip set up sympathetic spasms in his diaphragm and, inevitably, he began to be sick all over the nets from which he protruded.

Up in the bows, Hawk, who was that much thinner than Kestrel, was being far more successful. It still took him a while to extricate himself, though, and as he pulled the last twists from his ankles, he heard above the wind one of his colleague's pitiful moans. He turned his head quickly and, peering back down the deck, began to inch along towards the source of the cry.

The postman, too, had been much more systematic in his dealings with the nets and since he'd wasted no time in shouting, was already well clear. After sitting in the darkness under the wheelhouse for a while to familiarise himself with his immediate surroundings, he took out and primed the syringe and was about to move forward when he too heard Kestrel's moan coming from around the wheelhouse behind him to his left.

He edged quietly to peer round the corner and saw Kestrel's upper half bending to and fro. He moved closer, hoping to find it was Sparrow, his target, so that his business could be concluded at once. He came close enough to hear the whimperings but Kestrel's rocking and his posture kept his features well concealed. The postman was forced to move from his shelter. He leapt forward, grabbed Kestrel's hair and yanked his head back to look at his face, the syringe poised ready for a quick jab. He was disappointed as eyes belonging to someone other than Sparrow stared at him from the lime-green face. Kestrel tried to say, "Please, just let me die," but instead began pouring yet more of his contents from his mouth.

At the very moment the postman let the head fall back, Hawk came close enough to register the scene and gagged in horror. Kestrel's little nest was just under the port navigation light and its red glow fell on him and on the substances he'd ejected in such a way that Hawk, expecting the worst, deduced that his colleague had been severed at the waist and his top half had been plonked on the nets by the postman with blood still streaming from it.

Momentarily, revulsion overcame his natural fear and he screamed "You vile bastard" as he stumbled down the deck towards the postman. The latter was startled and whirled quickly round to face the lunging Hawk, who, on his approach, flapped an aggressive hand at him. As the slap was aimed, however, Hawk was already beginning to realise the peril into which he was hurtling and his body was so quick to over-ride the commands of his over-stimulated brain that the hand stopped short of actual contact.

The postman had instinctively adopted a defensive posture, his head ducking, his shoulders hunching forward and down and his hands coming together over his genitals. Of all these reflexes it was the last that was the most regrettable since the syringe in his right hand penetrated the serge of his trousers, embedded its point in the base of his penis, and forced most of its contents into his bloodstream.

His seizure was as rapid and conclusive as that of Detective Constable Baxter in Machin's garden but infinitely more bitter. There was just enough time before he died for realisation of the location of the puncture to sear through his horrified mind.

He fell at the feet of the already retreating Hawk just as Eagle made his appearance from the starboard side of the wheelhouse. He'd seen Hawk's lunge, the postman's demise, and now the sawn-off, apparently bleeding trunk of Kestrel also came into

170

view. He looked in astonished admiration at his subordinate.

"Christ, Jim," he said. "You're a deep one."

The two men stood warily apart from one another, Hawk overwhelmed by the atrocities that surrounded them and convinced they were all products of his chief's jangled brain. Eagle was uncertain how to approach his deputy now that he'd shown himself to be so effectively homicidal. They were both startled by another moan which gurgled up from Kestrel's deep nausea. Eagle had a rare rush of compassion.

"Jesus," he said, "you've left the poor bastard alive." And with the double intention of stopping Kestrel's misery and relieving some of his own emotion, he stepped over the postman and delivered a rabbit punch to the side of Kestrel's neck that sent him into merciful unconsciousness. Hawk moved nearer to hysteria.

"You murderous bastard!" he screamed.

"You can talk," shouted Eagle, reasonably.

"You're insane," went on Hawk. "Off your bloody head. You ought to be locked up."

"Oh, and I suppose you expect a medal?" countered a heavily satirical Eagle, whereupon both men shed a little of their tension by settling into the preamble to another of those childish exchanges which they took to be righteous indignation and mature rationality.

CHAPTER NINETEEN

The skipper and crew of the Katherine Jo Ross were in the wheelhouse where they'd clustered at first simply to chat away the hour or so of what they imagined was to be a routine trip. They'd witnessed the emergence and these first contacts of their passengers with much amusement. Since they couldn't, from their position, see that the postman was in fact dead, the seriousness of the developing saga wasn't yet apparent to them.

They chuckled, snorted and giggled at the imprecations Eagle and Hawk yelled at one another, rejoicing in the fact that their trip was bringing them not only remuneration but also entertainment. But the spectre at their particular feast was fast arriving and the gentle pleasure of these guiltless spectators was suddenly split and shattered by an eruption.

Lodgedale had arrived.

As the deceased postman had proved, the process of disentanglement required thought and studied movements. Lodgedale's ignorance of such niceties had ensured that he was the last to emerge. As he'd thrashed towards his final freedom, his thoughts had temporarily moved from Sparrow and the others to coagulate around the identity of those responsible for tying him up in those bloody nets. He'd worked out that the skipper of a boat under way would probably be in the wheelhouse and he'd rushed from the last embraces of the ropes in the stern straight to the wheelhouse door to fling it open and dive, flailing, for the man at the wheel.

Below, the engineer was puzzled when the engine telegraph rang to him the information that his skipper wanted the engines switched from full ahead to full astern without the usual intervening steps. He couldn't know that the lever in the wheelhouse had been operated by the groin of one of his shipmates whom Lodgedale had hurled aside on his way to the skipper. It

172

was to prove the first of many contradictory instructions which related less to the progress of the boat than to that of the brawl which was filling the wheelhouse with bits of flesh and teeth.

The crew were all strong men but the element of surprise and a long acquaintance with refined destructive techniques gave Lodgedale the initial advantage. He began humming to himself and marking the tempo of his tune by punching the faces around him and adding contrapuntal rhythms with his knees and feet. Progressively, he became totally absorbed in the work and settled into a medley of slow fox-trots, Souza marches, and even, with a rare flash of humour, a snatch of the Anvil chorus from *Il Trovatore*.

The fight clattered on around the enclosed space amongst shreds of charts, fragments of echo-sounding equipment and compass, splinters of the internal fittings, various tide-tables, navigational aids and all those sensitive modern devices that are necessary to ensure the safe passage of ships at sea.

The little boat responded sweetly to every pressure on the helm and every change of speed and direction which the ricocheting bodies conveyed to the puzzled but obedient engineer via his telegraph. To the lunging induced by the swell was added a zig-zagging and shunting which gave a ride far beyond the imaginings of the most inventive theme park innovator.

The wheel eventually locked tight in a position which sent the boat hard to starboard and the Katherine Jo Ross began to heel into the first of many revolutions that churned it round to chase its own stern at a spot several miles out in the North Sea.

Simultaneously, the engineer decided that the rush of unaccustomed orders he'd been receiving deserved some explanation and clambered up from his engine room. As he came out on deck he noticed the boat's pronounced heel and, through the wind, caught a snatch of screamed conversation.

"Oh yeah? Well, who sent a budgie to Cardiff without millet?"

"Well, at least I don't build nests in bloody Dundee."

"Oh no?"

"No."

He clutched his way forward to where Eagle and Hawk still faced up to one another amongst the spray. Beside them, he saw the lolling trunk of Kestrel and a fourth figure which stretched his credulousness to the limit. Under the navigation light the figure lay still on its back. From between its legs jutted something rigid and cylindrical which, in the dim red glow, the engineer took to be a very creditable erection.

The scene confirmed the uneasy suspicions which had come to him in his engine room and he quickly hauled himself up to the wheelhouse door, slid it open and was immediately sucked into the chaos which whirled around inside. In the confined space his arrival couldn't have the immediate impact on the battle that would have been expected elsewhere.

Lodgedale was heavily outnumbered, but panic and a reflex of self-defence was causing everyone in the wheelhouse to strike at anything which seemed to threaten so that the contest had become one-sided. At an early stage, for example, the engineer found his head on the floor beside that of Mouse Laurence. He shouted, "What the hell's going on Mouse?" and Mouse, in reply, bit into his ear-lobe.

It was some time later, as the contestants tired and blows and kicks got marginally less frequent that, one by one, they became aware that the wheelhouse was filled with a harsh white light. Also, part of the chorus of hatred and terror in which they were all involved was being screamed in Russian.

Even Hawk and Eagle on the deck outside hadn't immediately been aware of the approach of the huge Russian factory ship since they were well into details of one another's perversions. But the searchlight which had suddenly flooded the deck and the repeated calls from a loudhailer for them to heave to had dragged them from their confrontation to stare in fear at the illuminated castle which wallowed in the darkness a little way off.

The Russian ship, acting on instructions passed to it from the ubiquitous Big Snake, had been waiting to rendezvous with the trawler along the bearing she'd followed until Lodgedale's invasion of the wheelhouse. Her radar had picked it up very early and by monitoring its direction had established that it was the ship that they were supposed to meet.

When the blip on their screen started behaving in a way that seemed to defy all normal maritime laws, the Russian skipper had decided to investigate. His ship was brought to within hailing distance, its floodlights turned full on the cavorting trawler, and the order to heave to was transmitted and duly ignored. The Russian then sent a boarding party consisting of three crew members across in a dinghy.

It was the voice of one of these unfortunates that was distracting the individuals packed into the wheelhouse from their homicidal activities. He and his two shipmates had climbed aboard and when he'd opened the wheelhouse door to investigate and immediately disappeared, as into a giant vacuum cleaner, his colleagues had instantly called up on their radios for reinforcements.

When the latter arrived, the wheelhouse was already so full that it only needed three of them to force their way in for all activity to cease. It wasn't that Lodgedale's fury had abated, or even that the unexplained presence of four Russian sailors on board distracted some of their attention from the struggle; the simple fact was that no-one in the wheelhouse could move.

****

Since Russia had jumped so eagerly into the Western ways of personal, as opposed to institutional, greed and profit, their citizens had become progressively more adept at creating their own enterprise culture. Talks with some of the skippers on The Cage's rota had opened up the possibilities of lucrative little trips to Oslo and even, given the scope of their vessels, longer voyages to more exotic ports. The skipper of the factory ship had a network of contacts in Scotland and was always ready to do favours for people who might put some interesting contracts his way.

This time, his remit was simple. When contact had been established with the Katherine Jo Ross, he was to take custody of her five passengers and transport them eventually to Russia for interrogation and imprisonment, rebriefing or whatever else he fancied. Since he was assured of the co-operation of the crew of the Katherine Jo Ross, he'd foreseen no difficulties.

The unexpected manoeuvres of the British boat and the manner in which it was still chasing doggedly round and round to starboard, however, suggested the presence of factors of which he was ignorant. Before committing himself to any course of action, he decided to contact the control from whom he'd received his instructions.

He radioed the necessary call-sign, explained the situation and waited for confirmation from the person Tessa knew as Big Snake, but who to his Russian friends was simply 1812.

The skipper's bewilderment grew as he watched the churning little trawler with its crew and passengers so bizarrely disposed. Business, he knew, was a sinister pursuit, but to add such complications to the process of handling men and ships at sea seemed to him particularly perverse.

His puzzlement helped to prepare him for 1812's eventual instructions. If things had been normal, they'd have sounded weird, but instead, in these circumstances, they seemed natural. He surveyed his personnel, selected those that best suited the requirements of his orders, briefed them, dealt with their very reasonable objections to his absurd requests, and sent them across in another dinghy to begin the transfer.

He watched with interest as his people climbed aboard and began to perform the actions they believed to be an obscure test of their allegiance to Vladimir Putin. An engineer, whose task was straightforward, went below and stopped the engines. A cook approached Hawk, rolled up his sleeves and, smiling, shook him by the hand. The burly bosun slapped Eagle's face, put a beefy arm round his waist, hoisted him and began to bite his neck.

Meanwhile four of his largest foredeck hands were up at the wheelhouse door trying to prise and lever the occupants free and preparing to pinion Lodgedale, whose description they'd been careful to memorise. The easiest task had fallen to the two individuals who'd been briefed to contact Kestrel and the postman since their charges were, respectively, unconscious and dead.

As the skipper had anticipated, most of the trouble came from Lodgedale. Despite the size of the four men who'd untangled him from his adversaries and bound him with several yards of their best sisal, his body bucked and heaved with them across the deck. Before they managed to secure him in their dinghy, two of them had lost various strips of skin, one could only see out of his left eye, and the fourth would never father any more children.

While the cook and the bosun developed their particular encounters with Hawk and Eagle, apparently oblivious to what was going on around them, the postman's body and the lolling Kestrel, still secure in his little nest of nets, were hoisted aboard the dinghy which then returned to the mother ship to unload them all. Hawk and Eagle were invited to climb into the other dinghy, did so with alacrity, and the crew of the Katherine Jo Ross were at last left to recover their senses and equilibrium and gratefully prepare their boat for the return trip to Peterhead.

Before leaving the little trawler, the Russian skipper sent another party of his men across to make the statutory exchanges of spirits and cigarettes. This was normally a courtesy much enjoyed by both parties but on this occasion the formalities were rushed through as quickly as possible by the Scotsmen, who were terrified the Russians would discover the little insanities of their passengers and return them immediately. As the dinghy finally cast off from alongside, the Katherine Jo Ross's engines throbbed up through the revs and she headed quickly back to normality.

The factory ship turned north-east and made for the little gaggle of trawlers which were waiting to transfer their catches to its sumptuous holds for transformation into various instant fishy delicacies. The skipper was secretly impressed at the accuracy of the instructions which had made collecting his passengers so relatively easy. He would have no problems with either the postman or Kestrel but, as predicted, Lodgedale might take some persuading.

The havoc the policeman had wreaked on his own crewmen had confirmed reports about his character and it was now the skipper's job to show him that there was a place for men of his talents in the Russian police. He would be offered the usual privileges awarded to those most equal in the state and, in addition, be given the promise of his own interrogation block in the Lubyanka with *carte blanche* in its organisation and operation and a constant supply of criminals on whom to experiment. An elevated rank and decorations would satisfy his need for power, a working day totally dedicated to inflicting pain would ensure job satisfaction, and since rape was an option open to him in his interrogation sessions, all his wildest dreams would be accessible.

The skipper was confident that, if he could be restrained long enough to listen, Lodgedale would see the attractiveness of such a package.

Hawk and Eagle seemed already only too grateful for the opportunity of a new life that was being offered. The personality profiles the Big Snake had given the skipper had been minutely accurate and, for them, the massive pill of exile had been hugely sweetened by the potential for personal gratification their contacts had uncovered.

The cook who had approached Hawk had been chosen by the

skipper for his forearms and remarkably smooth elbows, which were devoid of the scrotal puckering which disfigures normal ones. As well as this youthful, pleasing abnormality, the man conveyed a general feeling of shiftiness, had a rather oblique way of walking, which was enhanced by the motions of a heaving deck, and squinted at Hawk through furtively narrowed eyes. Although he was a perfectly normal husband and father, he looked guilty. His smile was that of Sardanapalus on a bad day.

On board the Katherine Jo Ross, Hawk had been confused. The 'deaths" of Kestrel and the postman, the slanging exchange with Eagle, and the disorientation caused by the Russian searchlight and personnel had drained from him anything resembling resistance. As the cook had approached, he'd crooked his elbows provocatively, smiled his seemingly lascivious threat and extended a hand doubtless steeped in atrocities.

Hawk wanted only refuge. In blind terror he'd taken the proffered hand and as its fingers gripped his own, he suddenly felt a special, almost forgotten pressure at the base of his thumb which immediately catapulted his senses from despair to elation. The evil painted on the man's person was instantly explained, the shelter from the incomprehensible happenings on this absurd boat was offered and Hawk's tortured inadequacy was flooded with gratitude.

The cook had been instructed by his skipper, who was as mystified by the order as he was, to bend the bottom knuckle of his forefinger in a particular way and simultaneously alter the angle of his hand so that the normal handshake became distorted. The cook was assured by his skipper that this was the recognition signal of members of an international society for the appreciation of *articulatio cubiti*.

Hawk had lived for years with what he imagined was his secret guilt but, despite the promises in the personal columns of his monthly magazine and the Internet, he'd never actually met anyone who'd returned the signal his anxious hand always transmitted. And now, in the hour of his greatest trial, here was that little clutch of promise, the tiny pressure that signified there was after all a God.

As his wide, grateful eyes looked into the cook's hideously smiling face, the cook nodded confirmation that Hawk had made no mistake. They began an eager conversation full of references to triceps, ginglymoid joints, and the erotic potential of funny bones, all of which delighted Hawk with its implications and the cook for

178

the idiomatic English expressions he was being given the chance to practise.

Hawk was thrilled to discover that, in one of the smaller countries of the former Soviet Union, Eroto-Cubital Sociopathy was a major discipline at the University and the techniques which kept gymnasts so young for so long were rigorously researched and validated.

Having dangled such a bait before him, it was a simple matter for the cook to encourage his expatriation by suggesting he bring his British expertise to Russia and set up his own combined clinic and gymnasium, where he wouldn't be interfered with even though his charges would. At that, the two men had exploded into laughter, Hawk at the joy of such a giddying prospect, and the cook because he'd risked a joke in colloquial English and it had apparently worked. They shook hands again, the bent forefingers deliriously confirming the reality of their contact, and Hawk was ready to leave The Cage and a society which, sexually, was still in the Middle Ages.

Eagle's emigration was prompted by similar principles although the details were clearly different. Size had been foremost in the skipper's mind when he'd chosen his bosun for this particular approach. The need to subdue and dominate Eagle demanded biceps, pectorals, trapezoids, deltoids, and all the other bulging excrescences that signify power. The squat, chunky bosun had all these in abundance. She was also a woman.

Eagle's lack of interest in sports had prevented him ever watching them on television and he'd therefore never registered the fact that the true egalitarianism of the old Eastern bloc was most obvious in its refusal to distinguish between the sexes. The mountainous creatures, fresh from their breakfasts of anabolic steroids, who threw the shot about like a tennis ball, made Bad Boy Jackson look like a pansy. And yet they could all have been called mummy, if any man had ever mistaken them for a sex object or if the resultant foetus had ever managed to force its way out of a uterus that was solid muscle. To admirers of the old Russia, Anna Kournikova was a travesty of what womanhood was supposed to be.

Like Hawk, Eagle had felt all his criteria crumble during the trip on the Katherine Jo Ross. His pursuit of Bad Boy had been totally unsatisfactory and the wrestler's failure to appear had compounded the doubts Eagle entertained about him. And yet the needs he'd aroused were still seething in Eagle's mind, desperate for a satisfaction consummate with their enormity.

He'd witnessed the efficiency with which Hawk had despatched the postman and seen the carnage he'd previously inflicted on Kestrel. A faint memory of silk and kingfisher blue carried with it the regret of a wasted evening, a promise unfulfilled because of the intervention of Bad Boy. But Hawk was such a wimp, and Eagle's somersaulting desires seemed even more hopelessly frustrating than they'd been before. Little wonder then that the virile approach of the hulking bosun, the painful, wordless embrace and the immediacy of the sexual connotations as teeth tore pieces from his neck, should seem like the answer to a prayer.

And then to discover that, under the reeking oilskin, the square pectoral muscle which jutted into his side was surmounted by a small conical mound filled him with wonder. This must be a woman. For the first time in his life, Eagle was locked in his version of a sexual embrace and the antagonist was female. He could discard all his preconceptions about femininity; here was a woman capable of tearing him apart. Suddenly, just as Hawk had been filled with the glorious identification of his legitimised fetish, so Eagle was dazzled by the recognition that he was a closet heterosexual.

"Oh my God," he yelled as he tried to fling his free arm around the bosun's massive shoulders, "I love you. I love you."

The bosun's command of English may have been tenuous but she'd seen enough films to know the meaning of such an outburst. And anyway, even if her comprehension was faulty, since no man had ever said anything remotely like that to her, she was determined that this American, repulsive though he was, would be made to behave as if he were expressing affection and desire. She loosened her hold on him, lowered him to the deck, turned him to face her and clamped him once more in her arms, pressing his body against her steel-like abdomen in a parody of sexual contact and gasping straight into his nostrils the latakia fumes left in her lungs by her big black pipe.

They remained in this fetid embrace until one of the Russian seamen came to tell the bosun it was time to return to their ship. Eagle made no protest. He was in a realm of self-awareness far beyond nationalism and had already determined to devote the rest of his life to hurling himself as frequently as possible into the iron arms of this rank Amazon.

CHAPTER TWENTY

In the few weeks that followed as the ship continued to process the fish which its brood of trawlers disgorged into it, the passengers eased themselves variously into their fates. The postman was incorporated in one of the stages of the processing operations and his carcass became part of an agricultural fertiliser that would soon contribute to another mediocre grain harvest.

Poor Kestrel settled into a rhythm of miserable ingestion and evacuation and prayed for the time when static Russian soil would reconstitute the physiological stability he'd previously taken so much for granted. Lodgedale spent many hours with the skipper drawing up plans of dungeons and designing cudgels. Hawk dreamed blissfully of gymnasia crammed with lithe young bodies in leotards stretching spindly arms under his tutorial hands. And Eagle followed the bosun around the ship marvelling at her virile femininity and irritating her sufficiently to be granted the occasional cuff from her gnarled fists. None of them had any time for regrets and they all looked forward to arriving in Russia and consummating their several desires.

****

The 18th was a day of sun and sparkle. When Machin woke up, after a solid sixteen hours sleep, he felt marvellous. Tessa was already up and moving quietly about the room preparing to leave. The sight of her and the memory of the unbelievable afternoon they'd spent increased the well-being he felt and, in a voice that he hoped had the resonance of George Clooney's, he called "Hey, come over here."

She paused to grin briefly at him.

"No. Too busy," she said. "We're going home today."

Residual drowsiness prevented him feeling that this was in any way a challenge to his virility, so he simply lay there, aware of his body on a day of sunshine and beautiful women.

Tessa, too, felt good. When the trawler had tied up alongside on its return, she'd checked that its passengers were no longer on board. As the skipper came ashore, she stopped him, identified herself, had to endure a surprisingly furious ten minutes of abuse about events whose significance she failed to catch, and eventually handed over the agreed amount. It had needed only a little extra to discover what had become of his cargo and from where the instructions which had superseded her own had come.

As she drove back to Inverness, she thought hard about it all. The voice and accent that the skipper had described had belonged neither to the Big Snake, nor to the postman's boss. But Tessa had systematically worked back over her own memories, looking for the extra element that she felt to be there. At last, with a sudden, dazzling realisation, she'd found it, and the whole box of fragments had fallen together to form a coherent, comprehensible picture.

She knew now why the Big Snake was organising such a wholesale clearance and how he'd managed to be so many steps ahead of her all the time. She was confident enough to feel also that her insights into the Big Snake's motives and methods of operation would make her even more valuable to him and that her own future was exciting and secure.

Her happiness communicated itself to Machin and, through breakfast and the loading of their luggage into the Mercedes, they were like the couple he'd always imagined he'd one day be part of. They joked, laughed, touched and kissed, and not even the arrival of Bad Boy and Eric, whose wrestling match had taken place the previous evening while the trawler was out in the North Sea, could lower their spirits. Machin, in his characteristic way of responding only to present experiences, had already banished the horror and pain of his short career at The Cage from his mind.

The four of them eventually drove out of Inverness in bright sunshine, and the red Toyota fell dutifully into place several cars behind the Mercedes as they sped along by the Moray Firth.

For Machin, the original ride up in the Mercedes had only become pleasurable in its later stages. On this occasion, however, having started at such an intense peak, it surpassed anything he'd

182

ever known. Beside him at the wheel lounged Tessa, her short fair hair blowing back from her beautiful brown face. The huge sunglasses she wore were straight out of a Paris Hilton photo shoot. Chuck Berry sang "With no particular place to go" on the radio, and the casual masculine hand which Machin had laid on Tessa's thigh gently molested her flesh and was allowed to explore all the areas that had supplied such unbelievable pleasure in yesterday's hotel.

Everything was worth it. He and Tessa had been brought together and the future, which two days before had looked attractive in an isolated Cornish hovel, now held the flashy promise of everything life seemed to have given to everyone else but somehow denied him.

He thought of telling Tessa he loved her, but decided that would strike the wrong note. He wanted to say something to her though, but just as he'd worked out a crisp quip about ley lines and vibrations, Chuck Berry's voice and his own internal monologue were both cut by the familiar ringing of her mobile.

Tessa smiled as she pressed the button.

"Good morning," she said.

"Morning, BW," said the Big Snake.

"What's on your mind?"

"Just wanted to know if you had a nice evening."

"Great. Couldn't have been better."

"Good. How's your little sparrow?"

Tessa looked across at Machin.

"He's fine," she said. "But you know that already don't you?"

"You know me, BW. OK then. Armadillo's been a bit of an earner for us. You can let your sparrow go."

"Good."

"But I think it's time for you to move on from Aberdeen. We're setting up a branch down in Dundee. How would you like to be part of that? Get it going for me?"

"I'd love it," she said.

"OK. Talk to you when you get back. Take care."

Tessa hit the button again and settled happily back into her seat. She was a member of the club. The Big Snake knew she knew, and she was being invited to join. She was part of the inner circle, part of the Third Way. Only there was no Third Way. Just one man, a man who wanted to take the oil and gas industry back

183

to the good old days, when it didn't use offices and files and stupid codes, but just set up scams in which other people did all the work and all he had to do was collect the profits.

Her first assignment was in Dundee, a big stopping point on the expansion south to the central belt and into England. And, of course, over into the Caspian Sea, Azerbaijan and, who knew? Venezuela, the Gulf of Mexico, anywhere there were platforms which needed to be serviced, run and scammed. The Big Snake had asked her to set it all up and she was excited.

At a filling station just north of Aberdeen, she pulled off the road, waited for the red Toyota to notice and follow her, then drove up beside the pumps.

"What a day," said Machin, easing himself out of the Mercedes. He stood beside the car, stretching his arms and taking a deep breath.

"Yes. Beautiful," said Tessa, a big smile on her face.

She opened the glove compartment, took out a purse, counted out several twenty pound notes and handed them to Machin.

"What's this for?" he said.

"You'll need a taxi," she said. "Bye Chris. Look after yourself."

He stared at her, his world crumbling again. She smiled, blew him a kiss and accelerated away, followed by Bad Boy and Eric in the Toyota.

****

As the discarded Sparrow stood clutching his suitcase and wondering what to do, the man behind it all was enjoying himself. Mary sat in his chair at The Cage listening as the music loop changed from *The Skye Boat Song* to *Flower of Scotland*. He reached for his phone, dialed and turned his head to look out at the blue sky as he waited for it to be answered. He heard the click on the line and said, "Hey, Two-toes. This is Big Snake. How you doing?"

ABOUT THE AUTHOR

Bill Kirton was born in Plymouth, England but has lived in Aberdeen Scotland for most of his life. He's been a university lecturer, presented TV programmes, written and performed songs and sketches at the Edinburgh Festival, and had many radio plays broadcast by the BBC and the Australian BC. He's written three books on study and writing skills in Pearson's 'Brilliant' series and his crime novels, Material Evidence, Rough Justice, The Darkness, Shadow Selves and the historical novel The Figurehead, set in Aberdeen in 1840, have been published in the UK and USA. His short stories have appeared in several anthologies and Love Hurts was chosen for the Mammoth Book of Best British Crime 2010. Recently, as Jack Rosse, he's started producing children's books. The first two are Stanley Moves In and The Loch Ewe Mystery.

His website is http://www.bill-kirton.co.uk and his blog is at
http://livingwritingandotherstuff.blogspot.com/

More Great Books from Pfoxchase

DANCING IN THE DARK:
AN ANTHOLOGY OF EROTICA,

edited by Nya Rawlyns

Eight authors from around the globe, unite to bring you a cornucopia of delights. Stories to titillate, enthrall, enrapture. Explore, if you dare, dark, dangerous worlds where passion reigns supreme, where lust and love meet in a *pas de deux* of wanton desire and longing.

Sip from a frothy mix of delicious seduction. Eyes blind, your senses fly free, yearning, seeking, believing. Savor the re-imagining of ancient tales, brought to life with a modern twist and often bawdy humor. Tread carefully down a dangerous path of deadly seduction. Open your mind to new possibilities, indulge the senses.

Welcome to *Dancing in the Dark*—feel the subtle sway, the press of hot flesh to hot flesh, embrace the intricate weave of pleasure and pain, body and soul, heart and mind. Do you know the steps? Are you sure?

When the music starts, who will lead, who will follow?

Hard Workers by Kate Rigby: Hard work and dedication should count for something, shouldn't it?

Dance Macabre by Diane Nelson: Angel, former mob enforcer, damaged body and soul, finds release from her demons. What happens when you dance with the devil—who leads, who follows?

Delectable Deviations: An Erotic Adaptation of Hansel and Gretl by Noelle Pierce: Getting lost in the woods is more wicked than you think.

Stella and Bailey by Robb Grindstaff: Stella cooks dinner every night. Bailey, a Goth fantasy writer, stays out all night. What's the only thing these two sisters have in common? Me.

Headboards by Kate Rigby: A professional love consultant puts an ad in the paper and gets more than she bargained for.

Wintersong by Sessha Batto: In the winter of their love, all Armand wants is to reconnect with Peter. In the end, some obstacles are too big to easily overcome.

Suckers Sometimes Get Lucky by John Browne: When seven young men hire a stripper for a party, they never expected they would get Snow White.

Snapshots by S.A. Sayuri: The camera never lies ... or does it?

Sweet Seraphim by T.L Tyson: How do you learn to see when your blindfold can't be removed?

Reviews for Dancing in the Dark:

"This is the perfect erotica volume to have on your shelf. The stories are wonderfully diverse, running the gamut from funny to emotional to pulse quickening." —Marisu Fronc, Amazon

"Well my, my. I heard that this anthology was good, and that it was hot, but I had no idea it was that good and that hot! This anthology is loaded with erotica to suit every taste. Subtle or in your face, sweet or saucy, nice or naughty, this is the book to tempt your desires."
—Jessica Degarmo, Amazon

In print and eBook
Available now from: Amazon.com and other fine retailers.
www.pfoxchase.com

From Pfoxmoor Publishing

An Adult/Young Adult Paranormal Romance

LILY by LM DeWalt

Lily craves companionship, friendship, love. At 19 she has dreams and yearnings, and deadly secrets that make her anything but normal.

Ian, her maker, robbed her of choices and her very life, until a fateful encounter brought her hope and a family—and an unexpected, forbidden love for the human, Christian.

But will love be her undoing when Lily, and all she cares about, hurdle into a world of violence and mayhem? She and her new family face an enemy with an agenda that will tear her, and her world, apart.

Lily discovers that love comes at a price and a heart that never beats still echoes with passion and desire.

Rave reviews for Lily:

"*Lily* by LM DeWalt is a refreshing take on the Vampire mythology with a heroine struggling against her nature, determined to make a life out of the half-life she neither chose nor fully understands. Lily will have you on your feet, cheering her on, or reaching for a hanky..."
—Diane Nelson, Goodreads

"...I was totally taken with Lily's internal voice, her conflict borne of vulnerability. I was moved by her loneliness and her desire to connect with others and was suitably disturbed by the animal nature of what she is—a vampire." —Dean Mayes, Goodreads

In print and eBook
Available now from: Amazon.com and other fine retailers.
www.pfoxmoorpublishing.com

From Pfoxmoor Publishing

A Young Adult Fantasy-Adventure

DRAGON ACADEMY by Diane Nelson

With high school finished for the summer, Nick looks forward to visiting his aunt and uncle in New Jersey. What awaits him is a heat wave like no other—and two of the last Greywings on the planet. Nick has an innate ability to train horses but will he be able to translate his amazing skill to these teenage dragons?

The steaming soup of mid-summer heats up tempers and tests resolve as Nick vies with fellow trainers, Keith and Maxie, for mastery over their new charges. The dragons, Nikita and Michael, typical teenagers themselves, have other ideas.

Nick treads a torturous path through a minefield of competing demands: the expectations of his aunt and uncle, recalcitrant horses, the Academy's female students and the overwhelming egos of Nikita and Michael. One small mistake erupts into a conflagration that hurls everyone into a race against time and the overwhelming forces of nature.

Rave Reviews for Dragon Academy:

"…the read is engrossing, funny, sometimes an edge of your seat thing that is ridiculously entertaining." —Paul Neto

"As a teacher, I would definitely recommend my students read this book." —Laura DeWalt

In print and eBook
Available now from Amazon.com and other fine retailers.
www.pfoxmoorpublishing.com

New From PfoxChase

A SF/Romance

THE IRON ADMIRAL: CONSPIRACY

By Greta van der Rol

Politics. Hatred. Star systems on the brink of war.
A species under threat of extinction from a deadly virus.

Ex-Admiral Chaka Saahren goes undercover to discover the truth. Systems Engineer, Allysha Marten, takes one last job to rid her of debts and her cheating husband. On Tisyphor, deadly secrets about the past explode, as Allysha and the undercover agent scramble to prevent the coming holocaust and xenocide.

When the ex-Admiral's identity is revealed, she must come to terms with her feelings for a man she thinks caused the death of innocent civilians, including her father.

In a race against time, Allysha must set aside her conflicted emotions and trust a man she barely knows. Saahren must convince the woman he loves to find the truth as he once more assumes his position as …
The Iron Admiral.

In print and eBook
Available now from Amazon.com and other fine retailers.
www.pfoxchase.com